Sabrina® The Teen-Age Witch

Publisher / Co-CEO: Jon Goldwater
President / Editor-In-Chief: Mike Pellerito
Chief Creative Officer: Roberto Aguirre-Sacasa
Chief Operating Officer: William Mooar
Chief Financial Officer: Robert Wintle
Director: Jonathan Betancourt
Senior Director of Editorial: Jamie Lee Rotante
Production Manager: Stephen Oswald
Art Director: Vincent Lovallo
Lead Designer: Kari McLachlan
Associate Editor: Carlos Antunes
Co-CEO: Nancy Silberkleit

Published by Archie Comic Publications, Inc. 629 Fifth Avenue, Pelham, NY 10803-1242

Printed in Canada. First Printing. ISBN: 978-1-64576-895-1

Featuring the talents of

George Gladir • Dan DeCarlo • Rudy Lapick • Vincent DeCarlo

Bill Kreese • Jim DeCarlo • Chic Stone • Bill Yoshida • Dick Malmgren

Jon D'Agostino • Gus Lemoine • Harry Lucey • Marty Epp • Bob Bolling

Barry Grossman • Frank Doyle • Bill Vigoda • Dexter Taylor

Samm Schwartz • Stan Goldberg • Bill Golliher • Dan Parent

Mike Esposito • Mike Gallagher • Angelo Decesare • Dave Manak

Vickie Williams • Holly G! • Al Nickerson • Henry Scarpelli • Jason Jensen

Abby Denson • Tania Del Rio • Jim Amash • Jeff Powell • Ridge Rooms

Teresa Davidson • Tom DeFalco • Gisele • Rich Koslowski • Jack Morelli

Digikore Studios • Ryan North • Derek Charm • Kelly Thompson

Veronica Fish • Andy Fish • Nick Spencer • Mariko Tamaki • Jenn St-Onge

Matt Herms • Bob Smith • Glenn Whitmore

With introductions by

Jack Copley • Sweeney Boo • Stephanie Cooke • Gillian Swearingen

Vincent Lovallo • Tania Del Rio • Holly G!

Table of Contents

Sabrina 60 Magical Stories

ZAP!
?

Presenting Sabrina

Meet Sabrina, a teenage witch, who lives a typical teenage life, except she gets to hex her fellow teens. It all starts here! Two of Archie's best creators breathe life into another teenage world! They put a witch in the mortal world, made her a teen, and it looks like they borrowed from *Bell, Book and Candle*, the movie that inspired television's *Bewitched*.

✶ **Jack Copley**
Archie Historian

The very first introduction of Sabrina, you can't make it more special than that. She's cool, she's so well dressed, she's got powers, and we all want to be her! If there is one thing I really liked about Sabrina, is how much she loved fashion and seeing all her different and amazing outfits in these older comic strips!

✶ **Sweeney Boo**
Artist

Witch Pitch

So one thing that I love about the early Sabrina comics is how different she is from the modern Sabrina. Of course, there are still a few modern versions of her in between how she's portrayed in Archie Comics to the TV series *The Chilling Adventures of Sabrina*. But I love how mischievous Sabrina is early on. She's not concerned with using her powers for good or protecting mortals around her, she wants to be a "good" witch only in making her Head Witch proud through hexing and causing mayhem. It's such a fun way to portray the character and how her spells almost always backfire and do the opposite of what she intends, showing readers that even with magic, being a teenager can be a pain. With "Witch Pitch," it's so fun to have Sabrina be "on assignment" with something as menial as ensuring the school hockey team doesn't win their game... and having that all be thwarted by Sabrina developing a crush on one of the players. I love her unlucky in love (and magic) life!

✶ **Stephanie Cooke**
Writer

Originally presented in **Archie's Madhouse** #22, October 1962

George Gladir • Dan DeCarlo • Rudy Lapick • Vincent DeCarlo

NO... WE MODERN WITCHES BELIEVE LIFE SHOULD BE A BALL!

...BESIDES SOFT, GRACIOUS LIVING DOESN'T REDUCE OUR POWERS ONE IOTA!
KRAK

HOWEVER, WE MODERN WITCHES STILL HAVE OUR FAMILIARS!
A "FAMILIAR" IS AN IMPISH ANIMAL THAT HELPS PERFORM SMALL MALICIOUS ERRANDS!

MEET SALEM, MY FAMILIAR!

YESTERDAY SALEM GOT A GOLD STAR FOR TEARING UP THE NEIGHBOR'S PETUNIAS!

THERE ARE STILL OTHER WAYS YOU CAN SPOT A WITCH... **WE CAN'T CRY!**

ALTHOUGH SOMETIMES I COME REAL CLOSE TO CRYING WHEN THEY PLAY THOSE HORRIBLE TV COMMERCIALS!
2

ANOTHER PECULIAR TRAIT WE HAVE IS THAT WE CAN'T SINK IN WATER!

I REMEMBER THE TIME SOME FUN LOVING BOYS TRIED TO THROW ME INTO THE WATER...
THIS HIP PIP IS GOING TO TAKE A DIP!
WHETHER SHE LIKES IT OR NOT!

FOR A SECOND IT LOOKED LIKE MY SECRET WOULD BE DISCOVERED.
SABRINA, HOW COME YOU'RE FLOATING?
?

...BUT MY QUICK-THINKING SAVED THE DAY.
THAT'S BECAUSE I'M 99 9/10 % PURE!

STILL ANOTHER TRAIT WE HAVE IS THAT WE CAN MAKE OTHERS FALL IN LOVE.
50 EASY LOVE CHARMS
SHE'S SWIPING MY ACT!

...BUT WE'RE NOT PERMITTED TO FALL IN LOVE OURSELVES... THAT WOULD MAKE THE HEAD WITCHES VERY ANGRY!
SHE MUST BE WEARING A LOVE-PROOF VEST!
ZING
3

SPEAKING OF HEAD WITCHES, MY HEAD WITCH IS DELLA!

SHE'S FABULOUS! ONE OF DELA'S ROUTINE HEXING JOBS WAS INVENTING **THE TWIST!!!**

OW! MY ACHIN' BACK!
OOOOH! MY SACROILIAC!
HEY LET'S TWIST...

DELLA HAS ASSIGNED ME TO HEX THE STUDENTS AT SMALL HIGH SCHOOL... I FEEL LIKE A HEX AMONGST HICKS!

AS A CHEER LEADER I GET BEAUCOUP OPPORTUNITY TO CARRY OUT MY ASSIGNMENTS.
GOSH! ANOTHER FUMBLE!
40
B
B

SOMETIMES I WORK **FOR** MY TEAM!
3

...AND SOMETIMES **AGAINST**!
3

IT BREAKS UP THE MONOTONY THAT WAY!

MY BUSY HEX SEASON AT SCHOOL IS DURING EXAM TIME!
GOSH! I KNOW THE ANSWER BUT I JUST CAN'T THINK OF IT!

I'VE A PART-TIME JOB AT THE LOCAL SODA SHOPPE AND THIS GIVES ME EVEN MORE OPPORTUNITY TO CARRY OUT MY WICKEDNESS.

PSSST! IT'S SPIKED WITH LOVE POTION № 9!

SEE WHAT I MEAN!
WHAT DOES HE SEE IN HER?

EVERYWHERE I GO THE BOYS ARE SIMPLY WILD OVER ME!
OHHHH! SABRINA... SIGH
12

BUT YOU'LL NEVER CATCH ME FALLING IN LOVE... THAT WOULD MEAN I WOULD LOSE MY POWERS AND BECOME HUMAN...

...AND THAT WOULD BE BAD!

...I THINK!
THE END

MORE ADVENTURES OF SABRINA-THE TEEN-AGE WITCH-TO FOLLOW!

SABRINA The TEEN-AGE WITCH IN

SABRINA, YOUR WITCH'S ASSIGNMENT THIS WEEK IS TO PUT A SPELL ON YOUR SCHOOL HOCKEY TEAM!

MISS DELLA, **I'LL** SEE TO IT THAT BAXTER HIGH IS CLOBBERED!

A WITCH IN TIME SAVES NINE

MISS HEX APPEAL of 1962

Miss Della HEAD WITCH ASSIGNMENT DIVISION

B

BAXTER
VISITO
0
3
GOSH! WE'RE MISSING ONE EASY SHOT AFTER ANOTHER!
B

WHAT'S WRONG WITH YOU GUYS, ANYWAY?
COACH, THE PUCK JUST **WON'T** GO IN!!!
BAXTER HI

Originally presented in **Archie's Madhouse #24**, February 1963

George Gladir • Dan DeCarlo • Rudy Lapick • Vincent DeCarlo

WELL, MAYBE YOU SECOND-STRINGERS WILL DO BETTER IN THE NEXT PERIOD!
HE'S SENDING IN THE SECOND TEAM ?!

NOW I CAN CONSERVE MY WITCH'S POWER!
...THEY'LL LOSE BY THEMSELVES!

MY BUT THAT BLONDE BOY ON OUR TEAM IS CUTE!
* MURR! ME-URR!
* CAT LANGUAGE FOR.. "STEADY SABRINA"!

YIPPEE
YAY!
DONALD!
BAXTER HI

NOW WHY DID I **DO** THAT ?
?

...I'M SUPPOSED TO MAKE OUR TEAM LOSE!
* MEOWRR
* I SMELL TROUBLE

IT'S ANOTHER GOAL FOR DONALD!
OOPS! I **DID** IT AGAIN!
2

GREAT WORK, DONALD! YOU'RE MAKING FANTASTIC SHOTS!
DON'T ASK ME HOW I DO IT, COACH!
BAXTER HI
BAXTER 3
VISITOR 3
DONALD DID IT AGAIN!
THAT TRICK SHOT WINS THE GAME FOR BAXTER!

SABRINA, YOU GOOFED!
* MURR!
* AND HOW!

!?
GRRRR

UH, OH! IT'S "SPOTS" THE HEAD WITCH'S FAMILIAR!
* GRREOW! MEOWRR!
* LEOPARD LANGUAGE FOR "BOY, ARE YOU IN TROUBLE, KID!"

* GROWW! REOWRRR! RAMA RRAMA!
OH, ME! (GULP!)
* DELLA WANTS TO SEE YOU RIGHT AWAY AND YOU BETTER HAVE A GOOD ALIBI!

MAYBE DELLA WILL PUNISH ME BY TAKING AWAY MY RAINPROOF BROOMOBILE!

BAXTER HIGH WAS SUPPOSED TO LOSE! WHAT HAPPENED?
ER...AH.. I GUESS I GOOFED!

YOU'VE DONE SOMETHING WORSE THAN GOOF!
YOU'VE FALLEN IN LOVE!

...WITCHES ARE NEVER SUPPOSED TO FALL IN LOVE! YOU KNOW THAT!!!
WITCHES' HEADQUARTERS UNAUTHORIZED DEMONS KEEP OUT

I'M ASSIGNING YOU TO THE NORTH POLE FOR PUNISHMENT!
PLEASE, ANYTHING BUT THAT!

...I'M ALLERGIC TO LONG WINTER UNDERWEAR!
ALL RIGHT, I'LL GIVE YOU ONE MORE CHANCE!

BAXTER HIGH MUST LOSE THE STATE CHAMPIONSHIP!
I'LL TAKE CARE OF IT! I PROMISE!

NO, I DON'T THINK I CAN TRUST YOU!... I'LL HANDLE THE JOB MYSELF!
4

THE DAY OF THE CHAMPIONSHIP GAME:
HERE COMES OUR TEAM NOW, MISS DELLA!
BAXTER HI
WHO'S THAT DREAMBOAT... ER... I MEAN - THE MAN WITH THE PLAYERS!
THAT'S COACH RICHARDS!

I'VE CHANGED MY MIND, SABRINA!
HUH?

I THINK BAXTER HIGH SHOULD WIN THIS GAME!
GOSH! THAT'S PEACHY OF YOU, MISS DELLA!

BAXTER 2
VISITORS 0
YAY! THE COACH'S PLAY WORKED AGAIN!

BAXTER 5
VISITORS 0
IT'S AMAZING THAT I SHOULD SUDDENLY THINK OF SO MANY TRICK PLAYS!
BAXTER HI

WE WON!
THANKS TO THE COACH!

ER.. SABRINA, HOW ABOUT A DATE FOR TONIGHT, TO CELEBRATE OUR VICTORY?
DONALD, I'D LOVE TO...
ER... I MEAN I CAN'T!
!?
BAXTER HI
OH, SOMEONE ELSE, HUH?
NO, YOU BIG FOOL! I'M NOT ALLOWED TO DATE!
BAXTER HI
BEING A WITCH ISN'T ALL IT'S CRACKED UP TO BE!
GOSH, SALEM! I WISH I WERE MORE LIKE DELLA!
SHE NEVER LETS ANYTHING TEMPT HER!
SHE'S A REAL WITCHES' WITCH!
RESTAURANT
?
The End

Originally presented in *Archie's Madhouse* #37, December 1964

George Gladir • Dan DeCarlo • Vincent DeCarlo

SABRINA, YOU HAVE THE LOWEST EFFICIENCY RATING OF ANY WITCH IN THE DISTRICT!
PROGRESS REPORT

LAST MONTH, YOU ADMINISTERED ONLY 3 POTIONS, 2 BREWS, AND 1½ SPELLS!
IT'S NOT MY FAULT!

CAN I HELP IT IF PEOPLE DON'T HAVE ANY CONFI-DENCE IN ME AS A WITCH?

THEY WOULD HAVE CONFIDENCE IN YOU IF IT WEREN'T FOR YOUR LOOKS!
LOOKS? WHAT'S WRONG WITH MY LOOKS?
POTION LOTION

PLENTY! FOR A WITCH YOU'RE DOWNRIGHT UGLY!
I AM?

YES! YOU DON'T HAVE ANY OF THE ATTRACTIVE FEATURES WITCHES ARE FAMOUS FOR!
LIKE STRAGGLY HAIR, WARTS ON THE CHIN, BLOODSHOT EYES!

AND I AIM TO DO SOMETHING ABOUT IT!
(GULP!) WHERE ARE YOU TAKING ME?
2

HERE WE ARE!
HOME OF
PROF. TRANSISTOR
WORLD'S GREATEST MAD SCIENTIST
CUSTOM MADE MONSTERS TO YOUR EXACT SPECIFICATIONS

BE WITH YOU IN A SECOND!
...I'M WORKING ON MY LATEST INVENTION... X-RAY EXAM GLASSES!

TELL ME WHAT YOU SEE!
ALL I SEE IS A BUNCH OF EXAM QUESTIONS!
EXAM QUESTIONS
1. WHEN WAS AMERICA DISCOVERED?
2. GIVE THE SQUARE ROOT OF 29,929
3. HOW DO YOU SPELL "CAT"?

NOW WHAT DO YOU SEE?
GOLLY! NOW I SEE THE EXAM ANSWERS! THAT'S FABULOUS!
EXAM ANSWERS
1. 1492
2. THE SQUARE ROOT IS 173
3. C.A.T.

NOW WHAT'S YOUR PROBLEM?
SHE'S TOO UGLY!

UGLY?
YES!

I WANT YOU TO MAKE HER BEAUTIFUL LIKE ME!
!?
3

WELL, THIS LOOKS LIKE A JOB FOR MY BEAUTIFYING MACHINE!
BEAUTIFYING MACHINE? HOW DOES IT WORK?
BEAUTY
UGLY

WATCH! I PUT THE BEAUTIFUL OBJECT IN HERE!
BEAUTY

NEXT I PUT THE UGLY OBJECT IN HERE!
UGLY

... THEN I ADD A LITTLE JUICE!
BEAUTY
UGLY

YOU SEE! THE PIG HAS COPIED THE MOST BEAUTIFUL FEATURES OF THE POODLE!
SPLENDID!

SABRINA, GET IN THERE, AND BE PREPARED TO COPY MY MOST ATTRACTIVE FEATURES!
YES, AUNT HILDA! (SOB!)
BEAUTY
UGLY
4

READY?
I'M READY!
SO AM I! (SOB!)
BEAUTY
UGLY

BLAM!

W-WHAT HAPPENED?
I MUST HAVE MADE A LITTLE BOO BOO! ARE YOU ALL RIGHT?

I GUESS I'M OKAY!
BUT I'M NOT!

BOO HOO! LOOK WHAT THE PROFESSOR'S MACHINE DID TO ME! IT'S RUINED MY WITCH'S CAREER! (SOB)
5

...IT'S MADE ME LOOK AS UGLY AS SABRINA!
The END

Originally presented in Archie's Madhouse #48, August 1966

George Gladir • Bill Kreese

PLOP!
WILL YOU LOOK AT WHAT THE WAVES DRAGGED IN!
HA! HA!
HI, SABRINA!
GULP! IT'S DONALD WITH MY FINKY RIVAL, ROSALIND!
I'D INVITE YOU TO JOIN US BUT I ONLY HAVE FOOD FOR TWO!
HMPH! WHO NEEDS HER CRUMMY CRUMBS!
ER, THAT'S ALL RIGHT -- I HAVE MY OWN FOOD BASKET!
ZAP!
HAVE A HOT DOG, DONALD!
THANKS SABRINA!
ECH! THIS HOT DOG IS A COLD DOG!
OOOPS! I GOOFED!
2

TRY MY FOOD, I GUARANTEE IT'S TASTY!
I'LL FIX THAT!
ZAP!
(GULP!) SNAILS!
OH, BOY! THEY'RE MY FAVORITE DELICACY!
HEY, KIDS! COME ON AND DANCE WITH US!
WONDERFUL IDEA! SABRINA CAN WATCH OUR SNAILS!
SNACK B
I LOVE DANCING THE PONY!
ME TOO!
HMM! I'LL MAKE DONALD THINK HE'S A REAL PONY!
3

--THAT WAY HE'LL STEP ALL OVER ROSALIND'S FEET!
ZAP!
DONALD, WHAT'S WRONG? YOU'RE WHINNYING LIKE A REAL PONY!
(TEE!) (HEE!)
WHEE!
YEOW!
HA! HA! THAT WAS CLEVER, DONALD! DO IT AGAIN!
I'M SORRY SABRINA! I DON'T KNOW WHAT'S COME OVER ME!
I GOOFED AGAIN!
FORGET SABRINA! LET'S DO THE MONKEY!
HMPF! I'LL MAKE A MONKEY OUT OF HER!
WHAT'S THE MATTER, ROSALIND?
UGH!
ZAP!
TEE! HEE! I MADE HER LOSE CONTROL OF HER DANCING!
?
4

WOW! LOOK AT ROSALIND'S FABULOUS NEW DANCE STEPS!
MAN! SHE'S OUT OF SIGHT!
ANOTHER GOOF! MAYBE I OUGHT TO GO BACK TO WITCHCRAFT KINDERGARTEN!
HEY, GANG, SURF'S UP!
LET'S GO!
LAST ONE IN IS A SABRINA! HA! HA!
VERY FUNNY!
SINCE ROSALIND LIKES WAVES, I'LL GIVE HER WAVES EXTRA BIG ONES!
ZAP!
OH, DONALD!
HOLD ON ROZ!
5

HANG ON, ROZ, I'VE GOT YOU!
DONALD! MY HERO!
OH, NO! NOT ANOTHER GOOF!
OOPS, I FORGOT TO CALL OFF MY BIG WAVES!
GLUB! GLUB! SOMEBODY SHOULD TELL THIS OCEAN THAT WITCHES AREN'T SUPPOSED TO DROWN!
IT'S OKAY YOUNG LADY! YOU'RE SAFE!
TSK! TSK! CHALK UP STILL ANOTHER GOOF FOR SABRINA!
LIFE GUARD
BUT (SIGH!) AT LEAST IT'S MY BEST GOOF OF THE DAY!
6 THE END

Originally presented in **Archie's Madhouse #53**, April 1967

George Gladir • Dan DeCarlo • Jim DeCarlo • Vincent DeCarlo

I BETTER ASK JIMMY TO TAKE ME TO THE DANCE CONTEST!
HOME ECONOMICS
SNIFF! SNIFF!

THAT'S AN ODD SMELL, SABRINA! LET ME SAMPLE YOUR WORK!
ER..SURE, MISS THOMPSON!

SLURP!

? ! ?

EEAGH!!
?

LET'S SEE YOU PUT IT IN THE BASKET, SABRINA!

YOU MEAN LIKE THIS, MISS HASKINS?

I'M GOING TO ASK JIMMY TO TAKE ME TO THE DANCE CONTEST!
NOT IF I CAN HELP IT, BRENDA!

BALL, INTERCEPT ANYONE WHO TRIES TO TALK TO JIMMY!
OH, JIMMY!

EXCUSE ME, BRENDA! THE COACH WANTS TO TALK TO ME!
YES!
COACH

POW!
?
3

THAT WASN'T QUITE WHAT I PLANNED, BUT I BETTER ASK JIMMY TO THE DANCE BEFORE BRENDA!
COACH
OH, JIMMY!
KA-POW!
DARN. I FORGOT TO CALL OFF THE BALL!
THERE'S THE BELL, JIM! LET'S LEAVE HER, SHE WILL BE ALL RIGHT!
AND NOW I'LL BE LATE FOR MY ENGLISH CLASS, UNLESS, ...
POOF!
WHERE IS SABRINA?
RIGHT BEHIND YOU, MR. JENKINS!
4

GO TO THE BLACK-BOARD AND WRITE THE COMPOSITION YOU DID FOR HOMEWORK!
YES, SIR!

ONLY I DIDN'T WRITE ANY COMPOSITION FOR HOMEWORK, BUT THAT SHOULDN'T STOP ME!

SHALAMAZAM! CADABRA! WATUSI !!
POOF!

?? SABRINA, YOUR COMPOSITION IS BACKWARDS!
GULP! I MUST HAVE SAID MY INCANTATION BACKWARDS!
MY VACATION
I SPENT MY VAC
TRAVELING
THROUGH

WELL, HERE'S YOUR GRADE!
OH, BOY! A HUNDRED!
100

NO, IT'S 001! I WROTE YOUR GRADE BACKWARDS!
100

AND THERE'S THE CAUSE OF ALL MY TROUBLE - BRENDA!

LET BRENDA DISAPPEAR INTO A HOLE IN THE WALL! BAZAM!!
POOF!

AH! AND THERE'S JIMMY BY HIS LOCKER! I'LL ASK HIM ABOUT THE DANCE!
67

?? BRENDA!!
LET'S GO TO THE DANCE TONIGHT!
OH, NO!!
67

LATER:
WHO SENT YOU HERE TO BE PUNISHED, SABRINA?
NO ONE!
DETENTION ROOM
6

I DECIDED TO PUNISH MYSELF!
?
I SHALL NOT USE WITCHCRAFT IN SCHOOL
I SHALL NOT USE
HCRAFT IN SCHOOL
SHALL NOT USE
The END

SAY, SABRINA! I DON'T LIKE THAT LOOK IN YOUR EYE!

BRINY! BRINY! BRINY! WE BOTH WANT TO BE *TINY! TINY! TINY!*

SLOT RACING TODAY!

WITCHES HANDBOOK OF INCANTATIONS 1968 EDITION

SABRINA *The* TEEN-AGE WITCH "TEENY-WEENY BOPPERS"

Originally presented in *Archie's Madhouse* #53, April 1967

George Gladir • Chic Stone • Bill Yoshida

SABRINA, OUR SIZE IS CHANGING!
NATCH!

I MEAN... WE'RE GETTING TALLER!
OOPS! I MUST PUT THE SPELL INTO REVERSE!

CAN'T YOU STOP? OUCH! WE'RE GETTING SO BIG!
WHERE DID I GO WRONG?

NIX WITH THE TALL! WE WANT TO BE SMALL!

POOPSIE COLA

LOOK, TOMMY! WE'RE NO HIGHER THAN A SNAKE'S CHIN!
YEAH, AND I FEEL JUST AS LOW!
WITCHES HANDBOOK OF INCANTATIONS 1968 EDITION
POOPSIE COLA
2

WHAT MADE YOU DECIDE TO BECOME A PARACHUTE JUMPER?
A PLANE WITH THREE DEAD ENGINES!
CHEER UP! NOW WE CAN GO BACK AND WIN THAT RACE!

HURRY! IT'S ABOUT TO START!

LOOK! YOUR BROTHER BOB IS AT THE CONTROLS!
HEH! HEH! LITTLE DOES HE KNOW WE'RE BEHIND THE STEERING WHEEL!
3

HOT DOG! WE'RE OUT-RACING EVERYBODY!
C

I TAKE IT BACK SABRINA! YOU WERE RIGHT!
OH, TOMMY I MAY BE VERY TINY...
3

... BUT I WANT TO GIVE YOU A VERY BIG KISS!
LET GO, SABRINA! THE RACE ISN'T OVER!
3

NOW YOU DID IT, SABRINA! WE'RE GOING OFF THE TABLE!

GULP! WE HIT THE WINDOW FRAME!
BLAM!

BRACE YOURSELF SABRINA!

IT'S SO DARK IN HERE!
RELAX, SABRINA! I HEAR SOMEONE COMING TO RESCUE US!

OH, TOMMY! IT'S A HUGE BIRD BEAK!
4

HELP ME, TOMMY!
DON'T DESPAIR, SABRINA! I'LL CLIMB OUT AND RESCUE YOU!
THIS EARLY BIRD WANTS TO MAKE ME ITS WORMS!
THIS SAFETY PIN MIGHT DO THE TRICK!

IF ONLY I CAN GET TO SABRINA IN TIME!
HURRY, TOMMY!

SABRINA, TRY TO THINK OF THE INCANTATION THAT'LL MAKE US NORMAL-SIZED AGAIN!

I'M TRYING, TOMMY! I'M TRYING!
WAIT! I THINK I HAVE IT!

TAKE US AWAY FROM THIS CRAZY GIG! WE WANT TO BE BIG! BIG! BIG!

A CENSOR IS ONE WHO PUTS HIS "NO'S" IN OTHER PEOPLE'S BUSINESS!
BLIP

LOOK! WE'RE GETTING BACK TO NORMAL!
?

PHEW! I DON'T EVER WANT TO BE ANY OTHER SIZE AGAIN!
NEITHER DO I!
SLOT
TODA

TOMMY WHILE YOU WERE AWAY I LOST WITH YOUR CAR AGAIN!
ER... THAT'S ALL RIGHT, BOB!

IF ONLY THERE WAS SOME WAY WE COULD GET A REAL DRIVER IN-SIDE THIS THING!

EEEAAGGHHH!!!
GOSH! WHAT'D I SAY?
THE END
6

Originally presented in **Archie's T.V. Laugh-Out #1**, December 1969

Dick Malmgren • Jon D'Agostino • Bill Yoshida

WELL, I DON'T WANT TO MEET THEM !... THEY'RE JUST COMMON EVERY-DAY PEOPLE WITH NOTHING SPECIAL ABOUT THEM... I FORBID IT !

BUT AUNT HILDA !... ALL THE KIDS THROW PARTIES !

SOB !...I GUESS I'LL NEVER BE LIKE OTHER KIDS !
CONSIDER YOURSELF LUCKY !

SOB ! SOB !
LET HER HAVE A PARTY, HILDA, ...A YOUNG GIRL HAS TO HAVE FRIENDS HER OWN AGE !

MAYBE SO, AMBROSE,... AFTER ALL... SHE DOES HAVE A HANDICAP BEING SO UGLY !
2

I GUESS SHE HAS TO HANG AROUND WITH OTHER UGLY KIDS... WHO ELSE COULD STAND LOOKING AT HER ?

CRACK!

I DON'T KNOW WHAT IT IS?... MY GOOD LOOKS KEEP CRACKING THESE CHEAP MIRRORS!

OKAY!... YOU CAN HAVE YOUR PARTY, SABRINA... BUT I STILL DON'T LIKE THE IDEA!

OH, THANK YOU, AUNT HILDA! YOU'RE A DOLL!
I KNOW!... I KNOW... I WASN'T VOTED MISS GHOUL OF 1812 FOR NOTHING!

NOW I WANT YOU TO PROMISE ME YOU WON'T USE WITCHCRAFT ON MY FRIENDS!
3

YOU MEAN I CAN'T TURN ONE OF THEM INTO A WARTY LITTLE TOAD? (HEE) (HEE)!
NO, AUNT HILDA, PLEASE!... I WANT THEM TO THINK THAT WE ARE JUST LIKE EVERYBODY ELSE!

YUCK!... WHAT A ROTTEN THING TO SAY TO YOUR AUNT!
PLEASE, AUNT HILDA!

SHE'LL BE AT HER BEST BEHAVIOR, SABRINA, I PROMISE,... RIGHT, HILDA?

YEESH!... WHAT A CREEPY PARTY THIS IS GOING TO BE!
THANK YOU, COUSIN AMBROSE!

I BETTER CALL THE GANG AND TELL THEM THE GOOD NEWS!
4

THAT EVENING...
HI, SABRINA!
HI, GANG!... COME ON IN,... I WANT YOU TO MEET MY FAMILY!
YOU DIDN'T TELL US IT WAS GOING TO BE A MASQUERADE PARTY?

THE WHOLE PAD LOOKS LIKE IT'S BEEN DECORATED FOR HALLOWEEN!

HA! HA!
WHO'S YOUR INTERIOR DECORATOR, DRACULA?

WHY THAT YOUNG WHIPPER SNAPPER!
AUNT HILDA!

ZAP!
5

REMEMBER, HILDA, I PROMISED!
OH, BATS!... I CAN'T HAVE ANY FUN!
KIDS!... IF YOU WANT ANY FOOD IT'S OVER HERE!
FOOD?

I DON'T KNOW HOW I EVER LET YOU TALK ME INTO THIS FREAK SHOW!

THEY'RE NICE KIDS, HILDA, I LIKE THEM!
?
CHOMP!
CHOMP!

DOESN'T YOUR MOTHER FEED YOU AT HOME, JUGHEAD?... DID IT EVER OCCUR TO YOU THAT THE OTHER KIDS MIGHT WANT TO EAT, TOO?

HA! HA!... THAT'S FUNNY... YOU'RE QUITE A GIRL THERE, AUNT HILDA!
6

WOULD YOU MIND PUTTING SOME PRETZELS ON TOP OF MY PLATE ?
WILL THIS BE ENOUGH ?
THAT WILL DO FINE!
ZAD!

THAT OUGHT TO FILL YOUR BIG FAT STOMACH!
GAK!

YIPES!... THEY'RE ALIVE!
OH-NO!
CRASH!

I'M GETTING OUT OF HERE!
WHAT'S THE MATTER, JUG ?
ZAP!

AUNT HILDA GAVE ME A BOWL FULL OF SNAKES AND A LIVE LOBSTER NIPPED MY NOSE!
I DON'T SEE ANY SNAKES!
7

THAT'S STRANGE!... I'M SURE I SAW THEM?
DON'T MIND HIM, SABRINA, ...THE WAY HE EATS HE'S LIABLE TO SEE ANYTHING!
YOU'RE A REAL CHARACTER, JUGHEAD!

COME ON, SABRINA, LET'S DANCE! ... LET ME SHOW YOU SOME FANCY STEPPING!
?

ONCE YOU'VE DANCED WITH ME YOU'LL NEVER DANCE WITH ANYBODY ELSE AGAIN!
OH, BROTHER!

THIS KID IS TOO MUCH!
OH DEAR ME!
HA! HA! HA!
OUCH!
OUCH!
OUCH!
ZAP!
THUMP!
THUMP!
THUMP!
8

WHAT DO YOU CALL THAT STEP, REGGIE, ... THE CAN CAN ?
HEE! HEE!
HOW DID THAT HAPPEN ?
?

ISN'T THAT A LOVELY DRESS SABRINA HAS ON, VERONICA ?
?

YES, IT LOOKS LIKE A COPY OF A PARIS ORIGINAL I ONCE THREW AWAY!
GREAT WITCHES BREW!

THIS ONE I HAVE ON CAME FROM PARIS, TOO!
YEECH! ... THE KID'S A REAL CREEP!
ZAP!

?
WHAT DID THEY DO, DEARIE, ... DRAG IT ALL THE WAY ?
MY GOODNESS! ... WHAT HAPPENED TO MY DRESS ?
HA! HA! HA! HEE! HEE!
9

OH DEAR, I BETTER STRAIGHTEN THINGS OUT!
HEE! HEE!
PER-ZAP!

WHAT'S GOING ON AROUND HERE?
?

THERE'S SOMETHING CRAZY GOING ON AROUND HERE ?
YEAH!...LET'S SPLIT!...THIS PLACE IS WEIRDSVILLE!

SOB!...COUSIN AMBROSE!...AUNT HILDA IS RUINING THE WHOLE PARTY WITH HER WITCHCRAFT!

DON'T YOU WORRY, SABRINA!
...I'LL FIX EVERYTHING FOR YOU!
10

LET'S BUG OUT OF THIS BUGGY JOINT!
HEE! HEE!

ZAP!

HEY, KIDS!... WHERE ARE YOU GOING ?
LET'S PLAY SOME MUSIC!... THIS PARTY IS STARTING TO DRAG!
?

YOU PLAY THE GUITAR ?
MAN, I DON'T PLAY IT... I MAKE IT SING!
?

YOU MAKE ME WANNA DANCE, YOU MAKE ME WANNA LAUGH AND BE HAPPY AGAIN!
COME ON, CATS! ...CUT IN!
11

GO, AUNT HILDA! GO!
MY HEART WENT BANG-SHANG-A-LANG!
YAHOO!
TAP! TAP!
Archies

LATER...
WE HAD A GREAT TIME, SABRINA!... THANKS FOR EVERYTHING!

YOUR AUNT HILDA IS REALLY ONE OF THE GANG!
?
ZAP!

THANKS FOR THE WONDERFUL PARTY, AUNT HILDA, WE HAD A BLAST!
I HAVE A FEELING I'VE BEEN GIVEN A WHAMMY?
YOU WERE GROOVY, AUNT HILDA, REAL GROOVY!
The End

SABRINA THE TEEN-AGE WITCH IN THAT OL' BLACK MAGIC

NO, HOT DOG, NO! LEAVE THAT POOR LITTLE KITTEN ALONE!... DON'T BE SUCH A BULLY!

ARF ARF

GEE I'M SORRY, SABRINA!
DON'T WORRY, JUGHEAD! SALEM CAN TAKE CARE OF HERSELF!
GRROWF!

Originally presented in **Archie's I.V. Laugh-Out** #2, March 1970

Dick Malmgren • Gus Lemoine • Jon D'Agostino • Bill Yoshida

I DON'T KNOW SABRINA! THAT'S A MIGHTY SMALL CAT!

EXACTLY WHAT GOLIATH SAID ABOUT DAVID!
HUH?

GAK! HOT DOG HOW DID YOU GET UP THERE?
SHAME ON YOU, SALEM!
HEEK! HEEK!

IT WASN'T AT ALL NICE OF YOU TO ZAP THAT POOR CLUMSY BEAST!
HOT DOG PURRS!

HYUK, YUK! I DIDN'T!... I ZAPPED HIS DOG!
2

HOT DOG JR.,... CHILI DOG! TAKE THE ADVICE OF AN OLDER AND WISER CANINE!
STEER CLEAR OF THAT CAT SALEM!

THAT'S A MIGHTY POWERFUL BUNDLE OF FUR!
THE OLD BOY'S SHOWING HIS AGE!

HAW! WE SHOULD BE AFRAID OF SALEM! HAVE YOU SEEN SALEM?
THAT'S A MIGHTY SMALL CAT!

THAT'S WHAT GOLIATH SAID ABOUT DAVID!
WHO'S GOLIATH?
WHO'S DAVID?

OLD HOT DOG IS GETTING SOFT IN HIS OLD AGE! IMAGINE BEING AFRAID OF A *CAT*!
HAH! THAT WHISKERY LITTLE WART BETTER NOT CROSS *MY* PATH!
ZAP!
3

YOU'VE BEEN UP TO NO GOOD, SALEM! I CAN TELL BY THAT WITCHY PURR OF YOURS!
(PURR) ONE GAL'S "NO GOOD" IS ANOTHER GAL'S "WELL DONE!"

OOOH! HARVEY'S CAR! COME SALEM, WE HAVE COMPANY!

HILDA! AUNT HILDA! WHERE'S HARVEY? I SAW HIS CAR OUTSIDE!
HE'S WAITING IN THE LIVING ROOM, CHILD!

REALLY, SABRINA, HE IS THE MOST UNFORTUNATE LOOKING BOY! UGH! WHAT UGLINESS!
AUNT HILDA! YOU DIDN'T?

OF COURSE I DID, DEAR! WHY HAVE POWERS IF YOU DON'T USE THEM? I ZAPPED HIM INTO A RIGHT NICE LOOKING BOY!
ERK!
4

AUNT HILDA! YOU UNZAP HARVEY THIS INSTANT!
WHAT?

I DID YOU A FAVOR! I PRETTIED UP THAT REVOLTING LOOKING BOY FOR YOU!
WHY DO YOU YOUNG PEOPLE KEEP BUCKING THE ESTABLISHMENT?
UNZAP HIM!

I WAS ONLY TRYING TO HELP! YOU MIGHT SHOW A LITTLE GRATITUDE!
ZAP

THAT'S BETTER!
YUCH! ALL YOUR TASTE IS IN YOUR MOUTH, SABRINA!

HELLO, HARVEY! HOW NICE OF YOU TO COME!
HI, SABRINA!
SMARTY PANTS KIDS! ALWAYS THINK THEY KNOW BETTER THAN THE OLD FOLKS!
GRUMBLE! GRUMBLE!
5

WORK YOUR FINGERS TO THE BONE FOR THEM AND WHAT DO YOU GET?

...INGRATITUDE! THAT'S WHAT YOU GET! OOH, WHEN I THINK OF WHAT I'VE DONE FOR THAT GIRL!

GEE, SABRINA! YOUR AUNT HILDA'S MAKING AN AWFUL LOT OF NOISE OUT IN THE KITCHEN!
BAM!
CLANK!
CRASH!
TINKLE!

SHE'S CLEANING UP THE DISHES, HARVEY! AUNT HILDA IS A VERY VIGOROUS HOUSEKEEPER!

WORK, WORK, WORK, SLAVE, SLAVE, SLAVE! AND WHAT THANKS DO I GET? NONE! - OH THE INJUSTICE OF IT ALL!
ZAP
WRRRR!
6

WHAT SAY WE WHEEL DOWN TO THE CHOCKLIT SHOPPE AND I'LL BUY YOU A MALT?
SOUNDS GROOVY!

UH, OH! HERE COMES OL' WISE GUY REGGIE! HE'S GONNA SHOW OFF AT MY EXPENSE AGAIN!
ROAR!

HEY, YOU WITH THE BUCKET OF BOLTS! ... WANNA DRAG?
SEE?

HMPH! TRY THIS IN YOUR FOUR BARRELED CARBURETOR, MR. MANTLE!
PUTT! PUTT!
ZAP!

ROAR!
ZOOOMM!!
7

KOFF! KOFF!
W-W-WHA HOP?
CHOKE! GASP!
FINE FOR SPEEDING

WOW! DID YOU SEE THOSE WHEELS TAKE OFF? WA-HOO!! - IT WAS LIKE BEAUTIFUL!!... I DIDN'T THINK SHE HAD IT IN HER!

HI, ARCHIE! HELLO, OPHELIA! WHAT'S NEW?
CHOCKLIT SHOPPE

(SIGH) NOTHING'S NEW!... THAT DREAMBOAT SPENCER STILL TREATS ME LIKE LAST WEEK'S NEWS!
HEY!... GUESS WHAT?

I'VE GOT A BRAND NEW DIET!.. THIS IS SURE FIRE! CAN'T MISS!
WHEN DO YOU GO ON IT, SPENCER?

AS SOON AS I FINISH THIS ONE LAST, FINAL, DOUBLE DIP, SUPER SCOOP SUNDAE, I'M GONNA START!
Special 60¢
8

OH, HIM AND HIS COCKAMAMIE DIETS! HE'S ALWAYS KIDDING HIMSELF!
I WISH THERE WAS SUCH A THING AS BLACK MAGIC!

OOH, I'D WHAP HIM WITH SUCH A SPELL OR AN INCANTATION...
HMMM!

I'D GIVE HIM SOMETHING LIKE... "HOKUS POKUS, MISBEGOTTEN, EVERYTHING YOU EAT TASTES ROTTEN!
ZAP!

BLECH!

BLECH! BLECH! BLECH!
WHAT HAPPENED?
SPENCER! WHAT IS IT?
9

OPHELIA! IT WORKED! YOU ACTUALLY MADE THAT SUNDAE TASTE AWFUL TO HIM!
?

BUT, BUT, I WAS ONLY KIDDING! I HAD NOTHING TO DO WITH IT!
WELL IT WASN'T MY ICE CREAM!
SODA 30¢

GAK! NO! DON'T COME NEAR ME! I HEARD YOU! YOU HIT ME WITH A VOODOO CURSE!
SODA 30¢

YOU'RE A WITCH! A WITCH IS WHAT YOU ARE! DO YOU KNOW WHAT YOU ARE? WHAT YOU ARE IS A WITCH!
NO, DARLING, NO!

LEMME OUT OF HERE! DON'T LET HER NEAR ME!! HELP! HELP!
CRASH
10

WAH
OMIGOSH!

THAT WAS VERY STRANGE! HAVE YOU ANY IDEA WHAT HAPPENED, SABRINA?
ME? WHAT WOULD I KNOW ABOUT ANYTHING?
JUG-A-LUG SPECIAL 60¢

I JUST DON'T UNDERSTAND IT! WE ALL KNOW THERE'S NO SUCH THING AS BLACK MAGIC AND WITCHCRAFT... AND YET...
YES ??

... WELL, POOR OPHELIA'S PRETTY UPSET! I THINK I'LL DRIVE HER HOME!... SEE YOU, SABRINA!
SOB!

EEK!- SALEM, I BLEW THAT ONE BUT GOOD!... I WAS JUST TRYING TO HELP!
HEEK! HEEK!- THAT WAS MY GIRL WHO DID THAT! BEAUTIFUL PIECE OF BUSINESS!
11

SABRINA, MY CHILD! CONGRATULATIONS!
HUH- ON WHAT, AUNT HILDA?

NOW DON'T BE MODEST! DELLA JUST DROPPED IN AND TOLD ME ALL ABOUT IT!
"DELLA"? MY HEAD WITCH?

I'M PROUD OF YOU MY DEAR! WHAT A LOVELY PIECE OF WITCHCRAFT! SOCKING IT TO YOUR BEST FRIENDS LIKE THAT!
AND TO THINK THAT I WAS WORRIED THAT SHE WAS TURNING INTO A GOODY-GOODY!

SHE'S GOT THE OLD FAMILY SPIRIT! SHE CAN ZING IT IN WITH THE BEST OF THEM!
AND IT WASN'T EVEN AN ASSIGNMENT! SHE DID IT OUT OF SHEER MALICIOUS PLEASURE!
MORE BATS' WINGS MY DEAR! FRESH BAKED LAST YEAR!
The End

The Tooth Fairy

Sabrina, Archie, and Jughead catch a poor boy stealing hubcaps to help support his family, so Sabrina conjures up a shoe shine box and they convince the boy he can work for money instead of stealing. Fitting Sabrina with the Archies created an unusual morality-based story. Sabrina just happened to be walking around the area when Archie and Jughead were returning to their wagon?

✶ **Jack Copley**
Archie Historian

Sell Out

After enlisting The Archies to open the local concert for pop superstar Cotton Flubbernote, his agent Colonel Flam skips town with all the proceeds until Sabrina magically turns them back to Riverdale. Sabrina only fits in smoothly with The Archies and all of Riverdale on pages 8 and 11 of the story!

✶ **Jack Copley**
Archie Historian

Monkey Business & A Good Sport

Reggie and Sabrina are a pair that don't interact together very often, but in both of these stories we get to see Little Sabrina teach Little Reggie a lesson when his pranks go too far. Little Sabrina is too adorable to be taken seriously when she's upset, but considering what she does to Reggie, I wouldn't underestimate her! Luckily her moral compass always leads her in the right direction and she fixes her wrongdoings. But gee! You think Reggie would've stopped with his practical jokes after these incidents!

✶ **Gillian Swearingen**
Archie Contributor

Originally presented in **Sabrina The Teenage Witch #2**, July 1971

Dick Malmgren • Harry Lucey • Marty Epp • Bill Yoshida

JUST WATCH ME AND LEARN HOW A POLISHED ATHLETE PLAYS THIS GAME!
BIG SHOW-OFF!

FEAST YOUR EYES ON THIS, ARCH!... SHEER POETRY IN MOTION!
PLOP!

SHOTS LIKE THIS ALWAYS LOOK SIMPLE WHEN YOU'RE AS GREAT AS I AM, ARCH!
ISN'T REGGIE GREAT, SABRINA?
HMPH!

YOU'RE JUST TRYING TO MAKE ME LOOK BAD IN FRONT OF RONNIE! I KNOW YOU!
HA! HA!... A THREE YEAR OLD KID WITH HIS FATHER'S SHOES ON COULD MAKE YOU LOOK BAD! LET'S FACE IT... SPORTS ARE JUST NOT YOUR THING!
2

HEE! HEE! HEE!
WHAT'S WRONG WITH ME?
WHY CAN'T I PLAY LIKE REGGIE?

IT'S VERY SIMPLE, ARCHIE! YOU JUST DON'T HAVE WHAT IT TAKES!
THANKS A LOT!

POOR ARCHIE! HE'S SO DEPRESSED! HE NEEDS CHEERING UP! MAYBE A TUG ON MY EAR WILL HELP!
ZAP!

HEY! SUDDENLY I FEEL CONFIDENT!... LIKE A TIGER!

GRRR! THROW ME THAT BALL, REGGIE!
SURE, ARCH! ANYTHING FOR A LAUGH!
3

?
SHEER POETRY IN MOTION, EH, REG?
SWISH!
?

THAT WAS LUCK! I'LL BET YOU CAN'T DO IT AGAIN!
JUST WATCH! THE POWER OF POSITIVE THINKING IS WHAT DOES IT!
COACH

OKAY! SEE IF YOU CAN BLOCK THIS BASKET!
PA-TAP!
PA-TAP! PA-TAP! PA-TAP!
PA-TAP!

C'MON, BIRDBRAIN! YOU'RE JUST BEGGING TO BE DUMPED!
NOW YOU SEE ME!
COACH

NOW YOU DON'T!
PLOP!

I DON'T BELIEVE IT!
WHAT'S NOT TO BELIEVE?

IT'S ALL IN THE WRIST ACTION! SEE? WITHOUT EVEN LOOKING!
WOW! WHAT A SHOT!
THE WHOLE LENGTH OF THE COURT!
PLOP!

ARCHIE, I DON'T KNOW WHAT GOT INTO YOU BUT IF YOU CAN PLAY LIKE THAT IN TONIGHT'S GAME YOU'LL BE OUR STAR PLAYER!
OF COURSE, COACH!

BUT, COACH! ...I'M YOUR STAR PLAYER!
NOT WITH PLAYING LIKE ARCHIE'S YOU'RE NOT!
5

IF YOU WANT TO BE A STAR, REG, YOU HAVE TO LEARN TO USE YOUR HEAD!
ZIP!
WHUMP!
PLOP!
FANTASTIC!
THUNK!

IF THAT'S HOW YOU'RE GOING TO PLAY TONIGHT YOU WON'T EVEN BE IN THE GAME!

I THINK YOU'D BETTER SIT DOWN AND LET ARCHIE TAKE YOUR PLACE!
BUT, COACH!...
PLOP!

HOW HUMILIATING! TO BE BUMPED OFF THE TEAM BY ARCHIE!
NOW I'VE MADE REGGIE DEPRESSED!
ARCHIEKINS, I'M GOING TO LET YOU ESCORT ME TO THE VICTORY DANCE TONIGHT IF WE WIN!
A WISE DECISION, RON!
6

WITH ME PLAYING, THE GAME IS IN THE BAG!
AND I GAVE ARCHIE SO MUCH CONFIDENCE HE'S ALMOST AS OBNOXIOUS AS REGGIE!
BOO HOO!

WHAT'S THE MATTER, BETTY?
ARCHIE WAS SUPPOSED TO TAKE ME TO THE DANCE BEFORE HE STARTED PLAYING LIKE A PRO!

(SOB!) AT LEAST WHEN HE WAS A LOSER I HAD A CHANCE!... NOW HE WON'T EVEN KNOW I'M ALIVE!
NOW BETTY IS DEPRESSED! I'D BETTER UNZAP THIS SPELL BEFORE THINGS GET ANY WORSE!
ZAP!

LET'S SEE A FEW MORE PRACTICE BASKETS, ARCHIE!
SURE, COACH!

BOP!
7

I'LL GET IT, COACH! IT JUST SLIPPED!
SPLAT!
I KNEW IT WAS TOO GOOD TO BE TRUE!
STAND STILL, WILL YOU, YOU STUPID BALL?
COACH
REGGIE! ON THE COURT! ARCHIE!... OUT!
I KNEW YOU COULDN'T DO WITHOUT ME, COACH!
THINGS ARE BACK TO NORMAL!
COACH
FORGET THE DANCE, ARCHIE! I'D BE AFRAID YOU'D STUMBLE OVER YOUR OWN FEET! ... OR MINE!
I CAN'T UNDERSTAND IT!
CHEER UP, ARCHIE! BE HAPPY YOU WERE DOING SO GREAT OUT THERE, EVEN IF IT WAS JUST FOR A SHORT SPELL!
NOW HOW DID SHE KNOW THAT?
END

Originally presented in **Sabrina The Teenage Witch #3**, September 1971

Dick Malmgren • Bob Bolling • Rudy Lapick • Barry Grossman • Bill Yoshida

OKAY, KID, STAY RIGHT WHERE YOU ARE!
GOSH!
COME BACK WITH THOSE HUB-CAPS, YOU THIEF!

HERE, MISTER! THERE'S YOUR HUB-CAPS, BUT DON'T HIT ME!

I'M NOT GOING TO HIT YOU, KID, BUT DO YOU MIND TELLING ME WHY SUCH A YOUNG BOY LIKE YOU WOULD WANT TO STEAL?

I DON'T LIKE TO STEAL, BUT MY FATHER IS VERY SICK AND OUT OF WORK, AND I THOUGHT I COULD STEAL THEM TO GET SOME MONEY!
AND WHAT ARE YOU GOING TO DO WITH THE MONEY?
2

BUY SOME MILK AND BREAD, SO MY BROTHERS AND SISTERS COULD HAVE SOMETHING TO EAT!

OH, BROTHER! YOU DON'T BELIEVE THAT STORY DO YOU, ARCHIE ?! THIS LITTLE THIEF IS NOTHING BUT A CON-ARTIST!

I AM NOT! IT'S THE TRUTH, I TELL YOU! I'M NOT A CROOK! IT'S JUST THAT MY DAD IS OUT OF WORK AND I'M TRYING TO HELP OUT!
WELL, WE'LL SEE IF YOU'RE TELLING THE TRUTH OR NOT! LET'S GET GOING!

I HAVE A FEELING HE'S TELLING YOU THE TRUTH, ARCHIE!
WHAT ARE YOU GOING TO DO, MISTER ?! TAKE ME TO THE POLICE ?

NO! I'M GOING TO BRING YOU HOME AND TELL YOUR PARENTS! NOW WHERE DO YOU LIVE ?
8

DON'T DO THAT MISTER, PLEASE! THEY HAVE ENOUGH PROBLEMS AS IT IS! I ALWAYS TELL THEM SOMEBODY GIVES ME THE FOOD OR MONEY I BRING HOME!
THAT STILL DOESN'T MAKE IT RIGHT TO STEAL! I'M SURE THEY WOULDN'T LIKE YOU DOING THINGS LIKE THAT!

HEY! COME BACK HERE!
I'LL GET HIM, ARCHIE!

LEAVE ME ALONE, MISTER! YOU HAVE YOUR HUB-CAPS BACK!

WATCH OUT FOR THAT BUSH!
OOF!
THUMP!
4

ARE YOU OKAY, SONNY ?
SOB! LOOK AT WHAT YOU MADE ME DO!
SNIFF! YOU WENT AND MADE ME LOSE A TOOTH!
OH, YOU POOR LITTLE FELLOW!

WELL, IF YOU DIDN'T TRY TO RUN AWAY, IT NEVER WOULD HAVE HAPPENED!
SNIFF! SNIFF! I DIDN'T WANT YOU TO TELL MY PARENTS WHAT I DID!

-- BUT YOU CAN'T GO ON STEALING ALL THE TIME! IT CAN ONLY GET YOU INTO MORE SERIOUS TROUBLE!
SNIFF!

ARCHIE IS RIGHT, BECAUSE IF YOU GOT PUT AWAY, THEN YOU COULDN'T BE OF ANY HELP TO YOUR PARENTS, NOW COULD YOU ?
?
5

I NEVER THOUGHT OF IT THAT WAY, BUT WHAT ELSE CAN I DO ? I CAN'T AFFORD TO BUY A SHOE SHINE BOX--- I DON'T HAVE ENOUGH MONEY FOR THE POLISH AND BRUSHES!
I KNOW WHAT YOU CAN DO!

LET'S FIND THAT TOOTH YOU LOST!
?

HERE IT IS!
WHAT DO YOU WANT ME TO DO WITH IT ?

YOU HOLD IT IN YOUR HAND AND MAKE A WISH TO THE TOOTH FAIRY FOR THAT SHOE SHINE BOX YOU WANT!
ARE YOU CRAZY LADY !? YOU DON'T THINK I BELIEVE IN THE TOOTH FAIRY STUFF DO YOU ?! THAT'S FOR SILLY LITTLE RICH KIDS!
6

HAVE YOU GONE BANANAS, SABRINA!?
SO! I SEE YOU'RE A NON-BELIEVER TOO, JUG!

WELL I'LL PROVE IT TO YOU, BUT YOU MUST SINCERELY BELIEVE WITH ALL YOUR HEART THAT MIRACLES CAN HAPPEN! NOW CLOSE YOUR EYES AND WISH!

WITCHCRAFT POWERS HEAR MY *PLEA*, AND CONJURE UP A SHOE BOX BEHIND THAT TREE!
ZAP!

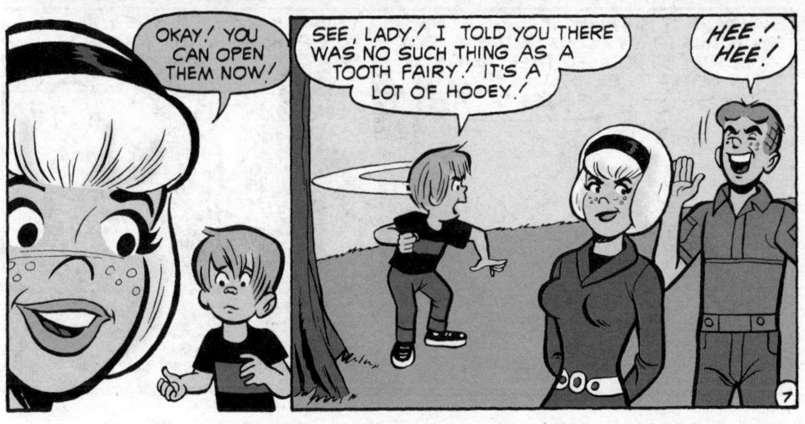
OKAY! YOU CAN OPEN THEM NOW!
SEE, LADY! I TOLD YOU THERE WAS NO SUCH THING AS A TOOTH FAIRY! IT'S A LOT OF HOOEY!
HEE! HEE!
7

IT IS ? WELL, THEN, WHAT'S THAT BEHIND THIS TREE!
?
WOW! IT'S A BRAND NEW SHOESHINE BOX!

--AND IT'S FULL OF BRUSHES AND POLISH! IT'S REAL COOL! BUT YOU CAN'T FOOL ME! ONE OF YOU GUYS PUT IT BACK THERE WHEN I HAD MY EYES CLOSED!

I KNOW I DIDN'T PUT IT THERE! DID YOU, JUG ?
DON'T LOOK AT ME! I HAD MY EYES CLOSED, TOO!

GOLLY! IS IT ALL RIGHT IF I GO HOME AND SHOW THIS TO MY MOM AND DAD ? BOY! WILL THEY BE PLEASED THAT THEIR SON IS GOING TO BE A MONEY-MAKING BUSINESSMAN!
WAIT, KID! WE'LL GIVE YOU A LIFT HOME IN THE WAGON!
8

GEE! ARE YOU GOING TO TELL MY FOLKS THAT I STOLE YOUR HUB-CAPS?

NO, KID, ONLY IF YOU PROMISE ME YOU WON'T STEAL ANY MORE!
I PROMISE I WON'T, MISTER! I PROMISE!
Archies

WE JUST WANT TO TELL YOUR DAD THAT YOU DIDN'T STEAL THAT SHOE BOX YOU HAVE!
WHERE DID IT COME FROM?
WELL IF I DIDN'T PUT IT THERE AND YOU DIDN'T, THEN WE'D BETTER START BELIEVING IN THE TOOTH FAIRY!

HA! HA! YOU'RE FUNNY, MISTER! YOU KNOW THERE'S NO SUCH THING AS A TOOTH FAIRY!

HEY, MOM! LOOK AT WHAT THESE NICE PEOPLE GAVE ME! NOW I CAN EARN A LOT OF MONEY TO HELP YOU AND POP!
9

I JUST DON'T KNOW HOW TO THANK YOU PEOPLE FOR DOING THIS FOR MY HAROLD! I WAS BEGINNING TO WORRY THAT HE WAS STEALING JUST TO HELP US OUT AND WE WOULDN'T WANT HIM TO GET INTO ANY TROUBLE! HE'S REALLY A GOOD BOY!

HAROLD WOULDN'T THINK OF STEALING! HE LOVES HIS FAMILY TOO MUCH! ISN'T THAT RIGHT, SON?
GULP! YES, SIR!

WE REALLY FEEL BAD THAT WE CAN'T GIVE OUR CHILDREN A BETTER LIFE THAN THEY HAVE! BUT THERE ARE TIMES IN LIFE WHEN THINGS JUST DON'T GO YOUR WAY!

BUT AS SOON AS THEIR FATHER GETS BACK ON HIS FEET, LIFE IS GOING TO BE A LOT BETTER!
RIGHT, MOM! AND NOW I'M GOING TO HELP OUT, TOO, BECAUSE I'M THE MAN OF THE FAMILY TILL DAD GETS BETTER!
10

WELL WE HAVE TO SPLIT, HAROLD! DON'T FORGET WHAT WE TOLD YOU!
I WON'T, SIR, AND THANK YOU!
AND IF YOU HAPPEN TO BE DOWN IN THIS NEIGHBOR-HOOD, THE SHOE-SHINE IS ON ME!

DIDN'T I TELL YOU HE WAS REALLY A GOOD BOY, ARCHIE?
I NEVER DOUBTED IT FOR A MINUTE, SABRINA!
YOU KNOW, ARCH! SOME THINGS ARE BLESSINGS IN DISGUISE!
The Archies

WHAT DO YOU MEAN BY THAT, JUG?
I MEAN THAT THE SCHOOL OF HARD KNOCKS SOMETIMES TURNS OUT THE MOST SOLID CITIZENS!

BECAUSE IF YOU EVER HAD TO DO WITHOUT THINGS WHEN YOU ARE YOUNG, MEANS YOU REALLY KNOW HOW TO APPRECIATE THEM WHEN YOU FINALLY GET THEM!
11

MAYBE IF EVERYBODY KNEW WHAT IT WAS LIKE TO SUFFER A LITTLE, THEY WOULD REALLY UNDERSTAND WHAT IT TAKES TO SUCCEED!
MY, BUT YOU'RE BEING PHILOSOPHICAL, JUG!
WHIRRR!

OH, HECK! THE CAR WON'T START!

NO WONDER, ARCH, SOMEBODY STOLE THE BATTERY!
SOMEBODY STOLE WHAT?

WELL, NOW WE'RE LEARNING WHAT IT'S LIKE TO SUFFER! NOW WHAT ARE WE GOING TO DO?
IT'S VERY SIMPLE, ARCHIE! I'LL KNOCK OUT YOUR TOOTH AND WE WISH FOR A NEW BATTERY FROM THE TOOTH FAIRY!
The End

Originally presented in **Life with Archie #113**, September 1971

Frank Doyle • Dan DeCarlo • Rudy Lapick • Barry Grossman • Bill Yoshida

HE'S THE HOTTEST THING ON THE PLANET, AT THE MOMENT!
I'LL BET HE'S SOLD A BILLION RECORDS IN THE LAST FEW YEARS!
RIVERDALE HOTEL
COTTON IN CONCERT

OH, MAN, HE'S ACTUALLY GONNA BE HERE IN TWO WEEKS!
IT WILL SEEM LIKE FOREVER!
COTTON IN CONCERT
$100.00 - RIVERDAL CIVIC CENTER

A HUNDRED BUCKS A TICKET! WE'D BETTER GET OURS EARLY!
A COTTON FLUBBERNOTE CONCERT WILL SELL OUT IN A DAY AT THE MOST!
COTTON IN

MORE LIKELY AN HOUR, YOUNG PEOPLE!
HOWDY! I'M COLONEL FLAM!

PRESIDENT AND ADVANCED AGENT OF FLUBBERNOTE ENTERPRISES, INC.!
GOLLY! YOU ACTUALLY WORK WITH COTTON FLUBBERNOTE?
2

FINE TALENT! LIKE A SON TO ME! A CREDIT TO THE ENTERTAINMENT INDUSTRY!
OH, MORE THAN THAT! HE "IS" THE ENTERTAINMENT INDUSTRY!
AND HIS GROUP THE FLUBBERNOTE FIVE -- THEY'RE GREAT, TOO!
(SIGH) WHO WOULDN'T BE GREAT ACCOMPANYING A SINGER LIKE THAT?
MAN! I WISH THE ARCHIES COULD BACK UP A MUSICAL GENIUS LIKE COTTON!
WOW! WOULDN'T THAT BE A GROOVE!
"THE ARCHIES?" YOU HAVE A GROUP?
OH, YES SIR! AND PRETTY GREAT, IF I DO SAY SO MYSELF!
OH, THERE YOU ARE, COLONEL FLAM! THIS TELEGRAM JUST ARRIVED FOR YOU!
WHY THANK YOU, EVELYN!
3

OH, DISASTER! OH, CHAOS! OH, CATASTROPHE!
TROUBLE, SIR?

THE FLUBBERNOTE FIVE! THE BUS WAS IN AN ACCIDENT! TWO OF THEM IN THE HOSPITAL!
HOW AWFUL!

COTTON CAN'T SING WITHOUT HIS GROUP! YOU'LL HAVE TO CANCEL THE CONCERT!
HEY! HEY! HAVE I GOT AN IDEA!!
THE ARCHIES!
EGAD!

COULD YOU DO IT? WOULD YOU DO IT?
WE CAN AND WILL!!

BRILLIANT! LOCAL GROUP PLAYING WITH COTTON! THE PEOPLE WILL LOVE IT!
I'LL GET SOME NEW POSTERS PRINTED UP!
4

AND SOON:
LOOK! THE ARCHIES ARE PLAYING WITH THE GREAT COTTON FLUBBERNOTE!
THIS WILL PUT RIVERDALE ON THE MAP FOR SURE!
I WOULDN'T MISS THIS FOR ANYTHING!
COTTON IN CONCERT with The Archies
$100.00
I WISH THE CIVIC CENTER WAS TEN TIMES LARGER! PEOPLE ARE OFFERING DOUBLE THE PRICE--- FOR STANDING ROOM!
GROOVY!
TOMORROW NIGHT IS THE CONCERT! WHEN WILL COTTON ARRIVE?
NOW BE BACKSTAGE BY SEVEN-THIRTY! IT WILL BE A BIG NIGHT FOR ALL OF US!
DON'T WORRY! WE HAVE TO BE VERY CAREFUL SNEAKING HIM INTO THESE SMALL TOWNS! HE COULD GET MOBBED!
SURE! THAT'S RIGHT!
THOSE BIG STARS CAN GET TORN TO PIECES BY THEIR LOYAL FANS!
I'M GOING TO GET HIS AUTOGRAPH!
5

THE FOLLOWING NIGHT---
OH, MAN! AM I NERVOUS!
I NEVER SAW SUCH A PACKED HOUSE!
I SURE WISH COTTON WOULD ARRIVE!
WHERE'S COLONEL FLAM?
The Archies

JUG, RUN OVER TO THE HOTEL AND TELL COLONEL FLAM IT'S ALMOST TIME TO START!
HE TOOK OVER THE WHOLE SEVENTH FLOOR!
OKAY!

SEVEN, PLEASE!
"SEVEN?"

THEY CHECKED OUT ABOUT AN HOUR AGO! AN OLD GUY AND A GROUP OF GROOVY GIRLS!
HE TOOK OFF IN A MINI-BUS, LOOKIN' REAL HAPPY!
URK!!
6

OMIGOSH! WE'VE BEEN HAD!
THE TOWNSPEOPLE HAVE BEEN HAD! THEY PAID THOUSANDS FOR THIS CONCERT!
I'M GOING TO SEE WHAT MY DADDY CAN DO!
The Archies
OH, HE USED YOU, ALL RIGHT! HE STOLE FROM YOUR TOWN AND LEFT YOU TO FACE THE MUSIC!
OOH! THAT MEAN OLD MAN!
THE PEOPLE ARE GETTING RESTLESS!
I'LL TELL THEM THE TRUTH! THEY'RE OUR FRIENDS AND NEIGHBORS! THEY'LL UNDERSTAND! THEY WON'T BLAME US!
STOMP!
STOMP
STOMP!
TRAMP
THAT ARCHIE! HE'S GOT A REAL KNACK FOR READING PEOPLE!
YOU DON'T OFTEN FIND TALENT LIKE THAT ANYMORE!
WONDER IF I'M GOING TO BE KILLED BY A FRIEND OR A NEIGHBOR!
SHUT UP AND RUN!
CIVIC CENTER
COTTON
7

ONLY ONE TRUE FRIEND OBSERVES THE PLIGHT OF THE FLIGHT OF THE ARCHIES--
TSK! SALEM, THAT CROOKED COLONEL FLAM HAS GOTTEN OUR FRIENDS INTO TROUBLE!
MEOWRR

BUT A VERY POWERFUL FRIEND INDEED, IS PERT, PUGNOSED SABRINA!
NOW I KNOW AUNT HILDA WILL NOT APPROVE, BUT I CAN'T LET THIS HAPPEN TO MY FRIENDS!

HOWLING GHOUL AND GHOSTLY WAIL,
SPREAD YOUR SPELL ACROSS THE TRAIL,
EYE OF NEWT AND LIZARDS TAIL,
LET ALL SIGNS POINT TO RIVERDALE!

AND ALL THE SIGN POSTS ON THE ROADS LEADING FROM TOWN DO AN ABOUT FACE!
SNAP!
RIVERDALE
SWOOSH!

COLONEL, YOU DUMB OL' GOAT! LOOK AT THAT SIGN!
YOU GOT US TURNED AROUND!
WATCH WHERE YOU'RE GOING!
WE'RE HEADING BACK TO RIVERDALE!
RIVERDALE
8

THAT'S IMPOSSIBLE! THE SIGN MUST BE WRONG!
WELL THERE'S ANOTHER! THEY CAN'T ALL BE WRONG!
RIVERDALE

AND SO THE BUS WHEELS ABOUT AND STREAKS BACK TOWARD THE FRIENDLY LITTLE TOWN IT HAD JUST LEFT!
CAN'T UNDERSTAND HOW I MADE THAT MISTAKE!
RIVERDALE

WONDER WHAT TOWN THIS IS? SOME SORT OF LOCAL CELEBRATION SEEMS TO BE IN PROGRESS!

HEY! IT'S FLAM THE CROOK!
GAK! IT'S RIVERDALE!!
GET HIM!
HE STOLE OUR MONEY!
LET ME GET MY HANDS ON HIM!

WE GOT IT! WE GOT ALL THE MONEY BACK!
RELAX EVERYBODY! WE'LL REDEEM ALL THE TICKETS!
THOSE THIEVES OUGHT TO BE PUT IN JAIL!
AND HOW ABOUT THE GREAT COTTON FLUBBERNOTE?
HE'S INNOCENT!
GROCERIES
SODA SHOPPE

HE KNEW NOTHING ABOUT THIS! I TRACKED HIM DOWN! HE'S ON TOUR IN SOUTH AMERICA!

I SPOKE TO HIM ON THE PHONE! HE'S SORRY THIS CROOK USED HIS NAME IN ORDER TO ROB YOU!
10

AND HE'S FLYING UP NEXT WEEK TO GIVE A FREE CONCERT FOR RIVERDALE WITH THE ARCHIES PLAYING!
HURRAY FOR COTTON FLUBBERNOTE!
HURRAY FOR THE ARCHIES!
SO, THANKS TO SABRINA, THE TEENAGE WITCH, EVERYBODY WAS HAPPY--EXCEPT SABRINA!
YOU DID IT AGAIN! YOU USED YOUR POWERS TO DO GOOD! WHEN WILL YOU EVER LEARN?
WE'RE WITCHES--- NOT LONE RANGERS!!
I'M SORRY, AUNT HILDA! REALLY I AM! I JUST COULDN'T RESIST HELPING MY FRIENDS!
W-ELL, I'LL FORGIVE YOU THIS TIME--- IF YOU GET ME A FRONT ROW SEAT AND AN AUTOGRAPHED PICTURE OF COTTON FLUBBERNOTE!
I REALLY DIG THAT GUY!
HA, HA! YOU GOT YOURSELF A DEAL, AUNT HILDA!
The End

Originally presented in **Archie's TV Laugh Out #14**, September 1972

George Gladir • Bill Vigoda • Chic Stone • Bill Yoshida

I'LL TELL YOU WHAT THE TROUBLE IS! IT'S THIS SOFT-HEARTED NIECE OF MINE! SHE WANTS TO THROW A PARTY FOR ALL HER DING-A-LING HUMAN FRIENDS AND I'M AGAINST IT!
BUT, AUNT HILDA! I GET INVITED TO ALL THEIR PARTIES!

WELL, WITCHES DON'T GO AROUND THROWING PARTIES FOR MORTALS! WE'RE SUPPOSED TO BE SCARING THEM!

BUT, I DON'T WANT TO SCARE MY FRIENDS! I JUST WANT TO HAVE A LITTLE GET-TOGETHER!

NOT IN THIS HOUSE YOU WON'T, BECAUSE I FORBID IT! IT'S JUST NOT OUR WITCHCRAFT WAYS!
OH, (SOB!) AND I WENT AND TOLD THEM IT WAS OKAY!
JUST A MINUTE, SABRINA!
2

IF YOU REALLY WANT THAT PARTY, I'M GOING TO LET YOU HAVE IT!
?
WHAT?

YOU MEAN I CAN, DELLA? GEE! THAT'S WONDERFUL!
HAVE YOU GONE SOFT ON MORTALS TOO?

WELL, SHE'S NOT GOING TO HAVE ANY PARTY IN THIS HOUSE! I'M SURPRISED AT YOU, DELLA, YOU'RE SUPPOSED TO BE OUR HEAD WITCH!
WELL IF YOU WON'T LET HER HAVE IT HERE, SHE'LL JUST HAVE TO USE OUR WITCH HEADQUARTERS UP ON GRAVEYARD HILL!

AND I'LL EVEN SUPPLY THE PARTY WITH SERVANTS AND ENTERTAINMENT! HOW DOES THAT SOUND, SABRINA?

OUT OF SIGHT, DELLA! I COULD JUST KISS YOU!
HAVE YOU GONE BANANAS, DELLA?
3

THANKS, DELLA! I'LL HAVE ALL MY FRIENDS THERE BY 8 O'CLOCK!
HOLY HALLOWEEN! WHAT HAS HAPPENED TO THE WONDERFUL WORLD OF WITCHES?

WILL YOU RELAX, AUNT HILDA! WE'LL MAKE A BONAFIDE WITCH OUT OF SABRINA YET!

WHAT ARE YOU TALKING ABOUT, DELLA?
I'M GOING TO SHOW HER THE PROPER WAY FOR A WITCH TO THROW A PARTY FOR MORTALS!

FIRST, I'D LIKE YOU TO MEET HUGO AND IGOR, THE SERVANTS FOR THE PARTY!
ZAP!
4

YIPE.!!

I THOUGHT YOU'D LIKE THEM, HILDA!
LIKE THEM? WHY (SHUDDER) THEY'RE BEAUTIFUL!

AND FOR THE ENTERTAINMENT OF THE EVENING THERE WILL BE COUNT DRACKO AND THE WEIRDO WOLF!
ZAP!

WOW! THAT'S FREAKY, DELLA! WHY DIDN'T I THINK OF SOMETHING LIKE THAT?

VERY SIMPLE, HILDA, BECAUSE I'M HEAD WITCH AND, YOU'RE NOT!
YOU REALLY TELL IT LIKE IT'S SUPPOSED TO BE, DELLA!
5

BUT WON'T THIS SCARE THOSE DING-A-LING HUMANS OUT OF THEIR MINDS ?
EXACTLY, HILDA! AND WHEN SABRINA SEES THE KIND OF FUN SHE'S MISSING SHE WON'T WANT TO BE LIKE THOSE SILLY MORTALS ANYMORE!

HA! HA! HA! HEE! HEE! DELLA, I'M GOING TO RECOMMEND YOU FOR A PROMOTION!

HEE! HEE! HEE! I WOULDN'T WANT TO MISS THIS FOR ALL THE TOAD'S LEGS IN A CAULDRON!
I KNEW YOU WOULD BE PLEASED!

LATER :
NOW NO CACKLING, HILDA, WE DON'T WANT TO GIVE ANYTHING AWAY!
HEE! HEE! HERE THEY COME NOW!
6

GULP! YOU MEAN THIS IS WHERE WE'RE GOING TO HAVE THE PARTY, SABRINA?

IT LOOKS LIKE A HAUNTED HOUSE! I DON'T KNOW IF I WANT TO GO IN THERE!
THERE'S NOTHING TO BE AFRAID OF, KIDS!

JUST THINK OF THE ROOM WE'LL HAVE FOR DANCING! JUST FOLLOW ME AND WE'LL COMMENCE WITH THE FESTIVITIES!
HOLD MY HAND, ARCHIE!
LET ME HOLD THE OTHER ONE!

EEEKK! EEYOW!

GASP! EEEEK!
7

HEE! HEE! THAT'S MUSIC TO MY EARS, DELLA!

LET'S GO AND SEE THE POOR FRIGHTENED HUMANS! THEY PROBABLY PASSED OUT FROM FRIGHT BY NOW!

WHAT A GREAT PARTY, SABRINA! WHO WOULD EVER THINK OF HAVING A SPOOK PARTY LIKE THIS? IT GIVES ME GOOSE PIMPLES!
IT'S GROOVY, SABRINA! WHO ELSE BUT YOU WOULD THINK OF HIRING ACTORS TO DRESS UP AS GHOULS? I WAS SCARED SILLY!
MY HAIR IS STILL UP ON END! THIS HAS GOT TO BE THE PARTY OF THE YEAR!
OH, DELLA, THANK YOU, YOU SURE KNOW WHAT KIDS ENJOY!
SHEESH! WHAT WERE YOU SAYING ABOUT MORTALS, DELLA?
-- I THINK IT WAS "WHAT FOOLS WE *IMMORTALS* BE"!
The End

Originally presented in **Little Archie #74**, October 1972

Dexter Taylor • Rudy Lapick • Barry Grossman • Bill Yoshida

HOW ABOUT WET PAINT? HA! HA!
?

T-THAT'S A TERRIBLE JOKE, REGGIE!
YEAH! IT'S TERRIBLY FUNNY! YUK! YUK!
HOP
HEE! HEE!
HA! HA!

D-DON'T YOU REALIZE I GOT PAINT ON MY CLOTHES?
SO WHAT? THE PAINT WASHES OFF!
·CANDY · ICE CREAM

SEE!
CANDY ·

HAR! HAR! DID ANYONE TELL YOU THAT YOU'RE ALL WET, SABRINA?

(SPUTTER!) I THINK YOU HAVE THE BRAINS OF A MONKEY, REGGIE MANTLE!
COOL IT, SABRINA! IT'S HOT TODAY! YOU'LL DRY OFF!
·CANDY · ICE CR
2

NOW I'VE GOT TO GO HOME AND CHANGE ALL MY CLOTHES!
HA! HA! YUK! YUK!
CANDY

OOOOOOH! WHAT I'D LIKE TO DO TO REGGIE MANTLE---
---AS A MATTER OF FACT, I THINK I WILL!
CANDY · ICE CREAM

REGGIE, SEE! REGGIE, DO! LET'S MAKE A MONKEY OUT OF YOU!

ZAP!
WOW!
· CANDY · ICE CREAM ·

THERE'S A MONKEY LOOSE OUTSIDE, LITTLE ARCHIE!
O'BOY! LET'S TRY AND CATCH IT!

YII!
THERE GOES EVERY CUSTOMER!
SHOP
3

DON'T YOU THINK THAT MONKEY LOOKS A LOT LIKE REGGIE, LITTLE ARCHIE?
NAW! THE MONKEY IS BETTER LOOKING!

MEANWHILE---
I SHOULDN'T HAVE PULLED THAT MEAN TRICK ON REGGIE--- WITCHES SHOULD NEVER LET THEMSELVES GET MAD!

I'D BETTER GO BACK AND TRY TO UNDO EVERYTHING!

OH, NO!
REGGIE'S GONE!
SHOP
SODA · CANDY · ICE CREAM
SCREECH!

D-DID YOU SEE REGGIE, POP?
HMPH! THAT'S THE ONLY ONE I DIDN'T SEE! EVERYONE ELSE LEFT TO CHASE A MONKEY!

ONE THING I DON'T NEED IS ALL THIS MONKEY BUSINESS!
CAN YOU SHOW ME WHICH WAY THEY ALL WENT, POP?
4

I GUESS I'LL JUST CLOSE FOR THE REST OF THE DAY!
DON'T, POP! WHEN I GET BACK, EVERYONE WILL WANT SOMETHING TO DRINK!

MEANWHILE, REGGIE'S ANTICS HAVE ATTRACTED QUITE A CROWD---
HIRAM! LOOK AT THE FUNNY LITTLE MONKEY!
COME ON! LET'S JOIN ALL THE KIDS!

AND AROUND THE CORNER ON THE NEXT BLOCK---
BUSINESS SHE'S A NO GOOD TODAY!
MAYBE IT'SA TOO HOT!

MOMMA MIA! ANOTHER MONKEY!
?
?

TWO MONKEYS!
THEY'RE GOING TO DANCE!

HA! HA!
THEY'RE GREAT!
CLAP! CLAP!
5

HERE! LET ME PUT SOMETHING IN YOUR CUP!
ME TOO!
T-THIS IS THE BIGGA DAY TONY EVER HAVE!
CLANK!

EVEN I FEEL LIKE DANCING NOW!
SO DO I!
CLAP! CLAP!

EVERYBODY DANCE!
?

MONKEY LEAVE! MONKEY GO! LET THE SHAPE OF REGGIE SHOW!

ZAP!
REGGIE!
Y-YOU SEEMED TO COME RIGHT OUT OF THIN AIR!

LOOK! REGGIE IS WEARING THE SAME CLOTHES AS ONE OF THE MONKEYS!
BRING BACK THE MONKEY! HE LOOKS BETTER!
LISTEN, LITTLE ARCHIE!
6

GEE.! ALL THAT RUNNING AND DANCING MADE ME THIRSTY.!
LET'S GO BACK TO THE CHOCKLIT SHOPPE FOR A SODA.!
GOOD IDEA.! (SMACK!)

I'M HOT TOO, HIRAM.! SUPPOSE WE JOIN THE CHILDREN.!
VERY WELL, MY DEAR.!

OPEN UP, POP.! WE ALL WANT SODAS.!
I WANT THE CHOK'LIT SHOP SPECIAL.! MR. LODGE IS TREATING.!
HUH ?

SAY, SABRINA.! HOW DID YOU KNOW ALL THIS WAS GOING TO HAPPEN ?
HEH.! HEH.! MAYBE A LITTLE MONKEY TOLD ME, POP.!

EVERYONE IS HERE EXCEPT REGGIE.!
I WONDER WHERE REGGIE WENT!

IT'S STRANGE.! ALL I WANT TO DO IS HANG FROM A TREE AND EAT BANANAS.!
THE END
7

Originally presented in **Little Archie #76**, January 1973

Dexter Taylor • Rudy Lapick • Bill Yoshida

VERONICA MADE A *DATE* WITH *BOTH* OF THEM!
THEY WERE FIGHTING TO SEE WHO TAKES HER OUT!

HERE'S WHERE I THINK I CAN HELP THEM OUT!
SECRET WORDS FOR WITCHES
ZELDA ZUMP

TO MAKE YOU HAPPY SO YOU'LL NEVER FEEL BLUE--- HERE'S A VERONICA FOR EACH OF YOU!

NOW YOU BOYS WILL NEVER FIGHT OVER ME AGAIN!
ZAP!
YIII! I WONDER IF MR. LODGE KNOWS HE HAS *TWINS*!

B- BUT, VERONICA, WE WERE FIGHTING OVER WHO HAS TO TELL YOU!
TELL ME WHAT?
(GULP!) NEITHER ONE OF US CAN TAKE YOU! *WE'RE BROKE!*

--- WELL ---?
THAT'S EASY! I'LL GIVE THEM BOTH SOME *SPENDING MONEY!*
SECRET WORDS FOR WITCHE
2

MAKE SOME MONEY--- COINS AND THE REST! PUT IT TOGETHER IN A TREASURE CHEST!

WOW!
QUICK! OPEN IT UP!
ZAP!

WE'RE RICH!
NOW YOU BOYS CAN TAKE VERONICA OUT!

ARE YOU KIDDING? I'VE WANTED TO BUY A BASKET-BALL FOR WEEKS!
I KNOW WHERE THERE'S A SWELL MODEL PLANE!

HUMPH! GOOD RIDDANCE!
I HOPE WE NEVER SEE LITTLE ARCHIE AND REGGIE AGAIN!

W-WHERE DID I GO WRONG NOW?
IT'S EASY FOR VERONICA TO SAY THAT! ALL I'D EVER WANT IS LITTLE ARCHIE!
3

GIVE ME SOMETHING--- STRONG AND WITH POWER, THAT WILL ATTRACT A BOY EVERY MINUTE AND HOUR!
ZAP!

A CHARM BRACELET!
IT HAS A SCENT THAT WILL ATTRACT THAT SPECIAL BOY FOR YOU, BETTY!

HERE COMES LITTLE ARCHIE! TRY IT!
OKAY!

AHEM! LITTLE ARCHIE!
SNIFF! SNIFF!
HEY!
AIRPLANE

I SEE YOU IN A NEW LIGHT, BETTY!
SNIFF!
YOU'RE WONDERFUL!
HUH?

YOUR ARM SMELLS LIKE A NICE JUICY HAMBURGER!
(SMACK!)
WHAT?
4

I CAN'T HELP MYSELF!
WAIT! WAIT! WILL YOU LET ME GET IT OFF MY ARM?
OH, DEAR! I DID IT WRONG AGAIN!
SNAP! SNAP!

WHEW! I ALMOST DIDN'T GET IT OFF IN TIME!
CHOMP! CHOMP!

I'VE GOT TO STOP ALL THIS MAGIC POWER!
THE BOOK SAYS TO TURN TO PAGE 73!

PAGE 73 HAS BEEN RIPPED OUT!

QUICK! I NEED HELP, AUNT ZELDA!
MERCY, SABRINA! WHAT'S WRONG?

I- I FOUND YOUR BOOK ON MAGIC! I TRIED TO HELP MY FRIENDS!
OH, MY! THAT BOOK IS POWERFUL!
5

IT WAS TERRIBLE.! EVERYTHING WENT WRONG.!
I THINK I CAN HELP YOU OUT, SABRINA.!

IT SO HAPPENS THAT I MEMORIZED EVERY WORD ON PAGE 73.!
GOLLY, Y-YOU DID?

YOU STAND ON ONE FOOT AND SAY, "CIGAM SDRAWKCAB" THREE TIMES.!

ZAP! ZAP! ZAP!
VERONICA'S GONE.!
POOF!
POOF.!
POOF!
POOF!

YOUR AUNT HILDA TORE THAT PAGE OUT MANY MANY YEARS AGO.!
WHY DID AUNT HILDA DO THAT?

WHEN I WAS YOUR AGE I TRIED THE VERY SAME THING.!
THE END
6

SABRINA THE TEENAGE WITCH in CARNIVAL CAPERS

WHAT'S GOING ON, LADIES?

WHEE! THERE'S A CARNIVAL IN TOWN!

WHAT FUN WE'RE GOING TO HAVE!

Originally presented in *Sabrina the Teenage Witch* #21, September 1974

Frank Doyle • Dan DeCarlo • Rudy Lapick • Bill Yoshida • Barry Grossman

KNOCK OFF THREE BOTTLES WITH ONE PITCH AND WIN A BIG DOLL!
COME ON! LET'S WIN SOME PRIZES!
HIT THE BOTTLES

NOW DON'T GET DISCOURAGED IF YOU DON'T DO WELL AT FIRST!

--- I'M GONNA USE MY SPECIAL CHARMBALL PITCH!
WINK!

WHEE! YOU KNOCKED OFF NINE BOTTLES WITH ONE PITCH! YOU WIN THREE BIG PRIZES!
2

BE CAREFUL, OL' LADY! THAT HAMMER IS HEAVY!

KLANG!

DADDY, LOOK AT THAT RED PROJECTILE!

HERE'S ANOTHER DOLL FOR OUR COLLECTION!

COVER UP THIS RED CIRCLE WITH THESE SIX SILVER DISCS AND YOU WIN ANY PRIZE YOU SEE!
PRIZ

HEH! HEH! THEY DON'T KNOW IT, BUT IT CAN'T BE DONE!

I DON'T NEED SIX DISCS TO COVER UP THE CIRCLE!
?

MY MAGIC WILL MAKE ONE DISC LARGE ENOUGH!

HERE, SABRINA! HELP US CARRY SOME OF THESE DOLLS!
PRIZES
4

WELL, I CAN SEE WHY YOU TWO LIKE CARNIVALS SO MUCH!

DON'T BE A SILLY TWIT, SABRINA!
THESE DOLLS AREN'T WHY!

HERE, DRIVER! GIVE THESE PRIZES TO YOUR ORPHANS!
OH, BOY!
THANK YOU, LADIES!
BUS
RIVERDALE ORPHANAGE

THAT'S WHY WE LIKE CARNIVALS SO MUCH!

LIKE I SAID BEFORE --- MY AUNTIES NEVER CEASE TO AMAZE ME!
END

Originally presented in **Sabrina the Teenage Witch #24**, February 1975

Frank Doyle • Dan DeCarlo • Rudy Lapick • Bill Yoshida • Barry Grossman

THE OLD ONES ARE SO SET IN THEIR WAYS.!

I'VE GOTTA BE ME, AND I FEEL GREAT AND I WANT TO SPREAD JOY TO EVERYONE.!
SO SUE ME, DELLA!

POOR OFFICER STARK.! THE WIND IS PRETTY BRISK, AND HE LOOKS CHILLY!
BAR
BA

IBBLE DE BIBBLE HE'S SURE TO FEEL BETTER, ALL BUNDLED UP IN A NICE COMFY SWEATER!
ZAP

WHAT THE ---?

EEP! SERGEANT!!
SO WHERE'S THE PIPE AND SLIPPERS, STARK? YOU WANT AN ARMCHAIR ON YOUR BEAT?
GET RID OF IT!!
2

OOPS! RAINDROPS ARE FALLING ON MY HEAD!!

THAT SWEATER WON'T DO OFFICER STARK ANY GOOD!
HE NEEDS A RAINCOAT AND AN UMBRELLA!
ZAP!!

OH NO!

ACK! THE SERGEANT!!

SIGH! MAYBE THE RAIN WILL MAKE YOU GROW! ALL MY TENDER LOVING CARE HAS HAD NO EFFECT ON YOU!!
3

NOW GROW, DARN YOU.!!

ISN'T THAT SWEET? SHE WANTS HER LITTLE PLANT TO GROW.!
ZAP

AIEEEEEEE!

YIKES! THERE GO MY EGGS.!!
THE DAIR PLAC
RIP!

HAVE NO FEAR.! HELPFUL SABRINA IS HERE.!
ZAP!

ULP.! THEY DIDN'T BREAK.!!
THE DAIR PLAC
BOING
CLUNK
4

FRESH, YOU CALL THESE EGGS, YOU CROOK? THEY ARE SO OLD, THEY'RE PETRIFIED!
FRESH EGGS
PROVOLON
CHEESE

EEP!
KRAK
SPLAT
SPLASH

TO THINK THAT I WAS WORRIED ABOUT THAT GIRL!

WELL, SHE PROVED HERSELF TODAY! SHE'S A REALLY GOOD WITCH!

SHE PRACTICALLY DESTROYED THE PEOPLE ON THAT STREET!
HEE, HEE! WHAT A DELIGHTFULLY WICKED SENSE OF HUMOR!
The END

Little Archie with Little Sabrina in ALL THOSE CHARMS

HI, KIDS! I GET LOTS OF LETTERS ASKING IF I EVER USED *MAGIC* TO HELP BETTY GET LITTLE ARCHIE !--- *HERE'S THE STORY* !

THAT LOAD LOOKS *HEAVY*, BETTY!

IT IS, LITTLE ARCHIE !

WHEEZE! PANT! PUFF!

Originally presented in **Little Archie #102**, January 1976

Dexter Taylor • Rudy Lapick • Bill Yoshida

AFTER ALL, YOU'RE NOT AS STRONG AS BETTY!
YES--- BETTY'S SUCH AN ALL-AMERICAN GIRL!

AFTER THIS, SHE'LL PROBABLY RUN UP TO THE GYM AND LIFT WEIGHTS!

THEN WHY AM I ALWAYS TREATED LIKE AN ALL-AMERICAN BOOB?
LOOK OUT!

CRASH!

ANY-THING HURT, BETTY?
O-ONLY MY FEELINGS, SABRINA!

POOR BETTY! SHE'S ALWAYS TRYING TO BE NUMBER ONE WITH LITTLE ARCHIE!

GOLLY, I'D LOVE TO HELP BETTY WIN LITTLE ARCHIE WITH MAGIC---

--NO--- I'D BETTER MIND MY OWN BUSINESS!
2

BUT WHY SHOULDN'T I USE MAGIC TO HELP BETTY ?
THIS SPECIAL CHARM BRACELET WILL MAKE ALL THE GUYS CRAZY ABOUT BETTY!

MAGIC! MAGIC! HEAR MY NOISE! HAVE THIS BRACELET ATTRACT THE BOYS!
ZAP!

WAIT, BETTY! I'VE GOT SOMETHING THAT WILL HELP YOU GET LITTLE ARCHIE!
EH ? WHAT'S THAT, SABRINA?

JUST WEAR THIS CHARM BRACELET FOR AN HOUR!
THIS CHARM BRACELET WILL ATTRACT LITTLE ARCHIE!

JUST TRY IT ON! YOU WON'T BE ABLE TO KEEP HIM AWAY!
GOLLY! I'D WEAR ANYTHING THAT WOULD ATTRACT LITTLE ARCHIE TO ME!

LATER---
WHAT'S WRONG, LITTLE ARCHIE ? YOU LOOK STRANGE!
I - I SUDDENLY FEEL CRAZY ABOUT BETTY!
3

HUMPH! THAT FEELING ISN'T STRANGE! IT'S RIDICULOUS!
YEAH! YEAH! S'LONG VICTOR!
ZAP!

WAIT, BETTY! LET ME WALK HOME WITH YOU!
I'M SORRY, LITTLE ARCHIE! I JUST DON'T FEEL UP TO CARRYING YOUR BOOKS TODAY!

NO! NO! I'LL CARRY YOUR BOOKS! I WANT TO WALK *ANYWHERE* WITH YOU!
OH, WOW! THIS CHARM BRACELET IS REALLY WORKING!

WAIT, BETTY! I'M CRAZY ABOUT YOU, TOO!
HUH?

BEAT IT, REGGIE!
YOU CAN'T TAKE *MY GIRL* AWAY FROM ME, LITTLE ARCHIE!
Y-YOUR GIRL?

MAN! THAT BRACELET SMELLS JUST LIKE A *HAMBURGER*, BETTY!
ZAP
JUGHEAD!
4

GET AWAY FROM MY GIRL, YOU CREEPS!
FANGS FOGARTY!

GOLLY, BETTY! I COULD JUST HUG YOU TO PIECES!
UGH! YOU'RE CRUSHING ME!
KERUNCH!

WAIT! THIS STUPID BRACELET IS THE CAUSE OF ALL THIS!

I NEVER WANT TO SEE THAT BRACELET AGAIN!

WHERE AM I?
NOW WHAT'S GOT INTO BETTY?

I'M SORRY, SABRINA! I---ER---AH--- SORT OF LOST THE BRACELET!
OH, DEAR! THAT CHARM BRACELET STILL HAS A MAGIC SPELL!

HI, DOLL!
SHE DATES ME FIRST!
OOOOH! I LOVE IT!
NO! ME!
THE END---OR IS IT JUST THE BEGINNING?
5

Sabrina *in* "GREEN-EYED MONSTER"

OH, IT'S YOU, HARVEY!--- I WASN'T EXPECTING YOU!

OH, AND WHO WERE YOU EXPECTING ?

Script & Pencils: Dick Malmgren / Inks: Rudy Lapick / Letters: Bill Yoshida / Colors: Barry Grossman

A DEAR OLD FRIEND OF MINE IS COMING OVER FOR A VISIT!

AND WHO'S THAT, SABRINA ?

Originally presented in Archie's TV Laugh-Out #48, April 1977

Dick Malmgren • Rudy Lapick • Bill Yoshida • Barry Grossman

GARY CORBET, WE WERE FRIENDS WHERE I USED TO LIVE!
?

GARY CORBET! YOU MEAN YOUR OLD FLAME, DON'T YOU ?! I'VE HEARD YOU TALK ABOUT HIM!

WELL, WE HAD A FEW DATES, BUT THAT WAS A LONG TIME AGO!

YEAH! BUT WHEN YOU TALKED ABOUT HIM, YOU ALWAYS HAD THAT LOVE HUNGRY LOOK IN YOUR EYES!--- I REMEMBER!

HOW COULD I FORGET GARY CORBET ? YOU AND YOUR AUNT NEVER STOPPED TALKING ABOUT HIM!

-- AND NOW YOU'RE SECRETLY MEETING HIM BEHIND MY BACK!
?
2

IF YOU DON'T WANT TO GO OUT WITH ME, JUST SAY SO! I'LL WALK RIGHT OUT OF YOUR LIFE!
BUT NO! YOU WANT TO EMBARRASS ME BY BRINGING YOUR OLD SWEET-HEART RIGHT HERE INTO YOUR HOME!
YOU'RE ACTING SO CHILDISH ABOUT THIS, I DON'T EVEN WANT TO DISCUSS IT!
GARY CORBET, HUH!
BING! BONG!
BING! BONG!
HI! YOU MUST BE HARVEY? I'M---
3

I KNOW WHO YOU ARE! AND IF YOU EVER SHOW YOUR FACE AROUND HERE, I'M GOING TO REARRANGE IT FOR YOU!
THUMP!

NOW GET LOST, LOVER BOY!

ZAP!

HARVEY! WAS THERE SOMEONE AT THE DOOR?
?
NOW WHERE DID HE GO?

THAT'S FUNNY! I COULD HAVE SWORN I HEARD HIM TALKING TO GARY!
SHE SURE HAS SOME WEIRD FRIENDS!
RIB-IT!
RIB-IT!
END

Originally presented in Little Archie #136, November 1978

Dexter Taylor • Barry Grossman

MODELING CLAY

NOW I'LL PUT A **HEX** ON OL' JUG AND SEE IF IT WORKS!
MAGIC DARK SECRETS

MAGIC! MAGIC! I'LL USE A PIN... MAKE JUGGIE FEEL IT ON THE CHIN!
MAGIC DARK SECRET
PINS

MEANWHILE, OUTSIDE IN THE HALL -
(SMACK!) SOMEBODY LEFT SOME FOOD!

SMACK! CRUNCH! GULP!
HEY!

WHADDAYA DOING WITH MY LUNCH?
2

TRY CHEWING ON THIS!

AT LEAST JUGHEAD DIDN'T EAT ALL OF IT!
OOOOH!

I-I HOPE I CAN STILL EAT FOOD!
I-IT WORKED! I DID IT!

NOW I'LL DO ONE OF LITTLE ARCHIE!
?

WITCHCRAFT? SO! REGGIE MUST THINK THAT LITTLE ARCHIE WILL FEEL IT WHEN HE STICKS PINS IN IT!

WELL, I THINK I'LL USE SOME MAGIC TO SEE HOW REGGIE FEELS!
3

MAGIC DOLL! DO YOUR THING! WHERE HE PUTS THE PIN, HAVE REGGIE FEEL THE STING!
ZAP!

AH, LITTLE ARCHIE!
HERE GOES!

YAAAAAG!

GEE! IS ANYTHING WRONG, REG?
I-I DON'T KNOW!

C'MON, VERONNY! LET'S MAKE THE SCENE AT THE CHOCKLIT SHOPPE!
OKAY, LITTLE ARCHIE!

I'LL GIVE LITTLE ARCHIE A DOUBLE WHAMMY THIS TIME!
4

YOW!
AGG!

I-I DON'T GET IT! WHEREVER I PUT A PIN, IT HAPPENS TO ME!

I'M GETTING RID OF THIS FAST!

WELL, I GUESS I CAN GO HOME NOW THAT REGGIE HAS BEEN TAUGHT A LESSON!
I'D BETTER HURRY... IT LOOKS STORMY!

JUST WHEN I THOUGHT I WAS BEGINNING TO KNOW EVERYTHING ABOUT MAGIC...

...NOW I FEEL LIKE I DON'T KNOW ENOUGH TO COME IN OUT OF THE RAIN!
THE END
5

Professor Pither's Pill

Pluto plans to ruin the Riverdale Regatta! Luckily Della the head witch assigns Sabrina the job of preventing it. Sabrina even shrinks herself to miniature size to foil his plan. I love this! It is just crazy! Bob Bolling is a master storyteller! Great maps, scenery, planes, underwater moments, varying panels, and even an "I'll get your for this, Sabrina" ending! A lot of the greatest Archie comics came from the stories by Mr. Bolling!

✶ **Jack Copley**
Archie Historian

Horrorvision

I've been a die hard Archie Comics fan since I got my first *Betty and Veronica Double Digest* when I was 9 years old, but I have never been able to pick a favorite character. That was until the last few years when I've realized that there's one character who has always been my favorite, I just didn't realize it! There's not a version of Sabrina that I don't enjoy! I absolutely adore the original comics, every animated show, the 1996 sitcom starring Melissa Joan Hart (and the corresponding comics), the manga series by Tania Del Rio, *The Chilling Adventures of Sabrina,* and now the newest series by Kelly Thompson.
I love every iteration of the character! "Horrorvision" was included in that first Double Digest of mine, and right away it stood out to me just because of how fun and goofy of a story it is. It was the perfect first encounter with a character who has ended up meaning so much to me.

✶ **Gillian Swearingen**
Archie Contributor

Sabrina in "THE GO FOR"

Originally presented in **Sabrina the Teenage Witch #52**, May 1979

Dick Malmgren • Rudy Lapick • Bill Yoshida • Barry Grossman

PUFF!
PUFF!
PUFF!
HE SAID HE WAS ONLY WALKING HER TO THE STORE.!
HOGWASH!
YOU TELL HIM THAT I SAW HIM GO INTO THE MALT SHOP WITH HER.!
WHO'S HE KIDDING ?!
PUFF!
PUFF! PUFF!
2

YOU TELL HER THAT SHE WAS BUYING SOME ICE CREAM FOR HER MOTHER AND SHE LEFT ALONE!
I STAYED THERE AND RAPPED WITH THE FELLOWS!
AND THAT'S THE TRUTH!
THIS IS DUMB, RUNNING LIKE THIS! I'M NOT A JOGGER!
SLAM!
ZAP!
NOW THIS IS MORE LIKE IT!
MUSH!
3

HE SAID HE WAS IN THERE WAITING FOR YOU!
I WILL NOT APOLOGIZE!
WHO DOES HE THINK HE IS, ANYWAY?
I'D BETTER ZAP SOMETHING MORE UP-TO-DATE, PEOPLE ARE STARING!
ZAP!
?
VA-ROOM!
GANG WAY!
RRRRRR
RRRRRRR
4

I WON'T APOLOGIZE EITHER!
I DIDN'T DO ANYTHING!
GOOD GRIEF!
THIS DARN HAT IS IN MY FACE! I CAN'T SEE!
THUMP!
THIS IS THE LAST TIME I'LL GET INVOLVED IN SABRINA'S ARGUMENTS!
END

SABRINA THE TEENAGE WITCH IN

HI, JASPER! GOT A NEW DOG?

YEAH, HARVEY! AIN'T HE A BEAUT?

Malmgren / D'Agostino

Originally presented in *Sabrina the Teenage Witch* #58, February 1980

Dick Malmgren • Jon D'Agostino

ACK!
WHAT'S WRONG, JASPER ?

THAT MOVIE ON TV LAST NIGHT! DIDN'T YOU SEE IT ?

THERE WAS THIS FELLA, SEE? EVERYBODY THOUGHT HE WAS MR. NICE GUY!
SO?

BUT THIS DOG IN THE PICTURE GROWLED AT HIM ALL THE TIME!

AND IT TURNED OUT -- THE GUY WAS--

-- A VAMPIRE!
2

HMMMPH! DO YOU KNOW WHAT HE'S THINKING?
I'M AFRAID I DO!

YAP! YAP! YAP! YAP!

IT'S A WELL KNOWN FACT!
ANIMALS KNOW THESE THINGS! THEY CAN SENSE IT!

SHE'S A VAMPIRE.!!

HA! YOU SILLY TWERP!
SABRINA'S MY GIRLFRIEND!

IF SHE WERE A VAMPIRE WOULDN'T I HAVE TEETH MARKS ON MY NECK?
3

HEY! YOU'RE RIGHT! IF SHE WERE A VAMPIRE SHE WOULDN'T PASS UP A PUSHOVER LIKE YOU!

FUNNY HOW OL' SPOT GROWLED AND BARKED AT HER, THOUGH!

HEY! HEY, SPOT! COME BACK HERE!
ARF!
ARF!

OH FOR--
ARF! ARF! YAP!
YAP! YIP!
SNARL!

OKAY! I GOT IT NOW! -- SHE'S NOT A VAMPIRE!!!

SHE'S A WEREWOLF!!!
4

JASPER! THAT'S EVEN SILLIER! IF SHE WERE, SHE'D TURN INTO A WOLF AT NIGHT!

AND BY THIS TIME I'D BE TORN TO SHREDS!
I'M WITH HER EVERY NIGHT!
ALIEN BEING!

THAT'S WHAT SHE IS, AN ALIEN BEING!!!
STOP BEING SO CHILDISH!
GRRRR!

HA, HA! OKAY, JASPER! I'VE GOT TO ADMIT IT! YOU'RE ON THE RIGHT TRACK!

I'M NOT A VAMPIRE OR A WEREWOLF!
THEN WHY DOES OL' SPOT...?

I'M JUST A COMMON OL' WITCH!!!
MFFP!
5

AHA! I KNEW IT! WHAT DID I TELL YOU, WISE GUY?

I KNEW OL' SPOT COULDN'T BE WRONG!
ANIMALS KNOW THESE THINGS!

ARF! GROWF!
SNARL!
C'MON, SPOT! YOU'VE MADE YOUR POINT!

FUNNEE! BEAUTIFUL, SABRINA! THAT WAS THE ONLY WAY TO GET RID OF THE LITTLE PEST!

HE'S HAPPY NOW AND HE'LL LEAVE US ALONE!--- THE LITTLE NUT REALLY THINKS YOU'RE A WITCH!
YUP! HE'S NEW! AND OL' SPOT IS NO ORDINARY DOG! NO SIRREE!
?
RIBBIT!
RIBBIT!
END

SABRINA
"CASTLE HASSLE"

AUNT HILDA SAID I SHOULD VISIT COUSIN AMBROSE'S FRIEND WHILE I'M VACATIONING HERE IN TRANSYLVANIA !
TRANSYLVANIA Hbf
COUNT VIKTOR

WOULD YOU TAKE ME TO COUNT VIKTOR'S CASTLE ?
COUNT VIKTOR'S CASTLE ?!

I WOULDN'T GO THERE IF MY LIFE DEPENDED ON IT... AND IT DOES!
?

Originally presented in *Sabrina the Teenage Witch #65*, February 1981

George Gladir • Bob Bolling • Rudy Lapick • Bill Yoshida • Barry Grossman

CASTLE VIKTOR
WHEW! THAT WAS QUITE A WALK FROM THE TRAIN STATION!

GOOD EVENING, CHILD! I VAS EXPECTING YOU!
YOU STARTLED ME, COUNT VIKTOR!
POP!

HEH! HEH! LET ME TAKE YOU INTO MY ARMS AND GREET YOU PROPERLY!

GEE! WHAT CREEPY LOOKING TEETH YOU HAVE! DIDN'T YOUR PARENTS EVER TAKE YOU TO AN ORTHODONTIST?

HERE! LET ME GET RID OF THOSE FANGS FOR YOU!
ZAP!

GASP! MY FANGS! THEY'RE GONE!
JUST LOOK AT THE IMPROVEMENT IN THIS MIRROR!
2

BUT I DO NOT REFLECT AN IMAGE!
BUT THIS IS A SPECIAL ENCHANTED MIRROR!

IT EVEN REFLECTS THE IMAGES OF GREMLINS AND LEPRECHAUNS!
NOT BAD! NOT BAD AT ALL!

BUT VIT OUT FANGS, HOW VILL I EXIST?... I CAN ONLY DRINK BLOOD!
THAT'S SHEER NONSENSE!

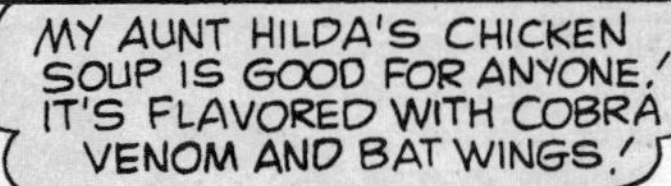
MY AUNT HILDA'S CHICKEN SOUP IS GOOD FOR ANYONE! IT'S FLAVORED WITH COBRA VENOM AND BAT WINGS!

CHICK SOUP

YOU'RE RIGHT! IT IS GOOD!
NO ADMITTANCE THE COUNT'S BEDROOM
SLURP

AND ANOTHER THING... YOU'VE GOT TO GET RID OF THIS DINGY BEDROOM ARRANGEMENT OF YOURS!
3

HAVEN'T YOU EVER HEARD OF A WATER BED?
ZAP!

OH, HEY! IT FEELS SO RELAXING AND COMFORTABLE!

AND NO WONDER YOU'RE SO PALE! YOU'VE GOT TO LET SOME DAYLIGHT INTO THIS GLOOMY PLACE!
NO! THE SUN IS RISING! I'M ALLERGIC TO SUNLIGHT! IT VILL DESTROY ME!

AUNT HILDA'S SPECIAL TANNING POTION WILL SOLVE THAT PROBLEM!
WITCHES CHICKEN FAT

YOU'RE RIGHT! I HAD NO IDEA THE SUN VAS SO BEAUTIFUL!
4

WHAT?! YOU SENT SABRINA TO VISIT MY FRIEND COUNT VIKTOR? DIDN'T YOU KNOW HE WAS A VAMPIRE?
NO!

GULP! I ONLY HOPE WE'RE NOT TOO LATE!

LOOK! THERE SHE IS!

THANK YOU FOR SENDING SABRINA TO VISIT ME!
?

SHE MADE ME SEE THE LIGHT IN MORE VAYS THAN ONE!
CASTLE ENTRANCE
THIS WAY, FOLKS!
TOUR GUIDE
I LOVE TRANSYLVANIA
FREE CASTLE TOURS
END

SABRINA

IN "TEAM EFFORT"

THAT DOES IT!

GIRLS' SUMMER BASEBALL

COACH SHADRON

GLADIR . BOLLING . LAPICK . YOSHIDA

Originally presented in **Sabrina the Teenage Witch #74**, July 1982

George Gladir • Bob Bolling • Rudy Lapick • Bill Yoshida

LATER, AT THE BOYS' PRACTICE FIELD---
CINDY REALLY HAS LOST HER CONFIDENCE --- I WISH I COULD HELP HER!
COACH

THIS CALLS FOR A **SPECIAL CREATIVE MAGIC**! THAT'S A LITTLE BEYOND ME!
COACH
6

OH, MAGIC MIRROR, IS THERE NO ONE I CAN TELL, THAT'LL PUT CINDY SAUNDERS UNDER A SUPER-CONFIDENCE SPELL?
2

ACK!
OW!
BUMP!
WELL, SABRINA! HOW NICE OF YOU TO DROP INTO MY DIMENSION!
GULP! IT'S THE HIGH PRIESTESS OF ANIMAL PROTECTORS.!!--- NO WONDER I HAVE BUTTERFLIES IN MY STOMACH!
3

WHAT BRINGS YOU TO THIS UNEARTHLY DIMENSION OF ANIMAL SPIRITS? SPEAK UP!! CAT GOT YOUR TONGUE?
MAYBE I SHOULD CHICKEN OUT--- BUT YOU OWE ME A FAVOR!

FAVOR? I DON'T RECALL—
CHECK YOUR RECORD BOOK!

BOOK-KEEPING WAS SUCH A BOAR, SO I WENT HOG-WILD AND BOUGHT A MULTI-DIMENSIONAL COMPUTER---
THERE'LL BE A SHORT PAUSE WHILE I FIND THE MEMORY BUTTON---

CLICK!
AH! THERE! OBSERVE THE FOG BANK OVER YOUR LEFT SHOULDER!

OH, YES, THE PUPPY ON THE ICE-BERG LAST WINTER!
-ON A DAY WHEN MY MAGICAL POWERS WEREN'T WORKING!

HOW MAY I HELP YOU?
WELL, IT'S CINDY SAUNDERS--- A GREAT BALL PLAYER, BUT NO CONFIDENCE--- ESPECIALLY WITH BOYS! CHECK IT OUT ON YOUR COMPUTER!
4

HMMM! I SEE! MY ANIMAL SPIRITS SHALL NOT FAIL YOU! JUST "ZAP" AT THE APPROPRIATE TIME!
I DON'T KNOW HOW TO–
THA-A-A-A-A
-ANK
-YOU!
OW!
BUMP!

SHE'LL NEVER TOUCH MY SUPER-SPEEDY SLIDER!
IT'S A TRIPLE!
SHE'S TRYING FOR HOME!
SHE'LL NEVER MAKE IT!

WOK!
ZAP!!

ZAZZZZZ!

SAFE!!!
SLITHER!

F-FOR A SPLIT SECOND THERE--- I THOUGHT CINDY LOOKED LIKE AN-AN ANIMAL!
I THOUGHT SO, TOO! SHE'S TERRIFIC!
CINDY, REPORT TOMORROW FOR OUR PRACTICE GAME WITH HASSELHEAD HIGH! YOU'RE IN THE STARTING LINE-UP!
LET'S CALL IT A DAY! I HAVE A BEASTLY HEADACHE!
I DON'T KNOW WHAT CAME OVER ME, SABRINA, BUT WHATEVER IT WAS-
IT'S GIVEN ME PLENTY OF CONFIDENCE!
AGAIN?!? NOW WHY HAVE YOU COME TO BADGER ME?
OW!
I DON'T PLAN TO HOUND YOU, HIGH PRIESTESS OF ANIMAL PROTECTORS, BUT-
BUMP!
7

I JUST WANTED TO THANK YOU FOR NOT LETTING THE BOYS MAKE A MONKEY OUT OF CINDY!
I'M RATHER SORRY--- THAT COULD HAVE BEEN AN IMPROVEMENT!

WELL, I NEVER GAVE A HOOT ABOUT BASEBALL, BUT I THINK IT'S GROOVY HAVING CINDY GO OUT FOR THE BOYS' TEAM!
LET ME SHOW YOU SOMETHING GROOVIER!
CLICK!

THE BOYS' BASEBALL TEAM GOING OUT FOR CINDY!
HAVE ANOTHER SODA, CINDY?
TOMORROW YOU'VE GOT TO SHOW US HOW YOU GRIP THE BAT!
HOW'D YOU LEARN TO SLIDE LIKE THAT?
THE END

BA-BOOM!

SABRINA

PART I

'PROFESSOR PITHER'S PILL'

Originally presented in **Sabrina the Teenage Witch #76**, November 1982

Bob Bolling • Rudy Lapick • Bill Yoshida • Barry Grossman

PROF. PITHER HAS ENDED HIS EXILE AND IS RETURNING TO EARTH!
PROF. PITHER FROM PLANET PLUTO?
PRECISELY!

AS YOU KNOW, HE'S ALWAYS LOOKING FOR MONEY TO FINANCE HIS PLANS TO DOMINATE THIS WORLD, INCLUDING THE FALKLAND ISLANDS! AND-
-HE FIGURED HIS ANTACID TABLET CREATION WOULD MAKE HIM WEALTHY, BUT -

- WHEN HE FOUND THAT NO REPUTABLE COMPANY WOULD BUY HIS ANTACID FORMULA, HE JUST COULDN'T STOMACH IT! FURTHERMORE -

- AN INSIDE SORCERER REVEALED TO ME THAT UNLESS THE RIVERDALE CHAMBER OF COMMERCE PAYS PROF. PITHER EIGHTY THOUSAND DOLLARS HE HAS THREATENED TO RUIN THE RIVERDALE REGATTA--- TOMORROW!
(GASP!) THE ANNUAL SAILBOAT RACE ON LAKE FLAKEY?! WHY, THE FIEND!

BUT, I DID HEAR THAT THE SECURITY AROUND LAKE FLAKEY TOMORROW WILL BE VERY TIGHT--- IN FACT, EVERY PRECAUTION HAS BEEN TAKEN!
THEY HAVE? THEN SHOULDN'T WE GET SOME MORE?

SABRINA! I'VE BEEN WATCHING YOU CLOSELY--- IF YOU CAN HANDLE PROF. PITHER IT WILL BE A BIG STEP UP THE LADDER FOR YOU!
I HOPE IT'S NOT THE RUNG IDEA TO PIT ME AGAINST PITHER!
2

YES, HE'S A WILY ADVERSARY!
NOT ONLY THAT, HE'S A VERY CLEVER FOE!
(GROAN!) I HOPE I'M NOT OVERDRAWN ON MY "ZAP" ACCOUNT!

REMEMBER, PROF. PITHER CAN ASSUME ANY FORM--- THE ONLY SURE WAY TO RECOGNIZE HIM IS BY HIS PECULIAR FONDNESS FOR AN AFTERSHAVE LOTION, "ESSENCE OF TASMANIAN SQUID"!
YECH!

I'LL CHECK BACK WITH YOU! I'M ON MY WAY TO A CAULDRON-WARE PARTY IN THE SEVENTH DEMENSION!

I'M MAKING MY EXIT NOW--- NO APPLAUSE, PLEASE-

BA-BOOM!
ONE LOUD CLAP WILL DO!
THUNDERATION! WHAT A FLAIR FOR THE DRAMATIC!
HOW DO YOU THINK SHE GOT TO BE HEAD WITCH?

NEXT DAY---
WHAT!? YOU'RE NOT COMING WITH US TO LAKE FLAKEY, SABRINA?!
NOT RIGHT AWAY, AUNT ZELDA! SOMETHING TELLS ME IT'S TIME TO PICK UP LITTLE COUSIN CLYDE'S BIRTHDAY GIFT! I'LL MEET YOU AT THE LAKE!
214

BUT, SA-
LET HER GO--- SHE MUST LEARN TO LISTEN TO HER INNER VOICE!
3

HI, PHIL! GOT ANYTHING HERE IN YOUR HOBBY SHOP FOR MY LITTLE COUSIN CLYDE?
I HOPE HE DOESN'T LIKE MODEL PLANES, SABRINA! SOME GUY JUST BOUGHT OUT MY ENTIRE STOCK!

UH HUH!
A REAL WEIRDO HE WAS--- HAD THE FRAGRANCE OF-ER-FISH!

FISH? FISH!? HOW ABOUT SQUID? ESSENCE OF SQUID?
UMM--- MORE LIKE AROMA OF MACKEREL? OR COULD IT BE SCENT OF STURGEON? NO, MAYBE-

TRACE OF TARPON? NO,--- HINT OF HALIBUT?--- WELL, TO ME IT WAS ALL SMELT!
MODEL PLANES!
KENIN'S HOBBIES

LAKE FLAKEY-

AT LAST!
(PUFF!) (PUFF!) PROF. PITHER'S IN TOWN, ALL RIGHT!
HE WON'T DARE SET FOOT AROUND HERE! POLICE DOGS HAVE BEEN TRAINED TO DETECT THE ODOR OF SQUID!
4

SOMEHOW HE'S GOING TO USE MODEL PLANES!
BUT THERE'S SECURITY FROM HERE ALMOST ALL THE WAY TO BONGO BAY!
BONGO BAY?
OCEAN
BONGO BAY
THRONGS OF SPECTATORS
LAKE FLAKEY
BADLANDS
KOOCHY CANAL
WHAMBAM DAM
MORE THRONGS
GOODLANDS
RIGHT ON, SABRINA--- FOR BENEATH THE PEACEFUL SURFACE OF BONGO BAY, SUNK TO A NEW LOW--- THE SUB ROSA AND ITS LONE OCCUPANT—
KYUK!
ROSA
PUDGY, PINT-SIZED PROF. PITHER ---
KYUK! KYUK! THOON LAKE FLAKEY WILL BE A THING OF THE PATHT!
PROFESSOR PITHER'S PILLS
PAT. PENDING
PROF
END OF PART I
5

SABRINA
"PROFESSOR PITHER'S PILL"
PART II
KYUK! KYUK!
RRRRRRRRRRRR
RRRRRRRP
ROSA
THERE THEY GO! EACH CARRYING A LOAD OF MY ANTATHID PILLTH!

GEESE?
NO, PLANES!
MODEL PLANES!

THEY'RE DROPPING HUNDREDS OF LITTLE OBJECTS!
PROF. PITHER'S MOISTURE-ABSORBING ANTACID PILLS!
LAKE FLAKEY IS SHRINKING! THE SAILBOATS ARE BECOMING STUCK IN AN ICKY MASS!
OH! I FEEL LIKE KEELING OVER!
THEY'RE LEAVING!
GOING BACK FOR MORE?
BAM!
GAS LINE PUNCTURED, THE MODEL GLIDES---
ZAP!
HMM! A PIECE OF MY HEAD-BAND WRAPPED AROUND THE GAS LINE SHOULD DO IT!
R-I-I-IP!
7

AH! IT STARTED!--- THE RADIO CONTROL SEEMS TO BE WORKING!
AMELIA LIVES!

WE'RE OVER BONGO BAY! (GASP!) A SUB!

KYUK! KYUK! ALL BACK THAFELY NOW!

—TO RELOAD FOR THE FINAL ATTACK ON LAKE FLAKEY THAT WILL THPELL THE END OF THE RIVERDALE REGATTA!
YECH! THE SUB REEKS WITH THE ESSENCE OF TASMANIAN SQUID!
I MUST STOP THIS MADMAN--- BUT HOW?
8

WAIT! THOSE PILLS! THAT VALVE!--- BUT I'LL HAVE TO RETURN TO NORMAL SIZE!

ZAP!
WH- ?

WHO ARE YOU? GET AWAY FROM THAT THEA-LOCK!
SABRINA IS THE NAME, AND "MUD" WILL SOON BE YOURS!

ACK! THE PILLTH ARE EXTHPANDING! THE THIDES OF THE THUB WILL BURTHT!

SLAM!
ZIP!

YOU CAN'T HIDE IN THAT CONNING TOWER, PROFESSOR! I'M GONNA ZAP THIS HATCH OFF ITS HINGES AND BRING YOU TO JUSTICE!
9

BLOOSH!

THO! FATE HATH CATHT A WITCH IN MY PATH TO WORLD CONQUETHT!

LATER...
WELL, SABRINA, YOU DID A FAIR JOB OF HANDLING PITHER--- BUT YOU DID LET HIM GIVE YOU THE SLIP!
(GROAN!) I SHOULD HAVE ZAPPED FIRST AND SPOKEN LATER!
HAPPILY, THE SAILBOAT RACES COULD CONTINUE WHEN THE FLOODGATES WERE OPENED!
WELL, ALL THAT'S WATER OVER THE DAM--- BUT I HAVE A FEELING WE HAVEN'T SEEN THE LAST OF PROF. PITHER!

CURTH YOU, THABRINA! MY NEXTHT TRIP TO EARTH WILL BE TO PUT YOU IN IT!
THE END--- FOR A WHILE

Sabrina in "QUICK CHANGE ARTIST"

WHAT'S THE MATTER, MIDGE? YOU LOOK A LITTLE DEPRESSED!

I AM, SABRINA! IT'S MOOSE AND HIS JEALOUSY, IT'S DRIVING ME BONKERS!

I CAN'T TALK TO ANY FELLOW IN SCHOOL WHEN HE'S AROUND!
IN FACT, NO GUY IS ALLOWED TO EVEN LOOK AT ME!

NOT UNLESS HE FEELS BRAVE BECAUSE HIS INSURANCE IS ALL PAID UP!

Originally presented in **Archie's TV Laugh-Out #88**, January 1983

Dick Malmgren • Jon D'Agostino • Bill Yoshida • Barry Grossman

I WISH HE WOULD CHANGE HIS WAYS!
I CAN'T TAKE MUCH MORE OF HIS JEALOUSY!
I FEEL LIKE ONE OF HIS POSSESSIONS!
POOR KID! SHE'S REALLY IN THE PITS!

MAYBE I CAN PICK HER SPIRITS UP WITH A LITTLE MAGIC!

DUH! IF MIDGE TELLS ME THAT YOU CALLED HER, YOU BETTER START SAYING YOUR PRAYERS, ARCH!
GULP! IT WAS ONLY ABOUT SCHOOL WORK, MOOSE!

ZAP!
?

DUH! WHAT DO I CARE IF YOU CALLED MIDGE, PAL?
HUH?
2

I MEAN, IF SHE WANTS TO TALK TO YOU, IT'S REALLY NONE OF MY BUSINESS, IS IT?
UH, ER,...

AFTER ALL, I DON'T OWN HER! YOU CALL HER ANYTIME YOU WANT, OL' BUDDY!
?

DUH!--- HEY, MIDGE! I'VE DECIDED THAT YOU CAN GO OUT WITH ANYBODY YOU FEEL LIKE, AND I'M NEVER GOING TO BE JEALOUS AGAIN!
HUH? DON'T YOU FEEL WELL, MOOSE?

DUH, I SURE DO! I FEEL LIKE A NEW PERSON! I SUDDENLY LOVE EVERYBODY!
OH, A DREAM COME TRUE!

IF THAT'S THE CASE, HOW ABOUT YOU AND I GOING OUT BOPPING TONIGHT, MIDGE?
?
?
3

ARE YOU SICK OF LIVING, REGGIE?
DON'T YOU SEE MOOSE?
WHAT ABOUT HIM?

DUH!--- THAT'S OKAY, MIDGE! IF YOU WANT TO GO OUT WITH HIM TONIGHT, WE'LL GO OUT SOME OTHER NIGHT!
GOOD THINKING, MOOSE!
HUH?

DUH! IT'S THE LEAST I CAN DO FOR A FRIEND!
I DON'T BELIEVE THIS!

WE CAN GO TO LOVERS' LANE LATER AND WATCH THE MOONLIGHT ON THE LAKE!
DUH! IT'S REALLY PRETTY THERE, REG!

WELL, IF MOOSE DOESN'T CARE ANYMORE, HOW ABOUT YOU AND I GOING OUT FRIDAY NIGHT, MIDGE?
HEY!
WHAT? YOU, TOO?

YOU GOTTA BE SICK! DID YOU FALL DOWN THE STAIRS AND LAND ON YOUR HEAD?
DUH, NO, MIDGE!
4

IT'S THE NEW ME!
WELL I DON'T THINK I LIKE IT!··· DON'T YOU CARE ABOUT ME ANY MORE?
?
I MISS THE OLD YOU, WHO WAS INSANELY CRAZY ABOUT ME!
IS THERE SOMEBODY ELSE YOU LOVE?
DUH! I LOVE EVERYBODY, MIDGE!
OH DEAR, THIS ISN'T WORKING TOO WELL!
POOF!
ZAP!
DUH!··· GRRRR, IF I EVER CATCH YOU GUYS TRYING TO MAKE DATES WITH MY MIDGE, I'M GOING TO BOP YOUR HEADS TOGETHER!
NOW, THAT'S MY OLD MOOSE!
I GUESS THERE ARE SOME THINGS THAT SHOULDN'T BE TAMPERED WITH!
END

SABRINA THE TEENAGE WITCH

WILD, WICKED WAYS

THERE IT IS... THE YOUNG WITCHES ACADEMY FOR YOUNG LADIES OF GENTEEL BREEDING AND REFINEMENT!

Y.W.A.

Originally presented in **Archie's TV Laugh-Out #102**, August 1985

George Gladir • Samm Schwartz • Barry Grossman

GIRLS, I WANT YOU TO GIVE SABRINA A WARM Y.W.A. WELCOME!
HELLO.
G..G.. OUCH
SOME WELCOME!
SOME OF THE LITTLE DEARS SHOW REAL TALENT FOR BEING MEAN LITTLE WITCHES!
FLIGHT REGULATION
NOW GIRLS, SINCE THIS IS YOUR FIRST FLIGHT, WE'RE NOT GOING TO GO UP HIGH! STAY CLOSE TO ME!
START YOUR BROOMS!
GRETCHEN, YOU'RE TOO CLOSE FOR COMFORT!
BUT NOT TOO CLOSE FOR MISCHIEF!
SNIP
SNIP
2

HAPPY LANDINGS!

AREN'T I THE LITTLE CUT-UP?

DID YOU SEE WHAT THAT KID DID?
I DID INDEED!

AND I'M AWARDING HER THE WICKEDEST STUNT OF THE WEEK AWARD!

YOU'RE GIVING HER A TROPHY FOR WHAT SHE DID?
YOU FORGET... WE'RE HERE TO TEACH OUR DEAR LITTLE TYKES TO *BE* WICKED!

I CAN SEE WHERE IT'S GOING TO TAKE SOME TIME GETTING USED TO AT THIS SCHOOL!
3

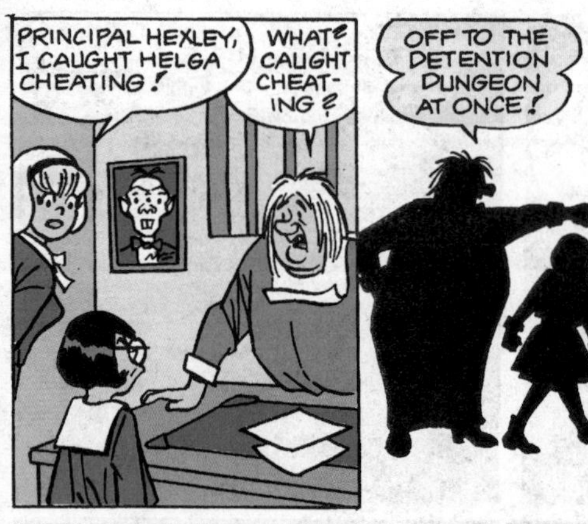
PRINCIPAL HEXLEY, I CAUGHT HELGA CHEATING!
WHAT? CAUGHT CHEAT-ING?
OFF TO THE DETENTION DUNGEON AT ONCE!

THAT'LL TEACH HER NOT TO GET CAUGHT NEXT TIME!... SOME KIDS NEVER LEARN!

WOW! THIS SCHOOL IS REALLY SOMETHING ELSE!
OH, MISS SABRINA, I'D LIKE YOU TO SEE WHAT I MADE!

WHAT DID YOU MAKE?
YOU'RE STANDING ON IT!
WAX DOLLS AND HOW TO MAKE THEM
LEARN TO SOUP UP YOUR BROOM

EEEEEEE

SABRINA, THANKS TO YOU, ALL THE GIRLS HAVE THEIR WINGS! I HOPE YOU ENJOYED THE EXPERIENCE OF TEACHING THEM!
BELIEVE ME, I'LL NEVER FORGET IT!

BYE! COME BACK SOON!
WHEN PIGS GROW WINGS!

NEXT DAY
IT'S NICE TO BE BACK IN A NORMAL SCHOOL!
VOTE

WHAT'S THIS?
TOMORROW IS "BACKWARDS DAY"! EVERYONE IS SUPPOSED TO DO THINGS BACKWARDS!
BACKWARDS DAY

BIG DEAL! I JUST CAME FROM A SCHOOL WHERE EVERY DAY IS "BACKWARDS DAY"!
BACKWARDS DAY
END

MAYBE WE SHOULDN'T HAVE KEPT SABRINA OUT OF SCHOOL FOR A WEEK SO SHE COULD CONCENTRATE ON HER WITCHCRAFT TRAINING!

... NOW SHE HAS SO MUCH TO MAKE UP IN ALL HER REGULAR SUBJECTS!

Sabrina -IN- "WORK QUIRK"

Originally presented in *Pep* #407, July 1986

George Gladir • Stan Goldberg • Rudy Lapick • Bill Yoshida • Barry Grossman

I JUST KNOW I'VE FOULED UP THIS RECIPE! I HOPE EVERYTHING GOES RIGHT!

OH, DEAR! SOMETHING IS TERRIBLY WRONG!

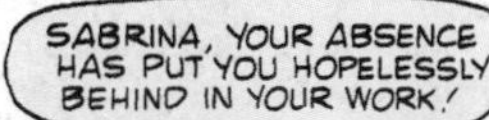
SABRINA, YOUR ABSENCE HAS PUT YOU HOPELESSLY BEHIND IN YOUR WORK!

CLEAN UP THIS MESS!
SABRINA'S EXHAUSTING WEEK HAS PROBABLY MADE HER MAGIC INEFFECTIVE!
I'LL HAVE TO USE MY OWN MAGIC!

ZAP

OH, DEAR! THE DISH SHE PREPARED IS PERFECT!
I FEEL SO ASHAMED FOR SCOLDING HER!

GYM IS MY NEXT CLASS! I'M OUT OF SHAPE! I WISH I COULD SKIP IT!
2

HURRY IT UP, SABRINA! YOU'RE LAGGING WAY BEHIND THE OTHERS!
GYM

I THINK SABRINA COULD USE A PAIR OF INVISIBLE FLYING SKATES!
ZAP!

SABRINA HAS A PROBLEM! SHE MISSED ALL THE POINTERS WE COVERED LAST WEEK!
IT COULDN'T HAVE HURT HER TOO MUCH!
GYM INSTRUCTOR
GYM INSTRUCTOR

... SHE'S ONLY LEADING THE PACK!
HOLY COW! SO SHE IS!

NOW IF I CAN JUST GET BY ALGEBRA I MAY SURVIVE THIS DAY!
214

SABRINA, GO TO THE BOARD AND DO PROBLEM NINE!
BUT, MISS SIMPKINS, I WAS ABSENT ALL OF LAST WEEK!
3

ABSENCE IS NO EXCUSE! YOU'RE REQUIRED TO KEEP UP WITH YOUR STUDIES!
OH, DEAR! IT'S ONE OF THOSE IMPOSSIBLE QUADRATIC EQUATIONS!

JUST AS I SUSPECTED! SHE DOESN'T KNOW A BLESSED THING!

CHALK, KEEP WRITING FOR SABRINA!
ZAP!

? WHY AM I SUDDENLY WRITING DOWN ALL THESE DUMB NUMBERS ?

REPORT TO THE PRINCIPAL'S OFFICE WHEN YOU'RE FINISHED!
YES, MISS SIMPKINS!

GOOD HEAVENS! HER ANSWER IS CORRECT!
...AND I SENT HER TO THE PRINCIPAL'S OFFICE TO BE PUNISHED!
4

OH, DEAR! I HOPE I GET TO THE PRINCIPAL BEFORE HE SPEAKS TO SABRINA!

UH, MR. WEATHERBEE, I SENT SABRINA TO YOUR OFFICE BECAUSE... SHE'S DOING SUCH OUTSTANDING WORK!
PRINCIPAL'S OFFICE

HOW ABOUT THAT? YOU'RE THE THIRD INSTRUCTOR TO TELL ME THAT TODAY!

YOUNG LADY, DO YOU KNOW WHY YOU'RE HERE?
SIGH! TO GET THE AXE!

I'M NAMING YOU STUDENT OF THE MONTH!
"STUDENT OF THE MONTH"?!
STUDENT OF THE MONTH

LATER:
THEY NAMED SABRINA "STUDENT OF THE MONTH"!
I HAVE ONE QUESTION, AUNT HILDA...
STUDENT OF THE MONTH
NAILS

HOW COME I DO MUCH BETTER WORK WHEN I'M ABSENT THAN WHEN I'M PRESENT?
5 END

Originally presented in Laugh #3, October 1987

George Gladir • Stan Goldberg • Rudy Lapick • Bill Yoshida

AREN'T YOU GOING TO STOP HER?
THERE'S MORE THAN ONE WAY TO SKIN A CAT!

SORRY, SALEM! THAT WAS JUST A FIGURE OF SPEECH!
MEOWRRR!

YOU FORGET WE HAVE OUR MAGIC TO TAKE CARE OF "LITTLE MISS REBEL"!

WHAT'S WRONG, SABRINA? YOU LOOK UPSET!
OH, MY OLD-FASHIONED AUNTS WANTED TO KEEP ME FROM ENTERING TODAY'S BEAUTY CONTEST!

OH, DEAR! SUDDENLY MY CAR IS OVERHEATING!
I'LL BET THIS IS THE WORK OF MY AUNTIES!

AND NOW IT'S COMING APART!
I'LL USE MAGIC TO REPAIR JENNY'S CAR LATER WHEN MY AUNTS AREN'T AROUND!
2

HI, GUYS!
C'MON, JENNY! WE'LL GET RUDY TO GIVE US A LIFT TO THE BEACH!
CREAMY BAR
ICE CREAM

I GUESS WE STOPPED SABRINA RIGHT IN HER TRACKS!
WRONG! SHE JUST GOT A FRIEND TO GIVE HER A LIFT!

WE'LL USE OUR MAGIC TO THWART HER AT THE BEACH!

GOSH! I HAD NO IDEA THE COMPETITION WOULD BE SO KEEN!

IT'S DIFFICULT PICKING THE WINNER!
YES! THEY'RE ALL SO BEAUTIFUL, IT'S DIFFICULT TO TELL THEM APART!
JUDGES STAND
3

I'M GOING TO PUT SABRINA INTO A RESPECTABLE 'THIRTIES-TYPE' SWIMSUIT!
ZAP!

OH, DEAR!

LOOK AT THE GIRL IN THAT OLD-FASHIONED SWIMSUIT!
SHE REALLY STANDS OUT!

ZELDA, IS THAT YOUR IDEA OF A RESPECTABLE SWIMSUIT?
IT'S STILL MUCH TOO SCANTY FOR MY MONEY!

ZAP!

OH, NO! THIS DEFINITELY HAS TO BE THE WORK OF MY AUNTIES!
I FEEL SO POSITIVELY HUMILIATED!
4

SOB! I HOPE THOSE TWO ARE SATISFIED!
THEY'VE DISGRACED ME IN FRONT OF ALL THESE PEOPLE!

MISS, THAT WAS A VERY CLEVER IDEA TO EXHIBIT SWIMSUITS THROUGHOUT THE AGES!
HOW DID YOU MANAGE ALL THOSE QUICK COSTUME CHANGES?
YOUR ROUTINE SET YOU APART FROM ALL THE OTHER CONTESTANTS!
FIRST PRIZE

LOOK! SABRINA WON THE CONTEST!
OBVIOUSLY BECAUSE SHE'S WEARING THE EYE-CATCHING SWIMSUIT I GAVE HER!

WHICH GIVES ME AN IDEA!
I'M GOING TO DO THE SAME FOR US!

ZAP!

HILDA, WE'VE BEEN HERE HOURS IN OUR SWIMSUITS, AND NOT A SINGLE GENT HAS APPROACHED US!
OBVIOUSLY THEY'RE AFRAID TWO GLAMOROUS TYPES LIKE US WILL TURN THEM DOWN!
END

Originally presented in **Laugh #9**, August 1988

Bill Golliher • Stan Goldberg • Rudy Lapick • Bill Yoshida

I HATE TO ADMIT IT, BUT THOSE TWO HAD A POINT! MY AUNTS SHOULD UPDATE THEIR WARDROBES!

HOME SWEET HOME!
THERE'S SOMETHING I NEED TO TALK TO YOU TWO ABOUT!

WHAT IS IT? DO YOU WANT US TO PUT A HEX ON ONE OF YOUR TEACHERS OR SOMETHING?
BEANS
BEANS
MILK

NO, IT'S NOTHING LIKE THAT!
IT'S ABOUT YOUR WARD-ROBES!

OUR WARDROBES? WHAT'S WRONG WITH OUR CLOTHES?
WE ALWAYS KEEP THEM NEAT AND MENDED!

THAT'S JUST IT! THE TWENTIETH CENTURY IS ALMOST OVER AND YOU TWO HAVEN'T CHANGED OUTFITS ONCE, YET!
2

I'LL HAVE YOU KNOW OUR CLOTHES AREN'T AS OUTDATED AS YOU MIGHT THINK!
IF I'M NOT MISTAKEN WE BOUGHT THEM IN 1655, GIVE OR TAKE A HUNDRED YEARS!

I REST MY CASE, LADIES!

I'M GOING TO THE MALL TO MEET THE GIRLS! I'LL SEE YOU TWO LATER!

YOU KNOW, HILDA, MAYBE SABRINA IS RIGHT! IT'S TIME WE GOT WITH IT!

HMMPH! I WOULDN'T KNOW WHERE TO START!
HOW ABOUT THIS? ONE OF SABRINA'S WAYOUT FASHION MAGAZINES!
UMPTEEN

ZELDA! YOU'RE A GENIUS! WE CAN ZAP UP ALL THESE FASHIONS AND HAIRDOS IN NO TIME!
OH WHAT FUN!
UMPTEEN MAGAZINE
3

LET'S SEE, I THINK I'LL TRY THIS ONE!
ZAP!
WELL, LITTLE SISTER, WHAT DO YOU THINK?
HAND ME THAT MAGAZINE!
MANY ZAPS LATER...
LET'S POP OVER TO THE MALL AND SHOW OFF TO SABRINA AND HER FRIENDS!
WE'LL SHOW THEM THAT WE'RE CAPABLE OF KEEPING UP WITH THE TIMES!
AH-HA! MY WITCH RADAR WAS RIGHT! THERE THEY ARE OVER THERE!
LET'S GO!
PIZZ
POOF!
SABRINA! GIRLS! IMAGINE SEEING YOU HERE!
AUNT HILDA? AUNT ZELDA? IS THAT YOU TWO?
ALOHA, KIDS!
4

WHY OF COURSE IT'S US, SILLY!
ZELDA AND I WERE JUST DOING A LITTLE CLOTHES SHOPPING!
VIDEO
SHOES
NEW RELEA

ONE CAN NEVER BE TOO MUCH IN VOGUE, YOU KNOW!

TOOT-A-LOO FOR NOW, GIRLS!
WHAT HAPPENED TO THEM?
A LITTLE FASHION ADVICE GONE HAYWIRE!
SHOES

NOW I'LL HAVE TO FIND A WAY TO GET THEM BACK IN THEIR OLD OUTFITS BEFORE SOMEONE TELLS THEM HOW RIDICULOUS THEY LOOK!

YOU'D BETTER WORK FAST!

AH-HA! I THINK I'VE GOT JUST THE IDEA!

I'M HOME!
YOU'RE JUST IN TIME TO SEE OUR LATEST OUTFITS!
ISN'T THIS WILD?
5

WHAT HAVE YOU GOT THERE, DEAR?
WHY IT'S THE ABSOLUTE LATEST IN FASHION DIRECTLY FROM PARIS!
GASP
I'M GOING TO RUN RIGHT UPSTAIRS AND PUT IT ON!
YEAH, AND THEN WE'LL ZAP US UP A FEW OF THEM!
MARVEY!
LATER:
TA-DA!
HERE'S HOPING THEY FALL FOR THIS!
HUH?
IT SEEMS I WAS WRONG ABOUT THE LATEST STYLE! THINGS HAVE SWUNG FROM THE '60s LOOK TO THE 1600s LOOK ALL OF A SUDDEN!
HMMM!
MY GOODNESS!
WELL, DON'T JUST STAND THERE, ZELDA! LET'S ZAP BACK THESE OUTDATED THREADS AND GET BACK TO OUR OTHER OUTFITS!
AMEN!
WELL, SALEM! MISSION ACCOMPLISHED!
YOU KNOW, ZELDA, IT'S HARD TO BEAT CLASSIC STYLE!
POSITIVELY, HILDA!
END

Originally presented in Archie Giant Series Magazine #587, October 1988

Samm Schwartz

Originally presented in **Laugh #17**, October 1989

George Gladir • Dan Parent • Jon D'Agostino • Bill Yoshida

ESMERALDA!
OKAY, OKAY, SABRINA! I BRING 'EM DOWN!
RIGHT DOWN INTO THE FOUNTAIN! YUK! YUK!
ZAP!
I DON'T KNOW WHY YOU DISLIKE THE MALL SO MUCH! THERE'S ALWAYS SOMETHING GOING ON!
Dickery Farms Cheese
WOULD YOU LIKE TO SAMPLE SOME OF OUR DELICIOUS SALAMI?
YOU'RE DARN RIGHT I WOULD!
THANKEE!
ESMERALDA!
CHEE! AT TIMES YOU CAN BE A REAL SPOILSPORT!
HERE'S YOUR SALAMI BACK, LADY! I WAS ONLY KIDDING!
THAT'S BETTER!
2

YOUR MOTHER WANTS ME TO GET YOU A PAIR OF ATHLETIC SHOES!
CRIMINY! I COULD SPEND HOURS TRYING ON ALL THESE SHOES!
$SALE
... SO WHY DON'T WE DO IT THE EASY WAY? I'LL CLONE MYSELF!
ZAP!
HUH?
I LIKE THE ONES ON THE END! THEY LOOK AND FEEL THE BEST!
YOU EMBARRASSED ME TO NO END!
HEY! YOU HAVE TO ADMIT MY METHOD WAS EFFICIENT!
HEY, GRAMPA! YOU ARE ONE FUNNY-LOOKING DUDE!
HA! HA!
La Chez Chic
3

THAT ROWDY CROWD IS TRYING TO SHOCK THE NICE OLD COUPLE WITH THEIR APPEARANCE!
SO TURNABOUT IS FAIR PLAY!
HAROLD, WHAT'S HAPPENING?
I DUNNO, MARTHA, BUT SUDDENLY I FEEL VERY YOUNG!
ZAP

OUTTA MY WAY, YOU DWEEBS! KING OF FEEDBACK IS RIPPIN'!

ESMERALDA!
HEY! YOU HAVE TO ADMIT THOSE ROWDIES HAD IT COMING!

I DON'T KNOW IF WE HAVE TIME TO PICK OUT A PAIR OF JEANS!
THE DRESSING ROOM IS ALWAYS SO CROWDED AT THIS HOUR!
4

I THINK YOU'LL HAVE ROOM!
DRESSING ROOM
ZAP!
EEAGH! THERE'S A HUGE SNAKE IN THERE!
ESMERALDA!! YOU DID IT AGAIN!
DRESSING ROOM
MY ESMERALDA AND YOUR SABRINA ARE BACK FROM THE MALL!
I LOVE THE MALL! IT WAS SUCH A GREAT EXPERIENCE! I'LL NEVER BE THE SAME AGAIN!
SWOOSH!
AND SIGH NEITHER WILL I!
END

SABRINA THE TEENAGE WITCH IN "HORRORVISION"

"WHEEL OF MISFORTUNE" IS ONE OF THE MOST POPULAR SHOWS ON WITCHES' TV!

SO SORRY! YOU JUST LOST THE MORTGAGE ON YOUR GINGERBREAD HOUSE! ...CARE TO SPIN AGAIN?

YOU OWE $30,000
TAX AUDIT
BANKRUPT
YOU OWE $30,000
BANKRUPT
BANKRUPT
YOU OWE $10,000
YOU OWE $30,000
LOSE
LOSE

1

Originally presented in **Laugh #19**, February 1990

Frank Doyle • Stan Goldberg • Rudy Lapick • Bill Yoshida

THAT SHOW IS TOO DEPRESSING, AUNTIES! LET'S TUNE INTO SOMETHING ELSE!
CLICK! CLICK!
GOOD EVENING! IT'S TIME FOR THE WITCHES' WEATHER REPORT!
WHAT CAN WE EXPECT IN THE WAY OF WEATHER, ROWENA?
I'M COOKING UP A HURRICANE FOR UPPER KLOPSTOCKIA!
WE'RE ABOUT TO GIVE YOU TV VIEWERS A FREE SAMPLE OF THAT HURRICANE!
...SO BATTEN DOWN YOUR HATCHES!
WOOSH!
2

QUICK, SABRINA! SWITCH CHANNELS!
I'M TRYING! I'M TRYING!
CLICK! CLICK!
WHEW! I'M GLAD WE DON'T LIVE IN UPPER KLOPSTOCKIA!

LOOK! A WITCHES' COMMERCIAL!
WE RECOMMEND YOU USE INSTANT COBRA VENOM IN YOUR BREW!

--- OTHERWISE WE'LL JINX YOUR TV SET... LIKE THIS!
BOUNCE! BOUNCE!

...AND WE'LL SEND POLTERGEISTS TO HAUNT YOUR HOME!
3

I'D BETTER ZAP THIS YUCKY COMMERCIAL BUT QUICK!

DON'T YOU DARE!
EEYOW!

AND NOW IT'S TIME FOR SISTER ABIGAIL'S COOKING HOUR!

ADD SOME NEWT AND WOOL OF BAT... A PINCH OF TOAD LIZARD'S TAIL... A DASH OF PYTHON SKIN... A STALE PIZZA PIE CRUST OR TWO... ALLOW TO BOIL AND BUBBLE!

I'M GOING TO LET A LITTLE OF MY BREW BOIL OVER INTO YOUR LIVING ROOM SO YOU CAN SAMPLE THIS DELICIOUS CONCOCTION!

STOP! WE HAVE ENOUGH OF YOUR SAMPLE!
4

TURN THE SET OFF, SABRINA!
I'M TRYING! I'M TRYING!

THE ZAPPER ISN'T WORKING! I THINK THE BREW HAS CLOGGED THE DIAL! GLUG! GLUG!

HELP!

LATER -
LOOK, AGNES! HILDA AND ZELDA ARE GIVING US THIS BRAND NEW WITCHES' TV SET!
AND I THOUGHT THEY WERE OUR ENEMIES!
THAT'S WHY WE'RE GIVING IT TO YOU!
END

SABRINA (IN) THE TEENAGE WITCH "A MAGICAL EXPERIENCE"

LOOK AT THOSE SILLY GIRLS FIGHTING OVER A MAGAZINE ABOUT AMERICA'S HOTTEST GROUP OF SINGERS!

IT'S THE LAST COPY OF THIS MAGAZINE!

I SAW IT *FIRST!* *GIVE IT HERE!*

ONE SNAP OF MY WITCHY FINGERS AND I CAN HAVE EVERY MAGAZINE EVER PRINTED ABOUT THE YOUNG DUDES!

SNAP!

Originally presented in **Laugh** #28, June 1991

George Gladir • Stan Goldberg • Mike Esposito • Bill Yoshida • Barry Grossman

HMPF! I DON'T NEED MAGAZINES TO FEEL CLOSE TO THE YOUNG DUDES!
VID

ONE SNAP OF MY MAGICAL FINGERS AND I CAN BE AT THE VERY HEALTH SPA WHERE THE YOUNG DUDES ARE VACATIONING!
SNAP!

GOOD GOSH! THERE'S ONE OF THEM RIGHT NOW!
SILVER DOOR HEALTH SPA

SORRY, MISS! YOU'RE IN DA MEN'S MASSAGE ROOM!

YOU BELONG IN DA VOOMAN'S MASSAGE ROOM!

DIS SHOULD MAKE YOU FEEL LIKE A NEW YOU!
2

(GROAN!) I WONDER WHERE PEOPLE GO TO RECOVER FROM A HEALTH SPA!
MASSAGE ROOM

SILVER DOOR HEALTH SPA
THE YOUNG DUDES JUST LEFT FOR A CONCERT THEY'RE GIVING TONIGHT!
YOUNG DUDES
SILVER DOOR HEALTH SPA

WHAT A COINCIDENCE! THAT'S EXACTLY WHERE I'M GOING!
?
SNAP!
SILVER DOOR HEALTH SPA

SILVER DOOR HEALTH SPA

THE CONCERT IS ALL SOLD OUT!
FORTUNATELY, WE WITCHES DON'T NEED TICKETS TO GAIN ENTRANCE!
TONIGHT
THE YOUNG DUDES
IN CONCERT
SOLD OUT

OH, EXALTED SPIRITS, TAKE ME AS CLOSE TO THE STAGE AS IT IS POSSIBLE TO GET!
SNAP!
3

OH, WOW! I'M RIGHT NEXT TO THE AMPLIFIERS!

YIIIII!!!

WHAT HAPPENED?
FOR SOME REASON, YOU BLACKED OUT DURING THE CONCERT!

I'VE GOT TO GET BACK TO THE CONCERT!
RELAX, DEARIE! THE CONCERT HAS BEEN OVER FOR HOURS!

I FEEL SO BLUE AND FRUSTRATED!
ICE CREAM
YOUNG DUDES 4-EVER
100 FLAVOR

I COULDN'T GET TICKETS TO SEE THE YOUNG DUDES PERFORM! HOW ABOUT YOU?
(SIGH!) I MISSED OUT, TOO!
4

WOW! THAT WAS SOME CONCERT!
TOO BAD WE DIDN'T GET A CHANCE TO TELL OUR FANS HOW MUCH WE APPRECIATE THEIR SUPPORT!
THE YOUNG DUDES

HEY! THAT LOOKS LIKE TWO OF OUR FANS!
ICE CREAM
100 FLAVORS

WE'D LIKE TO TELL YOU FANS HOW IMPORTANT YOU ARE TO US! WOULD YOU JOIN OUR TABLE?
IT'S... IT'S... THE YOUNG DUDES!
YOUNG DUDES 4 EVER

OH, SABRINA! THEY'RE GIVING US AUTOGRAPHS AND ALL SORTS OF SOUVENIRS! IT'S LIKE MAGIC!
NO, KAREN!

(SIGH!) IT'S A DARN SIGHT BETTER THAN MAGIC!
YOUNG DUDES
YOUNG DUDES
END

Originally presented in **Archie & Friends** #2, November 1992

Dan Parent • Bill Golliher • Henry Scarpelli • Bill Yoshida • Barry Grossman

OUCH
HEY! WHAT'S THE BIG IDEA?
WHO SAID THAT? WHO'S THERE?

I DID, CLUMSY! CLEARA, I'M AN INVISIBLE GIRL!
SLURP
SORRY! I DIDN'T NOTICE YOU!

SIGH! THAT'S OKAY! IT HAPPENS A LOT!
I'M SABRINA! A VISIBLE WITCH! NICE TO MEET YOU!

OW! YOU'RE SHAKING MY NOSE!
OOPS!
EXCUSE ME ...

...IS THIS SEAT TAKEN?
NO! UNLESS SOMEONE INVISIBLE IS SITTING THERE!

CUTE! JUST LIKE YOU...UH...
SABRINA'S THE NAME!
2

HERE'S YOUR SODA, CHIP!
HEY, I ASKED FOR A HEAD ON THAT!

I GUESS I HAVE TO DO EVERYTHING MYSELF!
EEEK!!
SCREECH!

I'M CHIP NOGGIN, GREAT GRANDSON OF THE ORIGINAL HEADLESS HORSEMAN!
DO YOU USUALLY GO TO THIS MUCH TROUBLE TO MEET A GIRL?
EYE OF NEWT 60¢
SUNDAE BLOODY SUNDAE 99¢

ONLY IF I WANT TO ASK HER OUT! WHAT DO YOU SAY TO SATURDAY NIGHT?
I DON'T KNOW YOU THAT WELL!
AHEM!

IF YOU GET A DATE FOR MY FRIEND CLEARA, WE'LL MAKE IT A DOUBLE!
SOUNDS GREAT!
ALL RIGHT!

OOPS! I'VE GOT A SOFT-BALL GAME TO GET TO! IT'S A DOUBLE-HEADER!
HERE'S MY NUMBER, CHIP! GIVE ME A SCREAM!
3

OH, SABRINA, I DON'T KNOW ABOUT THIS! I'M SO INSECURE ABOUT MY LOOKS!
WE CAN WORK ON A MAKEOVER FOR YOU! YOU'LL BE STUNNING!
THAT SATURDAY...
HELLO, CLEARA, COME IN!
I'M NOT SURE ABOUT THIS, SABRINA!
RIP
NONSENSE! I'VE BORROWED SOME OF THE BEST INVISI-COSMETIC PRODUCTS!
NOW A LITTLE BLUSH HERE, AND A LITTLE EYESHADOW HERE...
OH, STARRY NIGHT! YOU LOOK BOO-TIFUL!
LET ME SEE, LET ME SEE!
I DO LOOK RATHER BEWITCHING!
AND WE'LL ADD SOME REGULAR LIPSTICK TO ALLURE YOUR DATE!
I'M GOING TO KNOCK THEM DEAD TONIGHT!
THAT'S THE SPIRIT!
4

THAT NIGHT...
HI, SABRINA! THIS IS DRAC, CLEARA'S DATE!
H'LO!
HI!

HERE'S SOME BEAUTIFUL DEAD FLOWERS, SABRINA!
THEY'RE RAVISHED! I LOVE THEM!
HERE!
ER... THANKS!

IT SURE IS CHILLY OUT!
I CAN TAKE CARE OF THAT!

IT SURE IS CHILLY OUT!
YOU SHOULD'VE BROUGHT YOUR JACKET!

OH! THE CRYPT CAFE! I'VE ALWAYS WANTED TO COME HERE!
CRYPT CAFE
AND...
THE BAT WING FRICASSEE WAS DELICIOUS!
HOW WAS YOUR RARE LEG OF LOCH NESS MONSTER, DRAC?
ER... FINE!
5

OH, SABRINA! HE'S NOT INTERESTED IN ME!
I'M SURE HE'S JUST... UH...NERVOUS!
LET'S DANCE, SABRINA!
DO YOU WANNA DANCE, DRAC?
CARL AND THE DEADHEADS
ER- NO!
OH, WHY DO I EVEN TRY? YOU SEE THROUGH ME LIKE EVERYONE ELSE!
THAT'S NOT TRUE! I LIKE YOU! I'M JUST INSECURE ABOUT MY LOOKS!
WHY? YOU'RE SO DASHING!
HOW'S THIS FOR DASHING?
HAVE YOU EVER SEEN A VAMPIRE WITH BRACES?
I FIND THEM VERY ATTRACTIVE!
IN THAT CASE, WOULD YOU LIKE A BETTER LOOK AT THEM ON THE DANCE FLOOR?
IT LOOKS LIKE LOVE HAS BLOSSOMED!
AIN'T THAT THE TOOTH!
THE END

Originally presented in **Archie & Friends #4**, June 1993

Bill Golliher • Dan Parent • Rudy Lapick • Bill Yoshida

IT WOULD APPEAR THAT I'VE DROPPED MY HANKY!
ER, YES I SEE!
WELL!
MAYBE HE'S A BIT DENSE!
THE NEXT DAY IN SCHOOL...
H-HI, SABRINA!
OH, HI, MILTON! CAN I HELP-YOU?!
NO, I JUST LIKE LOOKING AT YOU!
'BYE MILTON'!
SO HE'S THE NEW MUMMY IN SCHOOL!
YES! BUT WHY CAN'T THAT HUNKY NEW VAMPIRE FALL ALL OVER ME LIKE MILTON DOES?
THAT'S THE WAY THE GRAVESTONE CRUMBLES!
THAT NIGHT...
IF THIS OUTFIT DOESN'T CAPTURE HIS ATTENTION, THIS GUY IS TRULY DEAD!
GO GET HIM, GIRL!
MIXED BUGS
2

♫ HMM! HMM! LA DE DA ♫ DA-
♫ LA DE DA DA DA! ♫
HIYA, CUTIE!
ER, HELLO! WELL, GOODBYE!
STRIKE OUT AGAIN?
YES! WHAT DO I HAVE TO DO? OFFER HIM A PINT OF BLOOD?!
THE NEXT DAY IN SCHOOL...
HO HUM! I FEEL SO DEFEATED!
CHEER UP, GIRL!
ER-UM, SABRINA... CAN I ASK YOU SOMETHING?
SURE, I GUESS SO!
WOULD YOU GO TO THE WINTER CARNIVAL WITH ME?
WHY NOT? I'VE GOT NOTHING BETTER TO DO!
PLOP!!
HE PASSED OUT!
3

I'M RATHER SHOCKED MYSELF THAT YOU ACCEPTED, SABRINA!
WELL, NOBODY ELSE HAS ASKED! WHAT HAVE I GOT TO LOSE?
AND AT THE CARNIVAL...
FUN
THIS GUY DANCES LIKE A CORPSE!
ONLY WITH LESS PERSONALITY!
OW! STOP STEPPING ON MY FOOT, MILTON!
I'M SORRY... I...
OH, YOUR HEEL IS STUCK IN MY BANDAGE...
FLOP!
MILTON, PLEASE TAKE ME HOME!
OKAY, SABRINA!
HA! HA! HA!
CARNIVA
THANK GOODNESS, MY VAMPIRE HEART THROB'S NOWHERE AROUND TO SEE ME! I'D BE SO EMBARRASSED!
4

SO...
MAY I KISS YOU GOODBYE, SABRINA?
WELL, I... ER... OH, SURE, WHY NOT!

I'LL JUST UNDO THESE BANDAGES AND...
GAK!!
IT'S YOU!

WHA... HOW... I DON'T UNDERSTAND!
WELL, AS YOU KNOW, VAMPIRES CAN'T BE OUT IN THE DAYLIGHT!

DURING THE DAY I DRESS AS A MUMMY SO I CAN ATTEND DAY SCHOOL LIKE EVERYONE ELSE!
BUT WHY DIDN'T YOU TELL ME?

WELL, I'M VERY SHY, AND IT'S EASIER TO TALK TO YOU WITH THE BANDAGES ON!
HOW SWEET!

DOES THIS MEAN YOU'LL SEE ME AGAIN?

ONLY THROUGH ROSE-COLORED BANDAGES!
THE End.

Our Spider, Have You Spied Her?

From a young age, I remember being enthralled by the idea of living skeletons, witches, ghosts, and creatures from outer space. These spooky characters were pretty much everywhere from cereal boxes, toys, TV shows, video games, comics and movies, and boy did I love every instance of it! When I learned about *Sabrina at Gravestone Heights*, which took Sabrina out of Riverdale High and into a school full of horror monsters, I was hooked! This quick story showcases the spooky and fun cast of monsters such as Eyeda, Cleara, Dr. Frankenstern, and more! Plus, it's all about a spider! Who doesn't love spiders?

✶ **Vincent Lovallo**
Archie Art Director

The Cleopatra Chronicles

Everyone knows and loves the *Sabrina the Teenage Witch* 1996 sitcom, but not as many people seem to talk about the corresponding comics. For a long time these '90s Sabrina comics were my favorite, and as a 2000s kid, I hadn't even seen the show! But I loved everything about these issues, with Dan DeCarlo's modernized Sabrina designs, the "Dear Sabrina" segments, interviews with the cast, and of course the covers that always included Melissa Joan Hart on them. Now the sitcom is one of my absolute favorites, and I collect all of the merchandise to display alongside my precious comics. The Cleopatra Chronicles is a 3-part series that kicks off these corresponding comics and it feels like a story that would've been perfect on the show.

✶ **Gillian Swearingen**
Archie Contributor

Oh, What a Knight

There's nothing quite like Sabrina Halloween stories! Not only does it feature the art of the inimitable Dan DeCarlo, this story also employs my favorite Sabrina conundrum: balancing real life with the magic world. In this case, Sabrina is trying to attend two parties at once with hilarious consequences. The best part about Halloween is that a witch can get away with a lot more than usual—because mortals will believe it's just a trick! This story inspired me when I wrote my own Halloween tales featuring Sabrina years later.

✶ **Tania Del Rio**
Writer/Artist

Originally presented in **Archie & Friends #8**, May 1994

Bill Golliher • Rudy Lapick

EYEDA! WHAT'S WRONG?!
WE'VE LOST THE GRAVESTONE HEIGHTS MASCOT, TESSIE THE TARANTULA!

HOW'D THAT HAPPEN?!
CLEARA AND I WERE CLEANING UP HER CAGE FOR THE BIG SCHOOL CARNIVAL WHEN SHE GOT AWAY!

WHAT ARE WE GOING TO DO? WE'RE GOING TO BE IN SUCH TROUBLE!
WHERE'S CLEARA, ANYWAY?

RIGHT HERE! SHE TOOK OFF HER LIPSTICK AND HAIRBOW SO NO ONE WOULD KNOW SHE WAS INVOLVED!
TATTLE TALE!!

BEING AN INVISIBLE GIRL HAS ITS PERKS!
OMIGOSH! IT'S FIFTEEN MINUTES 'TIL THREE!
2:45

IF WE DON'T FIND TESSIE BEFORE SCHOOL GETS OUT, SHE'LL WIND UP A GREASY SPOT IN THE HALLWAY!
EYEDA'S RIGHT! WE'D BETTER GET SNAPPING!
2

DIDJA HAVE TO SAY SNAPPING?!
SORRY, JEROME! GIRLS, YOU TAKE THE UPSTAIRS, WE'LL TAKE THE DOWN-STAIRS!
SOON...
HERE'S THE EMPTY CAGE, BUT NO SIGN OF TESSIE!
WHERE WOULD YOU GO IF YOU WERE A SPIDER?
DANCE CLASS, I GUESS!
DANCE CLASS?!
SURE! WITH EIGHT LEGS, JUST THINK OF ALL THE CRAZY STEPS YOU COULD DO!
OH, BROTHER!
IF ONLY SHE COULD HAVE LEFT US A TRAIL OR SOMETHING!
A TRAIL! THAT'S IT!
HOME ICK DEPT.
AH-HA! A STRAND OF SPIDER WEBBING! ALL WE HAVE TO DO IS FOLLOW IT TO THE OTHER END!
AND WHOOOMP, THERE SHE IS!
3

ANY LUCK, YOU GUYS?
YEAH! SABRINA FOUND A WEB TRAIL! C'MON!

IT GOES UNDER THE DOOR OF DR. FRANKENSTERN'S CHEM LAB!
DR. FRANKENSTERN!

YES?!
HAVE YOU SEEN THE SCHOOL TARANTULA? SHE'S MISSING!

IS SHE ABOUT THIS BIG, FUZZY, WITH A BIRTHMARK ON HER THIRD RIGHT LEG?
YEAH! THAT'S HER!

NOPE! HAVEN'T SEEN IT!! BUT EXCUSE ME WHILE I GET BACK TO WORK!

DR. FRANKENSTERN, I GET THE FEELING YOU'RE HIDING SOMETHING!
PREPOSTEROUS! NOW RUN ALONG BEFORE I GIVE YOU DETENTION!
4

C'MON, GIRLS! LET'S GO! BY THE WAY, DR. FRANKENSTERN...
YOUR FLY IS OPEN!
HUH?
CRASH!
DID YOU HAVE TO SAY FLY?!
SOON...
... SO I FOUND HER IN THE HALLWAY, AND FIGURED SHE'D BE THE PERFECT SUBJECT FOR MY GROWTH EXPERIMENT!
AND THEN YOU COULDN'T REDUCE HER BACK TO NORMAL SIZE!
SABRINA, WOULD YOU CARE TO DO THE HONORS?
SURE!
HOLD IT! I'VE GOT AN IDEA!
AND SO...
JEROME, WHAT A GREAT IDEA!
OUR BOOTH IS THE BUSIEST ONE AT THE CARNIVAL!
KEEP HOLDING UP THAT JAR OF FLIES, SABRINA! WE'VE GOT MORE RIDERS WAITING!
YES, SIR!
GIANT TARANTULA RIDE
$3.
THE END
5

Sabrina in the Homecoming!

AH, A NICE RELAXING EVENING! NOTHING TO DO BUT READ MY BOOKS OF INCANTATIONS AND CHANT FOR BAD LUCK FOR EVERYONE!
HELLO, GALS!
POOF
Teen GHOUL

Originally presented in **Archie & Friends #14**, May 1995

Dan Parent • Rudy Lapick • Bill Yoshida

IT'S THOSE SNEAKY HUMANS! I NEED YOU BACK THERE TO KEEP YOUR EYE ON THEM! THE WITCH WHO TOOK YOUR PLACE JUST MARRIED A MORTAL AND IS ON HER HONEYMOON!

BUT I'VE GOT THINGS GOING ON WITH ALL MY FRIENDS! WHAT ABOUT ALL MY PLANS?

YOU'VE GOT AT&T, MCI, SPRINT, NOT TO MENTION WITCHCRAFT TO HELP KEEP YOU IN TOUCH!
NOW PACK YOUR CAULDRONS AND HIT THE ROAD!

CAN'T I AT LEAST HAVE A GOOD-BYE BASH WITH MY FRIENDS?

OH, ALL RIGHT! BUT BE IN RIVERDALE BY SATURDAY!
OKAY, DELLA!

SO...
HAVE FUN IN RIVERDALE, SABRINA!
YOU CAN COME VISIT! I'LL FIX YOU UP WITH SOME HUMANS!
WOW! THAT'S WILD!
2

GEE, SABRINA! I THOUGHT WE HAD SOMETHING SPECIAL!
WE DO, CHIP! WE WON'T BE APART THAT LONG!

IT'S LONG ENOUGH FOR ME! HEY, I KNOW A WAY WE CAN BE TOGETHER!

I CAN STOW AWAY IN HER BOWLING BAG!
TALK ABOUT GETTING A-HEAD IN HER BOWLING! HAR!

AND BACK IN RIVERDALE...
GEE, I MISS GRAVESTONE HEIGHTS ALREADY!
ME, TOO!

BUT LET'S NOT JUST MOPE! LET'S GO OUT AND HAVE SOME FUN!
LET'S HIT THE BINGO HALLS!

-ER- I THINK I'LL TRY SOME BOWLING! SORT OF GET BACK INTO THE MORTAL THING!
SUIT YOURSELF!
3

HI, SABRINA! IT'S ME!
CHIP! HOW COULD YOU?
SUPER LANES

AW, I JUST WANTED TO BE WITH YOU, SABRINA!
THIS IS THE MORTAL WORLD! YOU CAN'T BE SEEN LIKE THIS!

IF PEOPLE SAW ME WITH A HEAD IN A BOWLING BAG, I'D BE ON EVERY TABLOID TELEVISION SHOW!
I - I'M SORRY!
LANES

BUT I WILL ADMIT, IT'S GREAT TO SEE YOU!
IF YOU STAY IN THE BAG, YOU CAN HANG OUT FOR AWHILE!

SOON...
I'VE GOT US SOME SNACKS, CHIP...
CHIP, WHERE ARE YOU? HEY, THIS ISN'T MY BAG!
Snacks

OH, NO! THAT LADY'S GOT IT! SHE MUST'VE MIXED IT UP WITH THIS SIMILAR BAG!
I'D BETTER GET CHIP BACK FAST!
ED'S TV SHACK
4

EXCUSE ME, MA'AM! YOU'VE GOT THE WRONG BAG! SEE, I'VE GOT YOURS!
WELL! LET'S OPEN IT AND...
ALLS
WE GOT 'EM!

NO! YOU CAN'T! PLEASE TRUST ME!
HMMPH! YOU NUTTY TEEN-AGERS! ALWAYS PULLING SOME KIND OF PRANK...
SHOES
WE GOT 'EM!

EEK! A HEAD! IT'S A HUMAN HEAD!
MA'AM! NO! IT'S JUST MY CUSTOM-MADE BOWLING BALL!

SEE! I'LL SHOW YOU!

WOW! A STRIKE!
SEE?
THE YOUTH OF AMERICA IS WARPED!
LANE

SORRY ABOUT THAT, CHIP! IT'S ALL I COULD THINK OF ON SHORT NOTICE!
AW- IT'S OKAY! YOU ALWAYS BOWL ME OVER ANYWAY!
END

Originally presented in **Archie & Friends #17**, February 1996

Bill Golliher • Jon D'Agostino • Bill Yoshida • Barry Grossman

UH-OH! IT'S DELLA THE HEAD WITCH!

OF COURSE! WHO ELSE MAKES THOSE KIND OF ENTRANCES?!

SO, SABRINA, YOU DON'T THINK THE OTHER WITCHES' OUTFITS ARE GOOD ENOUGH FOR YOU!

YOU DON'T WEAR THEM!

BEING HEAD WITCH HAS ITS PRIVILEGES!

NOW PUT ON THIS OUT-FIT BEFORE I REVOKE YOUR POWERS!

POOF!

OKAY! BUT THIS IS GOING TO BE EMBARRASS-ING!

AND SO...

MR. KLINE! WHAT DOES IT TAKE TO POPULARIZE A LOOK?

OH, I CAN MAKE *ANY* LOOK POPULAR!

APPEARING TODAY KELVIN KLINE DESIGNER

WHATEVER THE NEXT PERSON TO COME AROUND THE CORNER IS WEARING, I'LL BET I COULD TURN INTO THE NEXT RAGE!
THE GYP B
Bloomin Dales
8
2

UH-OH! IT LOOKS LIKE YOU COULD HAVE YOUR WORK CUT OUT FOR YOU!
EEP!
SIGH
G Y
8

NO, I SAID I'LL DO IT, AND I *WILL*!

HELLO, YOUNG LADY! I'M KELVIN KLINE THE DESIGNER! MAY I SPEAK WITH YOU?!
SURE!

AND IN A FEW MONTHS...
I PRESENT MY NEW *WITCH LOOK*, INSPIRED BY MY FRIEND SABRINA!
HE... EXPECTS US TO WEAR *THAT*?!
KELVIN KLINE

AND SO...
WOW! A BILLBOARD IN *TIMES SQUARE*... THIS IS THE GREATEST!
Kola
KELVIN KLINE
SUN
FILM
TICKETS
3

HERE'S ANOTHER ONE OF THOSE ANNOYING KELVIN KLINE ADS!
ADS?! WHO NEEDS ADS?
Kelvin Kline

JUST LOOK OUT THE WINDOW! EVERYONE'S DRESSED LIKE US!

AFTER HELPING POPULARIZE THIS LOOK, I DON'T MIND WEARING IT!
JUST WAIT 'TIL DELLA GETS BACK FROM HER GALAXY-WIDE BOOK TOUR! SHE'LL BE TICKED!

SHE WROTE A BOOK? WHAT'S IT CALLED?!
WHAT'S BREWIN', THE WITCHES' COOKBOOK OF COURSE!
WHAT'S BREWIN' Della

BOOM!
OOPS! THINK SHE'S BACK!

SO! WHAT HAPPENED WHILE I WAS AWAY?
NOTHING! IT'S BEEN VERY BORING!
4

YES! HORRIBLY BORING!
YOU'RE CLOSING ALL THE CURTAINS! WHAT'S GOING ON?!

ALL THE MORTALS ARE WEARING WITCH OUTFITS! THIS WON'T DO!
IT'S THE HOTTEST THING ON THE FASHION SCENE!

UH... IT IS?!
FUNNIEST THING! IT CAUGHT ON WHILE YOU WERE AWAY!

WELL, I CAN'T HAVE MY WITCHES WEARING THE SAME OUTFITS AS THE MORTALS!
?

DELLA! I DON'T KNOW ABOUT THIS!
I'M THE ONE WHO SHOULD LOOK FASHIONABLE!
HEY! THIS IS BETTER THAN SKIRTS! I'M OFF TO THE MALL!
The End

Sabrina®

DO YOU BELIEVE IN MAGIC?

CHAPTER 1

AS MY FANS HAVE *KNOWN* FOR YEARS, I'M A TEENAGE WITCH!

BUT, I WASN'T *BORN* WITH THESE POWERS! THEY WERE SORT OF THRUST UPON ME!

Originally presented in **Sabrina #1**, May 1996

Dan Parent • Dan DeCarlo • Bill Yoshida • Barry Grossman

HAPPY BIRTHDAY, SABRINA!
HAPPY SWEET SIXTEENTH, HONEY!
THANK YOU, AUNTIES!

AND THANKS TO ALL OF YOU FOR COMING!
YOU'RE OUR FRIEND, SABRINA!

BLOW OUT THE CANDLES AND MAKE A WISH!
A WISH! HMMM...

WOULDN'T IT BE GREAT IF THAT HUNKY BRAD THOMAS WERE HERE?
OH, WELL, I CAN DREAM, CAN'T I?

BOING
HEY, WHERE AM I?

HILDA, IT'S STARTING TO HAPPEN!
JUST AS WE FIGURED!
BRAD! WHAT ARE YOU DOING HERE?
2

I-I WISH I KNEW!
THAT'S ODD! HE APPEARED ALMOST MAGICALLY!!
AFTER THE PARTY...
OKAY, HILDA! NOW THAT SABRINA IS SIXTEEN, IT'S TIME FOR US TO TELL HER ABOUT ACQUIRING HER POWERS!
OKAY! LET'S DO IT!

SABRINA! WE'VE GOT TO TALK!
WHAT ABOUT, AUNTIES?

WELL, YOU SEE, WE'RE NOT LIKE YOUR EVERYDAY CITIZENS OF RIVERDALE!

WE KNOW YOU THINK WE'RE A LITTLE ODD...

WHAT WITH STRANGE THINGS ALWAYS POPPING UP AROUND US!
WELL, THERE'S A REASON, SABRINA!

AND NOW THAT YOU'RE SIXTEEN, IT'S TIME TO SPILL THE BEANS!
SABRINA, ZELDA AND I ARE WITCHES AND SO ARE YOU...
3

SOMETIME LATER...
WELL, SABRINA, WHAT DO YOU HAVE TO SAY?
ZZZ!

OH, DEAR, SHE MISSED OUR SPEECH!
PUT HER TO BED! WE'LL TELL HER TOMORROW!
Z

THE NEXT MORNING...
SABRINA, WE NEED TO TALK!
SORRY, AUNTIES! I'M LATE FOR SCHOOL!

OH, NO! HOW COULD I HAVE OVERSLEPT?
I WISH I WOULDN'T BE LATE!

HUH?
HOW'D I GET HERE SO FAST?
MUST'VE RUN FASTER THAN I THOUGHT!

OH, WELL, I'D BETTER GET TO CLASS...
SABRINA, SLOW...
W
4

BOF!
...DOWN.!!

OMIGOSH! I'M SO SORRY, MR WEATHERBEE!
I'M A MESS! THANKS A LOT, SABRINA!

I WISH THIS DIDN'T HAPPEN!
BOING

H-HUH?
HELLO, SABRINA! YOU'D BETTER GET TO CLASS!

THAT WAS STRANGE! DID I MAKE THAT HAPPEN?
SABRINA! WHAT WAS MY BOY-FRIEND BRAD DOING AT YOUR BIRTHDAY PARTY?
GYM

MAYBE COMING TO HIS SENSES!
HANDS OFF, SISTER!
5

I'D LOVE TO SEE HER GET WHAT'S COMING TO HER!
BOING
OOF!
HEY!!
WHO THREW THAT AT ME?
EEEEK!!
HELP! I'M BEING ATTACKED BY A ROPE!
GIGGLE!
BOING!
BOING!
BOUNCE!
TROUNCE!
I'M BEING DRIBBLED TO DEATH!
I DON'T KNOW WHAT'S HAPPENING, BUT I LIKE IT!
THIS IS SO STRANGE! EVERYTHING SEEMS TO BE GOING MY WAY!
SABRINA! FINALLY YOU'RE HOME!
TO BE CONTINUED— 6

Sabrina

DO YOU BELIEVE IN MAGIC?

CHAPTER 2

I'M A *WHAT*?

A *WITCH*, DARLING! A FULL-FLEDGED SORCERESS!

I KNEW WE WERE *ECCENTRIC*, BUT *NOT* SUPERNATURAL!
BUT I GUESS THIS EXPLAINS EVERYTHING THAT'S BEEN HAPPENING!

THIS COULD BE COOL! I CAN *CHANGE* THE WHOLE WORLD!
CAREFUL, SABRINA! IT'S NOT THAT *EASY!*

IT TAKES LOTS OF *PRACTICE!*
IT'S LIKE A BABY LEARNING TO WALK! YOU NEED TO START WITH BABY STEPS!

THIS BOOK WILL GUIDE YOU THROUGH!
ZAP!
YE OLD BOOK OF WITCH-CRAFT

AND WE'RE HERE TO *HELP* YOU, SABRINA!
SOB OUR LITTLE GIRL IS A WOMAN NOW!

AND SO...
SABRINA, YOUR LEVITATING IS GETTING PRETTY GOOD!
I'M STARTING TO GET THE *HANG* OF IT!
8

OH, HI, BRAD! THANKS FOR COMING TO MY PARTY!
OH, IT WAS... ER... INTERESTING!

9

WHAT A HUNK!
DID YOU WANT TO ASK ME SOMETHING, HARV?
ER-NO! NEVER MIND!

HEY! MAYBE I CAN MAKE BRAD FALL IN LOVE WITH ME!
IT'S GOING A BIT AHEAD IN MY WITCHCRAFT BUT IT'S WORTH A TRY!

I'LL NEED MY BOOK!
EEK!!
ZAP!

SHE'S DOING IT AGAIN! I'VE GOT TO CALL HARD COPY!
THIS SHOULD DO IT!

MAN OF MY DREAMS, HEAR MY PLEA... IT'S TIME FOR BRAD TO FALL IN LOVE WITH ME!
BOING

WHOA!!
FLIP!
OUCH!
10

HMM! HE FELL FOR ME, BUT IN THE LITERAL SENSE!
I'D BETTER GO TALK TO MY AUNTIES!

WHAT? WE CAN'T MAKE OTHERS FALL IN LOVE WITH US??
NOPE! WE CAN'T CONTROL LOVE! IT'S BEYOND EVEN OUR POWERS!

BUMMER!!
BUT YOU CAN DO NICE THINGS TO ATTRACT HIM TO YOU!

THANKS, AUNTIES!
HMM! MAYBE I SHOULD DO SOMETHING NICE FOR MY AUNTIES!

THEY'VE BEEN SO WONDERFUL WITH ALL OF THIS!
LET'S SEE... WHAT COULD I DO FOR THEM?

MY! WE'RE NOT GETTING ANY YOUNGER EH, ZELDA?
IDEA!
TO BE CONTNUED-11

Sabrina®

DO YOU BELIEVE IN MAGIC?

CHAPTER 3

A *MAKE-OVER!* I COULD GIVE THEM A *MAKE-OVER!*

PLUS, IT'LL GIVE THEM A NEW LOOK WHEN THEY HAVE TO COME TO MY CHEERLEADING EXPO AT SCHOOL!

AUNTIES! HOW ABOUT I GIVE YOU A *MAKE-OVER?*
W-ELL!! I DON'T KNOW!

C'MON, HILDA! WE COULD USE ONE!
OKAY! IT'LL BE *FUN!*
12

OKAY! SIT DOWN!
LET'S SEE ... YOU'LL NEED A SHAMPOO!

SLOSH!
WHOOPS! A BIT MUCH I GUESS!

NOW TO DRY...
SABRINA! WAIT!

WRRRRRR...
OUR HEADS ARE STUCK!

I CAN'T GET THEM LOOSE!
USE YOUR MAGIC!!

OH, YEAH! I KEEP FORGETTING! I'M A WITCH NOW!
ZAP
13

SABRINA! SKIP THE BEAUTY SCHOOL STUFF!
ZAP US WITH A DIRECT LOOK!

OKAY! HERE GOES!
ZAPPO

YIKES! THAT'S NO GOOD!!
ALTHOUGH YOU BOTH LOOK HEALTHY!!

NOPE! THAT WON'T DO!
RIBBIT!

WOW! I THOUGHT DODO'S WERE EXTINCT!

OKAY! I CAN GET IT RIGHT THIS TIME!
I'M GOING TO TALK TO SABRINA AND GET TO THE BOTTOM OF THIS!
14

HMM! THE DOOR IS OPEN...
HELLO!
ZAP!
EEK!!
DON'T HURT ME!!
YOU'RE NOT WORTH THE EFFORT, DEAR!
I CAN'T SEEM TO TOP THIS, AUNTIES!
ER...TRY ONE MORE!
OKAY! HERE GOES...
ZAP!
HEY! NOT BAD!!
YOU ACTUALLY LOOK LIKE YOU'RE FROM THIS CENTURY NOW!
LOOKING GOOD, HILDA!
NOT BAD YOURSELF, ZELDA!
15

WE LOVE IT, SABRINA!
THANK YOU SO MUCH!

NOW YOU BETTER GO PATCH THINGS UP WITH THAT FLAKY GIRL WHO JUST CAME IN!
RIGHT, AUNTIES!

DO YOU THINK SHE SUSPECTS WE DID THIS?
NO! AND LET'S NOT TELL HER!

SHE COULD USE THE MORALE BOOST!!
RIGHT! JUST LIKE WE NEEDED THIS NEW LOOK!!

EMILY! WAIT UP! YOU DIDN'T SEE WHAT YOU THINK YOU SAW!
OH, YEAH! WHAT WAS IT?

ER...UMM ... UH...
I'M WAITING, SABRINA!
CONTINUED-
16

Sabrina®

DO YOU BELIEVE IN MAGIC?
CHAPTER 4

...ER ...UH... WELL IT'S ...UH...

LOOK OUT!!

WHY CAN'T I DO ANYTHING RIGHT?
I CAN'T EVEN MAKE A SIMPLE PLANE WORK CORRECTLY!

THERE GOES MY SCIENCE PROJECT!
POOR HARVEY! MAYBE I CAN HELP HIM OUT?

ZAPP!
HARVEY, WHY DON'T YOU TRY IT AGAIN!

OH, WELL, I MIGHT AS WELL...
HEY!! WHAT DO YOU KNOW!!

IT'S WORKING BEAUTIFULLY!
I'M STARTING TO GET THE HANG OF THIS!

THE NEXT DAY...
AUNTIES, ARE YOU COMING TO THE CHEERLEADING EXPO?
R
18

OF COURSE! WE HAVE TO SHOW OFF OUR NEW LOOK!
LET ME DO THE HONORS!

ZAP!
THIS IS SO MUCH EASIER THAN TAKING THE CAR!
RIVER HIGH

GET OUT THERE, HONEY!
HI, SABRINA! I SEE YOU HAVEN'T LEFT MY BRAD ALONE!

YOU'RE NUTS, AMY!
OH WELL, GOOD LUCK ANYWAY, DEAR! BREAK A LEG!

LITERALLY!
LET'S GO!

GIVE ME AN...R...
GIVE ME AN... I...
RRRR
19

I...
ZOOM!
WHAT WAS THAT?
OMIGOSH! IT'S HARVEY'S PLANE! I FORGOT TO UNZAP IT!
IT'S IN THE AUDIENCE!!
ARCHIE... LOOK OUT!!
IT'S GOT GOT MY TOUPÉE!!
OH, DEAR! YOU'LL NEED A BUCK FOR ANOTHER!
IT'S COMING BACK AT...
...US!!
EXIT
I CAN'T UNZAP IT UNTIL I GET HOLD OF IT!
IT'S MOVING TOO FAST!
20

I BET SABRINA HAD SOMETHING TO DO WITH THIS!
OH, YEAH! IS THAT TRUE?
ER... UH!
AMY, LOOK OUT!!
EEK!!
OOF!!
WOW! THAT THING'S GOT POWER!
LOOK OUT FOR THE...
...POOL!
SPLASH
I DON'T KNOW HOW YOU DID THIS, BUT I'LL GET YOU FOR THIS!
SABRINA! DON'T TELL US! YOU ZAPPED THAT PLANE, DIDN'T YOU?
'FRAID SO, AUNTIES!
WELL, DON'T YOU WANT TO UNZAP IT?
ARE YOU KIDDING? THIS BOTCHED MAGIC IS REALLY WORKING IN MY FAVOR!!

Originally presented in **Sabrina #2**, June 1997

Bill Golliher • Dan Parent • Dan DeCarlo • Bill Yoshida • Barry Grossman

SABRINA OPEN THIS DOOR IMMEDIATELY BEFORE WE ZAP IT DOWN!!
WE JUST WANT TO MAKE SURE YOU SENT CLEOPATRA BACK WHERE SHE BELONGS!

AH! HERE IT IS! JUST WHAT I NEED ACCORDING TO THIS BOOK!
A CRYSTAL BALL!
SABRINA! I'M GOING TO COUNT TO FIVE!

ONE... TWO... THREE... FOUR...

OH, SPIRIT OF THE *NIGHT* HEAR OF MY *PLIGHT* AND *TRAP* THOSE I WISH IN THIS CRYSTAL BALL SO *BRIGHT*!

DO IT YOURSELF MAGIC SPELLS

SCRIPT: BILL GOLLIHER & DAN PARENT

ART: DAN DECARLO

LETTERING: BILL YOSHIDA

COLORING: BARRY GROSSMAN

Sabrina® in TROUBLE IN TIME! PART 1

FIVE! THAT'S IT!!
HILDA! WHAT'S HAPPENING TO US?

I WANTED TO LOSE SOME WEIGHT BUT THIS IS RIDICULOUS!

CLEOPATRA?! WHERE'S SABRINA?
ANCIENT EGYPT, OF COURSE! SOMEONE HAS TO KEEP AN EYE ON THINGS WHILE I'M AWAY!

LUCKY FOR ME I FOUND THIS MAGIC BOOK TO GET YOU TWO OUT OF MY HAIR!

OH, YEAH! JUST WAIT UNTIL WE GET HOLD OF YOU! YOU LITTLE...
FIZZLE
ACCORDING TO THE SPELL I USED, AS LONG AS YOU TWO ARE IMPRISONED IN THE CRYSTAL BALL, YOU'RE POWERLESS!
3

NOW, IF YOU DON'T MIND, I'M GOING TO LEAVE YOU TWO DOWN-STAIRS TONIGHT!
I WANT TO BE RESTED FOR MY FIRST DAY OF SCHOOL TOMORROW!

SALEM!
IT'S NO USE CALLING THE CAT! HE JUMPED THROUGH THE TIME PORTAL ALSO!

YOU'RE ALL ALONE NOW! GOODNIGHT!
THERE'S GOT TO BE SOMETHING WE CAN DO!

MEANWHILE 2,000 YEARS IN THE PAST...
SPEAK, WOMAN! WHAT ARE YOU DOING IN THE QUEEN'S CHAMBERS?
I DON'T KNOW! I DON'T EVEN REMEMBER WHO I AM!

LATER...
FOR THE LAST TIME... HOW DID YOU GET IN HERE WITHOUT THE GUARDS SEEING YOU?
I STILL DON'T KNOW!

ALL I DO KNOW IS THAT I'M HUNGRY AND I'D LIKE SOMETHING TO EAT!
HUH?
POOF!
4

THERE, THAT'S MORE LIKE IT!

HOW DID YOU DO SUCH A THING?

I DON'T KNOW!

CAN'T EVERYONE?

SURELY SHE MUST BE A *GODDESS*!

ALL BOW BEFORE THE GODDESS!

SHE MUST HAVE COME TO EARTH TO VISIT CLEOPATRA AND LOST HER MEMORY ON THE WAY!

?

THAT *MUST* BE WHAT HAPPENED!

LONG LIVE THE GODDESS! LONG LIVE THE GODDESS!

ARGGH!

PLOP!

MOTHER, LOOK! A CAT!
SOME THINGS NEVER CHANGE -- I'VE BEEN SPOTTED BY A BRAT!

I'D BETTER MAKE A RUN FOR IT!
HE'S SUCH A NOBLE CREATURE!

CAN WE TAKE HIM HOME AND FEED HIM EXOTIC FOODS AND PAMPER HIM?
IF HE WISHES!
?

I'M YOURS, KID!
COME, HONORABLE FELINE, WE WILL SHOWER YOU WITH LOVE AND AFFECTION!
SPRONG!

I FORGOT THE ANCIENT EGYPTIANS PRACTICALLY WORSHIPPED US CATS!
I'D BETTER NOT LET ON THAT I CAN TALK OR IT COULD REALLY SEND THEM OVER THE EDGE!

PURR!
I DESERVE THIS KIND OF TREATMENT! LET SABRINA FEND FOR HERSELF A LITTLE WHILE!
END PART ONE

Sabrina in TROUBLE IN TIME PART 2

...THE NEXT MORNING BACK IN THE PRESENT DAY!

HMM! *CLEOPATRA HIGH SCHOOL!* THAT WILL HAVE A NICE RING TO IT!

SO, CLEO, YOU SAY YOU'RE A NEW EXCHANGE STUDENT FROM EGYPT?
YES! HARVEY'S MET ME BEFORE! HAVEN'T YOU, DEAR?
HOMEWORK ASSIGNMENT PG 15 TO 35

UP... YES, CLEO'S A FRIEND OF SABRINA'S!
BUT, I'M AFRAID SHE AND HER AUNTS HAD TO GO OUT OF TOWN FOR A WHILE!
7

I DON'T KNOW IF YOU SHOULD BE HERE! I HAVEN'T SEEN ANY TRANSCRIPT FROM YOUR SCHOOL IN EGYPT!
PERHAPS THE SLAVE DELIVERING THEM WAS SLOWED BY A SANDSTORM!

HA! HA! HA!
SILENCE, INFIDELS! HOW DARE YOU LAUGH AT ME! I'M GOING TO THE ONE YOU CALL PRINCIPAL TO STRAIGHTEN THIS MATTER OUT!

DON'T JUST SIT THERE, BOY!!! CARRY MY BOOKS!!
YES MA'AM!

SOON...
SORRY, MS. CLEO FOR ANY INCONVENIENCE... GO AHEAD AND ATTEND YOUR CLASSES UNTIL YOUR PAPERS ARRIVE!
THAT'S MORE LIKE IT, PRINCIPAL! SEE IT MY WAY!

MEANWHILE...
GODDESS, SINCE OUR QUEEN HAS DISAPPEARED WE WANT TO NAME YOU OUR NEW CLEOPATRA!!
I'D BE HONORED! AT LEAST THEN I'D HAVE A NAME!

BUT I WILL NEED AN OUTFIT MORE BECOMING AN EGYPTIAN QUEEN!
8

HOW BEAUTIFUL!
IT'S JUST A LITTLE SOMETHING I WHIPPED UP!

LET'S CELEBRATE WITH A BANQUET FOR EVERYONE!
POOF!

I HAVEN'T HEARD OF MAGIC LIKE THIS SINCE THAT GUY SPLIT THE RED SEA!
YOU'VE GOT TO TRY THE DESERT BAR, IT'S DELISH!

LONG LIVE THE NEW CLEOPATRA!
OH, GO ON!

EXCUSE ME CLEOPATRA, BUT THERE'S A MARK ANTONY FROM ROME HERE TO SEE YOU!
HMMM! THAT NAME SOUNDS FAMILIAR! SEND HIM IN!

HELLO, MY...
HEY, YOU'RE NOT MY CLEOPATRA!
NO, I'M THE NEW ONE! THE OLD ONE TOOK A POWDER!
9

YOU SEE I'M A GODDESS WHO LOST HER MEMORY!
A GODDESS?

SURE! SEE, NO ONE ELSE CAN DO THIS STUFF!
AMAZING!
HELP!! LET ME DOWN!

YOU'RE CERTAINLY AS BEAUTIFUL AS A GODDESS! CAN WE GO OUT FOR PIZZA OR SOMETHING!
AH-AH! WATCH THOSE ROMAN HANDS, MARK ANTONY!

QUEEN, IT'S TIME FOR A ROYAL PARADE TO SHOW OFF OUR NEW CLEOPATRA!
SURE! WANNA COME MARK?

SOON...
AH! NOW THIS IS THE LIFE! ALL THE FISH I WANT!
BOOM! BOOM!

WHAT IS THAT RACKET?
LOOK! THERE'S A NEW QUEEN!
SHEESH! SOMEONE DIDN'T WASTE ANY TIME!
BOOM! BOOM!
10

SABRINA! THE NEW RULER OF EGYPT?
AND THAT MUST BE THE FAMOUS MARK ANTONY WITH HER!
BOOM! BOOM!

SHE'S IN GOOD HANDS! I'LL JUST ENJOY MYSELF A LITTLE LONGER!
SALEM!

I MUST BE FEELING GUILTY! I COULD'VE SWORN I HEARD HILDA'S VOICE!
YOU DID, YOU LAZY FLEABAG!

THAT IS HILDA! AND IT'S IN MY HEAD!
OF COURSE IT IS! ZELDA AND I ARE CONTACTING YOU TELEPATHICALLY FROM THE FUTURE! CLEOPATRA'S TRAPPED US IN A CRYSTAL BALL!

NOW GET OFF YOUR TAIL AND BRING SABRINA TO HER SENSES!
SHEESH! I WISH I HAD "TELEPATHY WAITING!"
WE HEARD THAT! NOW MOVE IT!
END PART TWO

Sabrina

-in-

"TROUBLE IN TIME"

PART 3

ER-MARK, I APPRECIATE ALL THE ATTENTION ... BUT I BARELY KNOW YOU!

I'M TRYING TO CHANGE ALL THAT, CLEOPATRA!

"SABRINA"?
GASP
A TALKING CAT!!

AREN'T YOU GOING TO BOW BEFORE A "TALKING CAT"? HE MUST BE A GOD!
NO! I'M NOT IMPRESSED!

HMPH! NOTHING LIKE A DOSE OF REALITY!
NOW LISTEN! YOU'RE A WITCH NAMED SABRINA FROM THE YEAR 1997!

SOMEHOW YOU DON'T COME ACROSS AS BEING VERY CREDIBLE!
I THOUGHT YOU MIGHT SAY THAT...

COULD I TROUBLE YOU TO ENCHANT THIS MIRROR FOR ME? IT COULD SHOW YOU WHO YOU REALLY ARE!
A MIRROR?! SURE, I'M GAME!

I DON'T HAVE A TV OR VCR! IT'LL HAVE TO DO!
WHAT'S A TV? OR A VCR?
ZAP!
13

LOOK! THIS IS WHERE YOU LIVE WITH YOUR TWO AUNTS AND ME, SALEM!

HMM! IT'S NOT RINGING A BELL!
THIS IS WHERE YOU GO TO SCHOOL!
RIVERDALE HIGH

THIS IS HARVEY, A GOOD FRIEND OF YOURS!
SORRY! NOTHING REGISTERS!

HMM! HE LOOKS FAMILIAR!
HIS EYES! I REMEMBER HIS EYES...

BOING!
I REMEMBER! I REMEMBER! HI, SALEM!
YOU'RE BACK! YOU'RE BACK!

NOW YOU CAN COME BACK AND SAVE YOUR AUNTS AND GET RID OF CLEOPATRA!
14

IF I RECALL, SHE DIDN'T WANT TO LEAVE, AND CAN'T BE FORCED INTO IT!
WE HAVE TO MAKE HER WANT TO COME BACK!

YOU'RE COMING WITH US! YOU'RE OUR BAIT TO MAKE HER RETURN!
I'LL FOLLOW YOU ANYWHERE!

MEANWHILE BACK IN RIVERDALE ...
OKAY, YOU CAN DROP ME OFF HERE ... BEGONE, PEASANTS!

HELLO, GIRLS! HOW'S IT GOING?
YOU'LL PAY FOR THIS!

NOW, NOW! AT LEAST I DIDN'T TURN YOU INTO TOADS!
AND I COULD'VE WITH THIS HANDY BOOK OF WITCHCRAFT!!
15

NOW LET'S SEE! THIS PLACE NEEDS A BIT OF DECORATING!
LET'S SEE IF I CAN FIND A SPELL FOR THAT!

AH, HOME REDECORATING!
IT SAYS, IMAGINE WHAT YOU'D LIKE TO SEE, AND SAY THESE WORDS...

THIS OLD HOUSE NEEDS A NEW LOOK!
THAT'S WHY I'M LOOKING IN THIS DUSTY OLD BOOK...

ZAP!!
WOW!

THIS IS MORE LIKE IT!
OUR HOUSE! OUR BEAUTIFUL HOME HAS BEEN SABOTAGED!
I DO LIKE THOSE TWO NEXT TO HER HOWEVER...
END PART THREE

Sabrina in "TROUBLE IN TIME" PART 4

I'VE GOT TO MAKE AN *APPEARANCE* AT SCHOOL!
TA! TA!
OH, DEAR! I HOPE SALEM'S GOTTEN THROUGH TO SABRINA!

WELL, I CAN'T SEEM TO REACH HIM *TELEPATHICALLY*!
THAT MUST MEAN THEY'RE IN *TRANSIT*!

I HOPE THEY HURRY! I'M *HUNGRY* AND I CAN'T ZAP ANY FOOD HERE!
WANT A COUGH DROP?
17

SO...
WHEE.!!! THIS IS FUN.!!
I'M GOING TO BE SICK!

WHY IS THIS TAKING SO LONG?
THERE'S A LOT MORE WEIGHT NOW THAN WHEN I ARRIVED!

LOOK.!! WE'RE HOME!
YOU LIVE IN THAT TINY HOUSE?

WOW! THIS IS MORE LIKE IT!
AUNTIES! WE'RE BACK!

OVER HERE! SABRINA GET US OUT OF HERE!
AND BRING SOME SNACKS!
ZAP!

AH, THAT FEELS BETTER.!!
NOW WHERE IS SHE?
18

SHE'S AT SCHOOL!
LET'S GET THERE BEFORE SHE CAN CAUSE TOO MUCH HAVOC!
CLEOPATRA HIGH
YIKES! TOO LATE!

SHE'S LEFT HER MARK IN HERE, TOO!
SABRINA! YOU'RE WEARING REGULAR CLOTHES!

NOBODY CAN EXPLAIN ALL THE EGYPTIAN STUFF INCLUDING OUR CLOTHES!
WHERE'S CLEOPATRA?

SHE'S HOLDING AN ASSEMBLY!

HELLO, COMMON FOLKS! I'M HERE TO ANNOUNCE MYSELF AS YOUR QUEEN!
19

NOT IF I HAVE ANYTHING TO SAY ABOUT IT!
WHAT? HOW DID YOU GET HERE?

I'M HERE TO SEND YOU BACK OR AT LEAST TO STOP THIS LUNACY!
WHAT? AND BLOW YOUR COVER AS A WITCH?

TAKE A LOOK! I'VE CLEARED OUT THE HALL! NOBODY CAN SEE OR HEAR THIS!
THE JIG IS UP!

I DON'T THINK SO! I'VE PICKED UP A FEW TRICKS FROM YOUR BOOK!
ZAP!

A CAGE! HA! THAT'S A GOOD ONE!
SHEESH!
ZAP!

DO WHAT YOU WANT ... BUT I'M NOT GOING BACK!
COME BACK HERE!
SHE'S RUNNING OUT TO THE FOOTBALL FIELD!
20

I'LL STOP HER IN HER TRACKS!!
ZAP!
EEK!!
TOUCHDOWN!!
BONK!
I'M STILL NOT GOING BACK!
NOT AS LONG AS I HAVE MY HARVEY!
MY CLEO... HOW I ADORE YOU...
WHAT HAVE YOU DONE TO MY HARVEY?
LET'S JUST SAY HE'S UNDER MY SPELL...
SABRINA! MY LOVE! ARE YOU OKAY?
MARK ANTONY! WHAT HAVE YOU DONE TO HIM?
HE'S UNDER MY SPELL, AND I DIDN'T EVEN HAVE TO USE MY MAGIC!
DEFINITELY NOT THE END

Sabrina in "OH, WHAT A KNIGHT"

SALEM, I'M EXPECTING GUESTS AT EIGHT FOR MY *HALLOWEEN PARTY!* BUT I SHOULD BE BACK BY THEN!

WHAT?! AREN'T YOU SUPPOSED TO SPEND THE EVENING WITH YOUR AUNTS AT A FAMILY GET-TOGETHER IN THE *OTHER REALM?!*

Originally presented in **Sabrina #8**, December 1997

Bill Golliher • Dan DeCarlo • Bill Yoshida • Barry Grossman

COME ON, SABRINA... OUR COUSIN VON LUDWIG IS EXPECTING US FOR DINNER AT HIS CASTLE IN THE OTHER REALM!!
AND I HEARD HE STOCKED THE MOAT WITH PIRANHAS, SO WE DON'T WANT TO UPSET HIM!

SURE THING, AUNTIES... LET'S GO!
SEE YOU LATER, SALEM!
WINK
YEP! THIS SHOULD BE AN INTERESTING HALLOWEEN!

ZELDA, YOU'RE POKING ME IN THE RIBS WITH THAT CASSEROLE DISH!
WE NEED A BIGGER TRANSPORTATION CLOSET!
SLAM!
POOF!

AND SO...
COUSIN VON LUDWIG!
LOOK! GHOSTS!
BOO!!

YES! I HAD THE PLACE SPECIALLY HAUNTED FOR THE OCCASION!
TAKE THEIR COATS, SIR GALAHAD!
BOO!

HEY, THERE'S NO ONE IN THERE!
YES, AREN'T SPIRITS THE COOLEST!
2

COME ON, EVERYONE, WE'RE HAVING HORS D'OEUVRES IN THE GREAT HALL!
GREAT!
RATTLE

SOON...
SO THEN I SAID TO MARIE ANTOINETTE, IT'S NOTHING TO LOSE YOUR HEAD OVER...
OOPS! IT'S 8 O'CLOCK... I'D BETTER EXCUSE MYSELF AND GREET MY GUESTS!

LATER:
I DON'T HAVE TIME TO WAIT FOR MY COAT, SIR GALAHAD! I'VE GOT TO GET TO THE OTHER REALM!
BUT...

I MUST GIVE THAT GIRL BACK HER COAT! IT'S THE GENTLEMANLY THING TO DO!
WELL, HURRY BACK! WE WERE ALL HIRED TO HAUNT THIS DRAB PARTY!

DING DONG!
SALEM, WHY DON'T YOU LET THEM IN?
I'VE GOT THIS LITTLE PROBLEM WITH DOOR KNOBS! NO OPPOSING THUMBS!

SABRINA, WE WERE BEGINNING TO THINK THE PARTY WAS CALLED OFF!
NO WAY! I WAS JUST DOING A LITTLE DECORATING!
ZAP!
3

COOL JOB!
I'LL BE RIGHT BACK! I'VE GOT A FEW SNACKS TO WHIP UP!

THIS SHOULD DO IT!
ZAP!

NOW WHERE COULD SHE BE?
HI, WHO ARE YOU?

SIR GALAHAD'S THE NAME, M'LADY!
MY NAME IS AMY! YOU SOUND CUTE! WANNA DANCE?!
KISS

SABRINA! WHERE HAVE YOU BEEN?
THE LITTLE WITCHES ROOM! I THINK I GOT AHOLD OF A BAD BATWING!

MEANWHILE...
WHAT'S TAKING SIR GALAHAD SO LONG? MAYBE WE SHOULD GO TO THE OTHER REALM AND FETCH HIM!
YEAH! C'MON, GUYS, THIS SCENE IS GETTING KIND OF DULL ANYWAY!

MRS. ASTRALBERG HAS BEEN ASKING FOR YOU!
SO THIS IS SABRINA... WHAT A CUTIE!!
OUCH!

I KNOW A NICE WARLOCK I'D LIKE TO INTRODUCE YOU TO! MY GRANDSON!
I HAPPEN TO HAVE SOME PICTURES!
SHEESH

SOON:
SABRINA! GET HOME IMMEDIATELY! THINGS ARE GETTING OUT OF CONTROL!
OH, NO! SALEM'S CONTACTING ME TELE-PATHICALLY!

GOT TO GO!
WELL! I THINK HE'S CUTE!
5

SHE'S GOING BACK TO OUR REALM!

SOMETHING'S UP! WE'D BETTER FOLLOW!

MEANWHILE...

COOL! THE POLTERGEISTS ARE BREAKING THINGS!

NOW THIS IS A *PARTY!*

CRASH!

BOO!

SIR GALAHAD, I JUST HAVE TO SNEAK A PEEK!

EEK!!!

BOO!!

AHHH! THE *CHEESE DIP* IS *HAUNTED!!*

WHAT IN THE WORLD?

Sabrina
-in-
"I'M GAME"

HI, HARVEY! WANT TO CATCH A MOVIE?

SORRY! BUT I DON'T HAVE TIME! I'VE GOT TO GET HOME AND TRY OUT MY *NEW VIDEO GAME!*

Originally presented in **Sabrina #13**, May 1998

Bill Golliher • Dan DeCarlo • Bill Yoshida • Barry Grossman

SABRINA, I THOUGHT I JUST SAW YOU OUTSIDE WITH HARVEY!
YOU DID! BUT HE HAD ANOTHER NEW VIDEO GAME TO TRY OUT! NO TIME FOR ME!

THAT'S BOYS FOR YOU! IN YOUR DAY IT'S VIDEO GAMES, IN OUR DAY IT WAS THE CRUSADES!
THOSE DARNED OLD MIDDLE AGES!

YOU MIGHT AS WELL GET USED TO IT!
THERE ARE SOME THINGS GIRLS JUST CAN'T COMPETE WITH!

HMM! BUT MAYBE I CAN COMPETE IN A VIDEO GAME! THEN HE'LL HAVE TO NOTICE ME!
SEE YA!
POOF!

WHAT DID THAT MEAN?
MAYBE IT'S BEST WE DON'T KNOW!

HERE IT IS GUYS!
LOOKS LIKE I'M IN TIME TO ZAP MYSELF INTO THE CARTRIDGE!
2

MONSTROUS COMBAT V! COOL!
I'LL TAKE SUMO SUE!
MONSTEROUS COMBAT V
IT SEEMS LIKE THIS IS THE ONLY CHARACTER I CAN PICK!
SO FAR SO GOOD!
SUPER SAB? SOUNDS CHEESY!
PLAYER 1
PLAYER 2
MEANWHILE...
OMIGOSH! THIS IS ONE OF THOSE FIGHTING GAMES!
SUE CRUSH!
SUE GET YOU GOOD!
NOT IF I MAGICALLY MOVE OUT OF THE WAY!
BOING!
OH, NO! MY POWERS DON'T WORK IN HERE!
OF COURSE NOT! YOU HAVE TO WIN THE MATCH FIRST!
URF
I JUST ASSUMED THIS WOULD BE ONE OF THOSE GAMES WITH A CUTE HEDGEHOG!
3

THAT'S ODD! MY CHARACTER IS NOT RESPONDING!
YEAH, RIGHT! WHAT A LAME EXCUSE!
WHAT CAN I DO? THERE'S NO WAY I CAN WIN THIS BY FORCE!
HMMM! THIS IS A LONG SHOT, BUT I'LL GIVE IT A TRY!
GITCHEE GITCHEE COO!
TEE HEE HEE!
AH-HA! SO YOU ARE TICKISH! EH, TUBBY!
STOP IT! HEE HEE!
TAKE THIS!
PLEASE NO!!
HA HA HEE HEE! I GIVE UP!
I CAN'T BELIEVE IT!
GAME OVER
4

YOUR CHARACTER JUST TICKLED SUMO SUE INTO SUBMISSION!
I DIDN'T EVEN KNOW THERE WAS A CONTROL FOR THAT!

WHAT A STUPID GAME... NOT EVEN A PUNCH OR A KICK!
I'M OUTTA HERE!

I'M BACK!
HOW'D IT GO?
POOF!

I WON! YOU SHOULD SEE THE OTHER GIRL!
SABRINA, TELEPHONE!

HARVEY? YEP! I STILL HAVE THE COOKIES! BUT WHAT ABOUT YOUR GAME?
POOF!

IT WAS PRETTY LAME! FUNNY THING THOUGH... ONE OF THE CHARACTERS REMINDED ME OF YOU!
AS LONG AS IT WASN'T SUMO SUE I'LL TAKE THAT AS A COMPLIMENT!
END

Sabrina in "A Monstrous Halloween"

HAPPY HALLOWEEN, AUNT HILDA!

SABRINA! YOU'RE NOT WEARING *THAT* TO THE FAMILY GET-TOGETHER IN THE OTHER REALM!

Originally presented in *Sabrina* #20, December 1998

Bill Golliher • Dan DeCarlo • Jon D'Agostino • Bill Yoshida • Barry Grossman

ZELDA! SABRINA REFUSES TO GO TO THE OTHER REALM!
OH, SHE DOES, DOES SHE?

THAT'S RIGHT, SHE DOES! FOR ONCE I'M GOING TO SPEND HALLOWEEN WITH MY MORTAL FRIENDS!
IS THIS DECISION FINAL?

IT CERTAINLY IS!
OKAY!

I FEEL KIND OF FUNNY!
ZAP!
THEN THE WAY YOU LOOK SHOULD BE DOWNRIGHT HILARIOUS!

EEK!!! I'VE BECOME A FREAK!
TO PUT IT MILDLY!

WHAT'S HAPPENED TO ME?
EXACTLY WHAT HAPPENS TO ANY WITCH WHO REFUSES TO ATTEND THE HALLOWEEN FAMILY FUNCTION!
2

YOU BECOME A MONSTER UNTIL THE STROKE OF MIDNIGHT!
THIS IS NUTS!

THAT'S THE BREAKS, KID! IT'S JUST AN OLD SPELLMAN FAMILY CURSE!
CAN I CHANGE MY MIND? HUH, CAN I?

I'M AFRAID NOT! ONCE YOU SAID THE DECISION WAS FINAL, THAT WAS IT!
YOU KNEW ALL ALONG AND YOU DIDN'T WARN ME!

SOMETIMES EXPERIENCE IS THE BEST TEACHER!

I GUESS YOU WON'T BE GOING OUT NOW!
HOW COULD I? LOOK AT ME!

JUST DON'T ANSWER THE DOOR! YOU DON'T WANT TO SCARE THE TRICK-OR-TREATERS!
HAH! HAH!
3

BOOM!
GOOD RIDDANCE!
HMPH! JUST LOOK AT ME! AND THAT PARTY AT HARVEY'S WOULD'VE BEEN SO MUCH FUN!
WAIT A MINUTE! I CAN GO!
MY VOICE IS STILL THE SAME! I'LL JUST CONVINCE EVERYONE THAT THIS IS AN ELABORATE COSTUME!
WHO KNOWS, I'D SAY I EVEN HAVE A GOOD SHOT FOR THE BEST COSTUME TROPHY!
THERE! AT LEAST THIS GIVES ME A BIT MORE OF A FEMININE LOOK!
SOON...
DING DONG!
I'LL GET THAT, HARVEY!
THANKS, GINA!
4

BOO!!
SHRIEK!!

SORRY, GINA! DID I SCARE YOU?
SABRINA?! THAT YOU IN THERE?

WHAT'S ALL THE COMMOTION?!
YOW! WHAT'S THAT?!
HARVEY, IT'S ME! SABRINA!

HEY, EVERYBODY! CHECK OUT SABRINA'S COOL COSTUME!
I DON'T EVEN SEE ANY SEAMS!

IT'S TOTALLY QUALITY WORK!
IT HAS TO BE THE FIRST PRIZE COSTUME FOR SURE!
THAT'S WHAT I'M THINKING!
SO MY AUNTIES WERE CONVINCED THIS WOULD BE A BUMMER, BUT I'M MAKING IT WORK FOR ME!
5

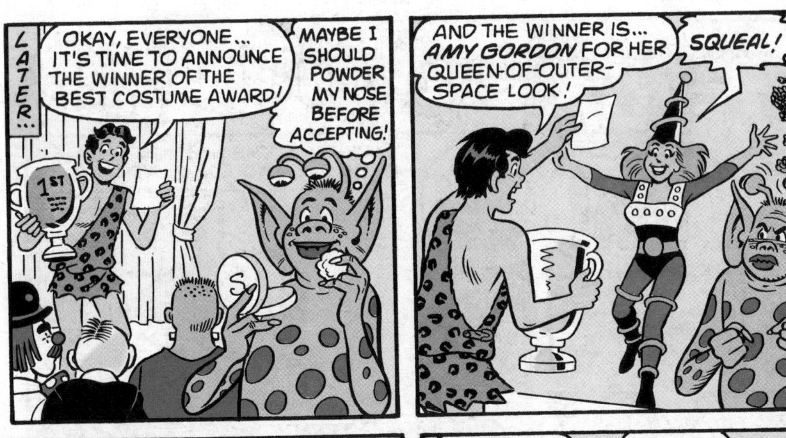
LATER...
OKAY, EVERYONE... IT'S TIME TO ANNOUNCE THE WINNER OF THE BEST COSTUME AWARD!
MAYBE I SHOULD POWDER MY NOSE BEFORE ACCEPTING!
1ST
AND THE WINNER IS... AMY GORDON FOR HER QUEEN-OF-OUTER-SPACE LOOK!
SQUEAL!

HOW DID SHE WIN? MY COSTUME IS MUCH BETTER THAN HERS!
YOU FORGOT ONE IMPORTANT DETAIL...

... ALL THE JUDGES ARE GUYS!
HMMPH!
JUDGES

THANK YOU ALL SO MUCH!
THIS CLINCHES IT! NEXT HALLOWEEN I'M HANGING WITH A FREAKIER CROWD!
MY FAMILY!
1ST
End

ZELDA™ in YOU DON'T KNOW JACK!

HA!
A LIKELY EXCUSE! DON'T EVER CALL ME AGAIN!
UH-OH! LOOKS LIKE THERE'LL BE ONE MORE FOR DINNER!
ZAP!
SLAM!

Originally presented in *Sabrina* #26, June 1999

Mike Gallagher • Dan DeCarlo • Jon D'Agostino • Bill Yoshida • Barry Grossman

THEY'RE ALL NO GOOD! JUST A CENTURY AGO, THEY WERE GENTLEMEN! BUT NOW...
CALM DOWN... COME EAT!

NO!
I'LL BE IN MY ROOM THINKING ABOUT WHEN THEY HAD MANNERS!
?
SLAM!
GOSH! SHE SURE IS MAD!
YUP!

LET ME GUESS... MORTAL MAN TROUBLE!
ZEL'S AN OLD-FASHIONED GIRL... LATE NINETEENTH CENTURY ENGLAND'S MORE HER STYLE!

HMM... JUDGING FROM THOSE SOUNDS, I'D SAY SHE'S ALREADY FEELING BETTER!
ZAP!
TEE HEE!
GIGGLE!

JACK, I'D LIKE YOU TO MEET MY SISTER, HILDA... MY NIECE, SABRINA... AND SALEM!
CHAHMED, I'M SURE!
ZELDA, YOU DIDN'T...
2

WE'LL TALK ABOUT IT LATER... DON'T WAIT UP! COME ON, JACK!
I SAY! NOTHING LIKE AN INVIGORATING CONSTITUTIONAL BEFORE DINNER!

AUNT ZELDA CONJURED HERSELF A DATE WITH A 19TH CENTURY ENGLISH-MAN, DIDN'T SHE?
YES...IS IT JUST ME, OR WAS THAT GUY CREEPY?
HE GAVE ME THE YIPS!

LET ME CHECK THE RESIDUAL MAGIC IN HER ROOM... HMM... LATE 1800s, ALL RIGHT... LONDON!
WE WERE JUST STUDYING THAT PERIOD!
WHAT DID SHE SAY HIS NAME WAS? JIM? JOSH?

"JACK," AS IN
JACK THE RIPPER!

HOLY ABALONE! DID SHE SAY WHAT RESTAURANT THEY WERE GOING TO?
NO... I'LL LOOK IN THE PHONE BOOK! OH, MY! THERE'RE PAGES OF THEM!
TEAR THEM OUT AND WE'LL SEARCH FOR HER ALPHABETICALLY!
YOU STAY HERE, SALEM!
3

MEANWHILE, AT RODOLFO'S RESTAURANT...
THERE'S YOUR TABLE!
MANY THANKS, MY GOOD MAN; HERE'S A LITTLE SOMETHING FOR YOU!
TSK!
MENU

NO, THAT'S NOT NECES... WOW! THIS COIN IS SOLID STERLING!
POUND STERLING, MY DEAR SIR!
PSSST... JACK!

OH, MY... WHAT EXQUISITE CUTLERY!
JACK, LISTEN... YOU'VE GOT TO STOP HANDING OUT THOSE RARE, OLD COINS TO EVERYONE, OKAY?
YOU TIPPED THE HOSTESS, THE BARTENDER AND TWO PEOPLE WHO DON'T EVEN WORK HERE!

HERE'S SOME WATER... A WAITER WILL BE RIGHT WITH YOU...UM...SIR?
GROAN!!
A JOB WELL DONE, MY BOY... HERE YOU GO!
STUFF!

JACK, KNOCK IT OFF! YOU'RE CAUSING A SCENE!
NONSENSE, MY DEAR! AH, LOOK THERE! ANOTHER DESERVING STAFF MEMBER!

I SAY! YOU'RE ALL DOING A SMASHING JOB! AH, THE KITCHEN... ALLOW ME TO SHOW MY APPRECIATION...
?
4

AT THAT MOMENT...
THEY'RE NOT IN THIS PLACE!
TSK! IT'S GETTING LATE AND WE'RE STILL IN THE "C'S"!
CANDACE'S KITCHEN

I'M GOING TO CALL HOME ON MY "SPELL-PHONE!"
ZAP

SALEM? ANY NEWS?
YES!
I DUMPED HER GARBAGE AND FOUND A CRUMPLED NOTE THAT SAYS RODOLFO'S!

RODOLFO'S! THAT'S OVER ON THE EAST SIDE! GOOD WORK, SALEM!
I'LL TELL YOU EXACTLY WHERE!

MOMENTARILY...
WE'RE HERE! LET'S GO INSIDE!
NO, WAIT! THAT SCREAM COMING FROM THE ALLEYWAY... IT'S ZELDA!
EEE!
NO, JACK! DON'T... NO!!
Rodolfo's
5

AUNT ZELDA!!
YOUR DATE'S NOT WHO YOU THINK HE IS!
(SIGH) YOU GOT THAT RIGHT!
AND YOU REMOVE THE RUBBISH? BULLY FOR YOU, SIR! PLEASE ACCEPT THIS TOKEN OF THANKS...
Rodolfo's KITCHEN

WHEW! THANK THE STARS, YOU'RE ALL RIGHT!
WE THOUGHT YOUR "JACK" WAS... UH... WHAT'S HE DOING?
GIVING MONEY TO THE TRUCK DRIVER!
PLOP

BUT WHY?
BECAUSE HE'S NUTS, LIKE ALL MEN! I SHOULD'VE KNOWN HE'D TURN OUT TO BE SOME NOTORIOUS CHARACTER!
YOU DON'T MEAN...
OH NO!
DON'T SAY IT!

YES! IT'S HIM... JACK THE TIPPER!
AND YOU DIRECTED THAT LARGE, HORSELESS CARRIAGE ONTO YON THOROUGHFARE ... MY COMPLIMENTS, CONSTABLE!
SCRAM, POPS!
Rodolfo's
OOFAH! I ASKED HER NOT TO SAY IT!
6
END

Originally presented in **Sabrina #3**, March 2000

Angelo Decesare • Dave Manak • Vickie Williams • Jon D'Agostino • Barry Grossman

SOON...
I KNEW THE ANSWER BECAUSE I WAS WATCHING THAT GAME AT THE HOSPITAL ON THE DAY MY COUSIN WAS BORN!
THIS IS SO COOL! I CAN'T BELIEVE WE'RE GONNA SEE THE MOST AWESOME BAND AROUND... THE ALUMINUM POTATO CHIPS!!! WHAT A TEAM WE MAKE, CHLOE!
I WONDER WHERE OUR SEATS WILL BE...
ROCKIN' 92
ROCKIN' 92FM
SEAT?! SINGULAR? AS IN ONE?
BUT THE D.J. SAID--
HE NEVER SAID HOW MANY. ONE TICKET, KIDS... TAKE IT OR LEAVE IT!
ON AIR
WELL, THAT WAS A SURPRISE!
YEAH...WHAT A SHAME ...I'LL TELL YOU ALL ABOUT THE CONCERT TOMORROW...
92FM
WHAT'RE YOU TALKING ABOUT? I'M THE ONE WHO GOT THROUGH TO THE RADIO STATION!
BUT I'M THE ONE WHO KNEW THE ANSWER! I WON THE PRIZE!
WELL, WHAT IF I DON'T THINK SO?
WELL, MAYBE I'LL JUST MAKE YOU THINK SO!
2

choke
sniffle

BOOHOOHOOHOOO
I'M SORRY!
NO, I'M SORRY!
I'D NEVER RISK OUR FRIENDSHIP!
sniff
sob
DIDN'T MEAN TO SNAP AT YOU!
ME EITHER!
gurgle

LET'S JUST BE PALS AGAIN AND FORGET ABOUT THE TICKET...
WELL, MAYBE WE CAN STILL SALVAGE THE SITUATION... AS A TEAM!

LET'S GO TO THE STADIUM... MAYBE WE CAN FIND SOMEONE TO TRADE US TWO FOR ONE...
MAYBE. IT *IS* A GREAT SEAT.
ENTRANCE
TODAY The ALUMINUM POTATO CHIPS

HI... CAN WE EXCHANGE ONE TICKET IN SECTION 'A' FOR TWO SEATS FURTHER BACK?
NO REFUNDS-- NO EXCHANGES-- NEXT!

Hmf-- THAT'S THAT!
Uh... AHEM, EXCUSE ME...
BOX OFFICE

SORRY--COULDN'T HELP OVERHEARING YOU...MY DATE MISSED HER PLANE, SO I'VE GOT TWO TICKETS AND I ONLY NEED ONE!
WHERE ARE YOUR SEATS?
CHLOE... DON'T TALK TO STRANGERS!

I UNDERSTAND HOW YOU FEEL...HERE, LOOK, SECTION 'B'...JUST BEHIND THE AREA YOU'RE IN NOW!
THEY SURE ARE!
WELL... OKAY!

IT'S A DEAL! HERE YOU GO, GIRLS... ENJOY THE SHOW!
THANKS...
YOU, TOO!

C'MON,... I CAN HEAR THEM WARMING UP!
HERE YOU GO!
WAIT A MINUTE! HOLD IT!!!

THESE ARE TICKETS TO NEXT WEEK'S TRACTOR PULL... NICE TRY, YOU LITTLE SNEAKS... SCRAM!
SPUTTER choke WH- WHAT ?
gasp THAT DUDE RIPPED US OFF!
B

C'MON--LET'S CATCH HIM! HE WON'T GET AWAY WITH THIS!
HE ALREADY HAS, CHLOE! WE CAN'T GET INSIDE!
A

snarl THEN ZAP HIM OUTSIDE... OR BETTER YET, ZAP HIM TO THE SOUTH POLE!
NOW, YOU KNOW I SHOULDN'T. AND I WOULDN'T!

GRRR...IT BURNS ME UP--THINKING OF HIM IN THERE ON OUR TICKET!
I'M NOT SAYING LET HIM GET AWAY WITH IT...I'M JUST SAYING, "NO WITCHCRAFT"...
TODAY the ALUMINUM POTATO CHIPS
STADIUM ENTRANCE

SO YOU HAVE A PLAN ?
I'M GETTING ONE... FOLLOW ME!
THRIFT STORE
ZIP!
5

A SHORT TIME LATER...
EXCUSE ME, SIR... IS THIS YOUR SEAT?
WE WANT THE CHIPS!
WE WANT THE CHIPS!
YEAH, WHAT ABOUT IT?
ADC

THEN, I SUPPOSE YOU'LL HAVE NO TROUBLE TELLING ME WHAT DAY WNBA ROOKIE, TAMIKA REYNOLDS SCORED HER FAMOUS "TRIPLE DOUBLE"?
HUH?
WHO?

I'M SORRY. THAT'S INCORRECT... MA'AM?
AS I SAID TO THE D.J. WHEN I WON THE TICKET... umm...
YOU?!
AUGUST 21ST!

RIGHT! WE CALLED THE RADIO STATION TO CHECK YOUR STORY, MA'AM... TAKE YOUR SEAT! COME WITH ME, PAL!
THANK YOU!
BUT
I
SHE

THAT WASN'T ONE MA'AM, IT WAS TWO KIDS!!!
TELL IT TO THE COPS, BUDDY...
I TOLD YOU THE OLD OVERCOAT TRICK WOULD WORK, CHLOE!
EXIT
DOWN IN FRONT!
TEAM POWER!
LADIES AND GENTLEMEN... THE ALUMINUM POTATO CHIPS!
The End
6

SALEM IN Bride & GLOOM

HAPPY BIRTHDAY, SALEM! WE MADE YOU A HEART-SHAPED FISH CAKE TO SAY THAT 'WE LOVE YOU'!

CUTE, SABRINA, BUT THE CAKE WOULD BE A LOT MORE APPETIZING IF IT WAS SHAPED LIKE A MOUSE!

HAPPY BIRTHDAY Salem WE LOVE YOU!

Originally presented in Sabrina #17, May 2001

Angelo Decesare • Dave Manak • Jon D'Agostino

SALEM, WHAT YOU NEED TO BRING SOME FUN BACK INTO YOUR LIFE IS A DATE! AND I KNOW WHERE YOU CAN GET ONE!
SABRINA, I HAVEN'T DATED SINCE I WAS A WARLOCK, A COUPLE OF CENTURIES AGO!

THIS IS "PURR-FECT PAIRS," AN ON-LINE DATING SERVICE FOR CATS! I'LL TYPE IN A DESCRIPTION OF YOU...
YOU'RE WASTING YOUR TIME, SABRINA!
PURR-FECT PAIRS

...AND UP POPS YOUR DREAM DATE!
HUH?!
Malicia

SABRINA! WHAT CAN I SAY? I'M... I'M BEWITCHED!
AWESOME! NOW ALL WE HAVE TO DO IS ARRANGE A DATE, SALEM!

DATE, SHMATE, SABRINA! START MAILING OUT THE WEDDING INVITATIONS! I'M... IN LOVE!
2

A FEW DAYS LATER...
ZELDA! HILDA! SABRINA! I'D LIKE YOU TO MEET MY FIANCÉE, MALICIA!
HI, MALICIA! AND CONGRATULATIONS!
YOU'LL ALSO BE PART OF OUR FAMILY, SO MAKE YOURSELF AT HOME!

I KNEW YOU'D FEEL THAT WAY, SO WE BROUGHT ALONG MALICIA'S LUGGAGE!

ZZZAP!!
MY DEAR, YOU'RE MARRYING A VERY TALENTED CAT!
Meow! Meow!

SOON...
THERE! THAT LOOKS LIKE EVERYTHING!
IT LOOKS LIKE EVERYTHING IN THE WORLD!
Paris
3

SALEM, WHERE ARE YOU GOING TO PUT ALL THIS STUFF?
WELL, UNTIL MALICIA AND I ARE MARRIED, I TOLD HER SHE COULD STAY IN YOUR ROOM, SABRINA!

MY ROOM?!! AND WHERE AM I SUPPOSED TO SLEEP?!

LATER...
THANKS FOR LETTING ME STAY IN YOUR ROOM TONIGHT, AUNT ZELDA!

YEAH, THANKS! SALEM IS USING MY ROOM TO STORE MALICIA'S COLLECTION OF STUFFED ANIMALS!

MORNING...
WHAT IS THAT TERRIBLE ODOR?

PHEW!
WHAT'S GOING ON HERE?!
OH, HI, SABRINA! MALICIA WANTED FISH FOR BREAKFAST, SO I CONJURED UP A FEW!
4

MROWR! ROWR!!
YOW! WHAT'S THAT HORRIBLE NOISE?!

MALICIA LIKES TO LISTEN TO CAT OPERA.
ROWR-MEOW-WROWR!

SALEM, WHY ARE YOU LETTING MALICIA TAKE OVER OUR HOUSE?!
I CAN'T HELP IT, SABRINA! I'M BEWITCHED BY LOVE!
PURRRR!

"BEWITCHED"... Hmmm! I THINK IT'S TIME TO DO A LITTLE RESEARCH!

LATER...
LOOK, AUNTIES! I FOUND AN ENTRY FOR MALICIA IN "WHICH WITCH IS WHICH"!
WHICH WITCH IS WHICH?

IT SAYS MALICIA'S A WICKED WITCH! SHE TURNS HERSELF INTO A CAT TO TAKE ADVANTAGE OF UNSUSPECTING CATS AND THEIR FAMILIES!
OH, NO! POOR SALEM!
5

YOU MEAN, "POOR MALICIA"! SHE TOOK ADVANTAGE OF THE **WRONG FAMILY**!

SOON...
MORE CREAM WITH YOUR CAVIAR, MALICIA ?
SALEM, SWEETIE, IT'S US, YOUR OTHER THREE WIVES !!
Caviar

WHY, YOU SNEAKY LITTLE FUR-BALL! I'LL TURN YOU INTO A **BUG**!
ZAP!
ZAP!
?
DON'T TRY IT, 'SISTER'! YOU'RE OUTNUMBERED!

I'M OUTTA HERE!
WH-WHAT HAPPENED ? WHERE AM I ?
THE SPELL IS BROKEN! SALEM IS BACK TO NORMAL!
Poof

YOU CAN SAY THAT AGAIN, SABRINA!
YIPEE! FOOD!
CHOMP! GLUG!
THE END

Hat Attack

I remember falling in love with Sabrina on the *Groovie Goolies* Saturday morning cartoon! My wee heart would pitter pat when she flew by on her broom every week! Even before I worked on Archie comics, I named my white ferret Sabrina the Teenage Ferret! So it was a little girl's dream come true to pencil and sometimes write Sabrina! I do believe I'm the first openly, high-functioning Witch to work on her title! Yeah, I'm proud of that!! So when I wrote, I wanted to bring some real and some fun of what being a Magickal Girl is like! I was indeed a teenaged Witch—and when I was a 30-something Witch I brought, hopefully, a dimension to her aunties! I loved creating a love triangle for Sabrina! I figured—Archie has one... sooooo, that's how Shinji was born! I wanted him to be a Magickal Guy... more fun! Oh and I loved penciling Abby Denson's stories!!! Especially "Hat Attack"! And could their be a more lovable scamp than Salem? I could do an all-Salem comic book easy peazy! What more can I say?! This crazy world NEEDS Sabrina and her wacky world of magical mayhem... So let's zap her up the biggest b-day cake and all of us make a wish that Sabrina will keep us giggling for another 60 years!

✶ **Holly G**
Writer/Artist

Charmed I'm Sure

I'm a huge fan of Holly G's run on Sabrina, especially her introduction of new character and love interest, Shinji, who later became a big part of my own run. What I love about this particular story was that it really ramped up the romantic tension! Not only does Shinji kiss Sabrina during their study session—despite her having a boyfriend—but a rival witch has set her eyes on Harvey as well! The story doesn't end with a typical gag, but with DRAMA, and I love that. One of the things I love about Sabrina as a character is that she's extremely adaptable–she can fit into any type of story from humor to romance to horror. Some might call it magic!

✶ **Tania Del Rio**
Writer/Artist

Originally presented in *Sabrina #40*, February 2003

Holly G! • Al Nickerson • Vickie Williams • Jason Jensen

HAIR...
ZAP
BOING!
MORNING, AUNTIES... ≡SIGH≡ MORNING, SALEM. WHAT DO YOU ALL WANT FOR BREAKFAST?
Scratch Scratch
Don't forget to Recycle
BRING ON THE BACON!
KITTY KOOKIES
MMM? MUFFINS, BLUEBERRY MUFFINS!
BLAH, BLAH, BLAH... MUFFINS!
ZAP
MMM... THEY LOOK GOOD!
E-OOO!
?
YUCK! BLAH-BERRY MUFFINS!
2

SABRINA, DEAR, YOUR "SPELL POSTURE" IS TERRIBLY POOR!
sniff sniff
YES, DEAR, JUST LOOK AT YOU!
tsk SOR-RY.
I'VE SEEN BETTER DRESSING ON A SALAD! HAR-HAR!
NO! SABRINA! THIS IS VERY SERIOUS...
...IF YOU DON'T CORRECT YOUR SPELL POSTURE NOW...
...YOU'LL HAVE MISSHAPEN MAGIC FOR THE REST OF YOUR LIFE!!
W-WHAT SHOULD I DO?!
THE BEST THING FOR POOR SPELLING IS 'SPELLING SCHOOL'!
THERE'S A WONDERFUL AFTER-SCHOOL SPELLING PROGRAM IN THE OTHER REALM!
ZAP
MAGIC
OTHER REALM
Be a Happy Witch
Yellow Pages
3

I'LL SIGN YOU UP FOR CLASSES STARTING TODAY!
DON'T WORRY, 'BRINA! WE'LL NIP THIS PROBLEM IN THE BUD!
LATER THAT AFTERNOON...
HEY, SABRINA! WANT TO HANG OUT AT THE PIZZA PARLOR AFTER SCHOOL?
OOH, SORRY, HARVEY. I'D LOVE TO BUT I'VE GOT SPELLING TUTORING AFTER SCHOOL!
SPELLING?! BUT YOU ACED YOUR VOCABULARY TEST THIS WEEK!
OOH, ER--UM--BUT MY FRENCH SPELLING STINKS!
BUMMER!
FRIDA NIGHT DANCE
WELL, IF YOU FINISH EARLY, MEET ME! OKAY?
SURE, HARV! SEE YOU LATER!
4

AFTER SCHOOL...
THIS IS A BUMMER! I COULD BE SHARING A SLICE WITH HARVEY RIGHT THIS MINUTE...
BYE, HAVE FUN!
SPELLING SCHOOL
BEEP BEEP
...BUT I DON'T WANT TO BE DOOMED TO A LIFE OF SLOPPY SPELLING!
SCHOOL OF SPELLING
HERE'S MY CLASS. PROFESSOR S. LE CHAT IS MY SPELLING MISTRESS.
EXCUSE ME...
22
DO YOU KNOW IF THIS IS THE SPELLING CLASS?
WOW! HE'S CUTE!
UH-YEAH, IT IS!
OH, GOOD! I COULDN'T READ MY HANDWRITING!
22
5

MY NAME IS SHINJI, HI! SO, WHY ARE YOU HERE? NOT THAT I'M COMPLAINING!
I'M SABRINA. 'SLOPPY SPELLING'! AND YOU?
OH, I HAVE 'SPELLEXIA'!
WHAT'S THAT?
WELL, IF I WISH TO CONJURE A CAT--I'LL GET A TACK!
THAT COULD GET TRICKY!
TELL ME ABOUT IT! MY LITTLE SISTER WANTED A DOG...WELL, LET'S JUST SAY THE GREEK GOD, ZEUS, WAS VERY CROSS WITH ME, NOT TO MENTION MY PARENTS!
ZAP
MISS SPELLMAN! WE'LL HAVE LESS LAUGHTER AND MORE MAGIC...
HA HA HA
I AM PROFESSOR LE CHAT, AND IT'S MY JOB TO PUSH YOU BUNCH OF LACK LUSTER WITCHES INTO SHAPE!
SO, LET'S GET SPELLING!
End of Part One
6

FIRST THINGS FIRST! ON YOUR FEET, CLASS!
Sabrina
SPELL TROUBLE PART 2
...YOUR CLASS UNIFORMS!
ZAP
VERY CUTE!
AND YOU, MR. YAGAMI!
wink
ZAP
HEY! MY HAIR!
WE MUST HAVE CLEAR VISION TO SPELL CLEARLY!
DON'T WORRY, SHINJI--IT'S VERY CUTE!
THANKS!
wink
7

I WANT YOU TO PAIR UP NOW!
SABRINA?
SURE!
HERE'S YOUR FIRST ASSIGNMENT!
THIS CLASS IS TURNING OUT BETTER THAN I EVER IMAGINED!
IT'S THE PONYTAIL! IT MAKES ME IRRESTIBLE, RIGHT?
WHA--!? NO-I-UM, WAS WONDERING IF YOU UNDERSTOOD THE ASSIGNMENT...
SURE, I THINK WE HAVE TO...
SABRINA, SNAP OUT OF IT!!
...I CAN'T GO CRUSHING ON SHINJI WHEN I'M DATING HARVEY!
HOW CAN I EAT? I MISS SABRINA!
AT THAT VERY MOMENT...
HARVEY, DUDE, YOU'RE THE ONLY GUY I KNOW THAT DOES PIZZA TWO HANDED!
PIZZA
CHOMP
8

ALRIGHT, WE HAVE TO CONJURE A FROG...
...I'LL TRY FIRST!
GREENIE, TEENIE, SITS ON A LOG, ON THIS TABLE, SHOW ME A FROG!
WHAT IN THE WORLD IS THAT?!
IF I'M NOT MISTAKEN, THAT IS A GORF!
BURP
SHINJI-- THIS IS ELEMENTARY CONJURING! HOW HARD IS IT ZAPPING UP A FROG?!
ZAP
THERE! NOW, THAT'S A FROG! EASY!
MEOW!
WELL, ALMOST!
9

DISTRACTED, MISS SPELLMAN, MR. YAGAMI? THAT'S BOTH OF YOUR PROBLEM--I WANT YOU TO WORK TOGETHER...FOCUS!
...CLEAR YOUR MINDS, NOW THINK FROG!
ZAP
IT WORKED!
WE DID IT!
RIBIT!
WE MAKE A PRETTY GOOD TEAM! HUH, SABRINA?
GOOD WORK, DARLINGS!
LATER THAT EVENING...
SOOO-- HOW WAS YOUR SPELLING CLASS?
UM--GOOD! IT WENT OKAY!
10

WELL, JUST WANTED TO SAY GOODNIGHT!
HOW SWEET! GOOD-NIGHT, HARVEY! SEE YOU TOMORROW!
I GUESS I'LL SEE SHINJI TOMORROW, TOO!
THIS IS SO WEIRD, I JUST MET SHINJI BUT I FEEL LIKE I'VE KNOWN HIM FOREVER!
≷YAWN≶ I AM BEING WEIRD! IT'LL ALL MAKE SENSE IN THE MORNING...
GOOD MORNING, SABRINA! HOW WAS SPELLING SCHOOL?
PICK UP ANY POINTERS?
NEED MILK
I DON'T KNOW! LET'S ASK SALEM!
≷BURP≶ MY COMPLIMENTS TO THE ZAPPER!
JUICE
the end

Sabrina in "Danger FROM THE Deep" part one

OKAY! OKAY! I KNOW YOU'RE HERE TO SEE A CERTAIN *WITCH*, BUT FIRST TAKE A MOMENT TO HEAR *MY* TALE!

YOU SEE, I'M NOT REALLY A *GOLDFISH*...

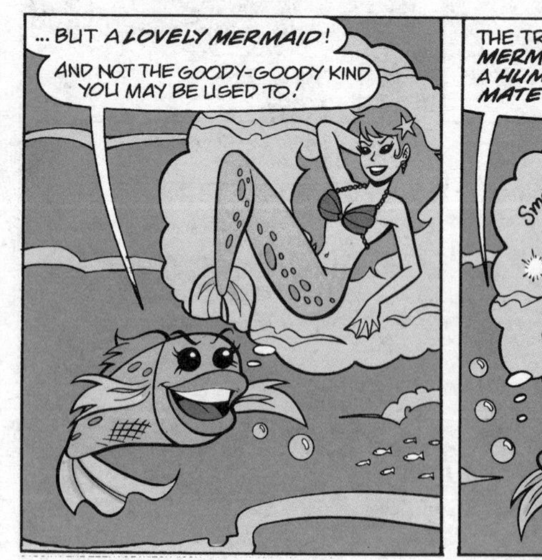

Originally presented in Sabrina #40, February 2003

Bill Golliher • Holly G! • Al Nickerson • Vickie Williams • Jason Jensen

THAT'S WHAT BRINGS ME TO THE CARNIVAL IN THIS LITTLE 'BURB...
WHOA! HERE COMES MY CHANCE!
HARVEY, I'M REALLY ENJOYING THE CARNIVAL!
ME TOO, SABRINA!
3 BALLS $2.00
FUN HOUS

YOUNG MAN, CARE TO WIN A GOLDFISH FOR THE LITTLE LADY?
JUST TOSS A PING PONG BALL INTO A BOWL!
FISH TOSS!
3 BALLS

HE'S A CUTIE!
WOW! IT SEEMED TO ALMOST JUMP INTO THAT ONE!
SPLASH
ZIP

TAKE GOOD CARE OF THIS FISH, KIDS! SHE'S A SPECIAL ONE!
IF ONLY THEY KNEW!

I'D BETTER GET THIS FISH HOME AND INTO A BIGGER TANK! IT LOOKS CRAMPED!
SABRINA!
COTTON CANDY
SODA
MOXIE
2

AUNT ZELDA ?! WHAT ARE YOU DOING HERE ?
I'VE GOT A DATE !
COTTON CANDY
ICE CRE
HELLO, SABRINA, HARVEY !
MR. HASTINGS ?!
OUR HISTORY TEACHER ?
YOU'RE DATING HIM AGAIN ? *
EVER SINCE MEETING HIM AT YOUR SCHOOL'S OPEN HOUSE, WE'VE BEEN REALLY HITTING IT OFF...
THIS COULD BE IT !
* SEE ISSUE #42 SABRINA.
AUNT ZEE, JUST BECAUSE YOU HAVE TO MARRY WITHIN A YEAR OR LOSE YOUR POWERS...*
... WHY DO YOU HAVE TO DATE MY TEACHER ?
GET OVER IT, SABRINA !
* SEE ISSUE #42 SABRINA, TOO.
C'MON, ZELDA ! WE'VE GOT TO RIDE THE TRIPLE LOOPS !
I'M THERE !
SEE YA, KIDS !
TWISTER
SOON...
GOODNIGHT, HARVEY ! THANKS FOR ALL THE FUN AND THE FISH !
HOW 'BOUT MAKING THE EVENING PERFECT WITH A KISS ?
3

Smooch!
GRRR!
HEY! I DON'T THINK THE FISH LIKED THAT!
GUESS IT'S NOT A KISSING FISH!
SPLASH
GOODNIGHT!
AH! A MIDNIGHT SNACK!
YOU SHOULDN'T HAVE!
NO! IT'S A NEW PET HARVEY WON FOR ME!
A TALKING CAT?! I WONDER...
HOW SWEET!
NOW TO GIVE THE FISHY A ROOMIER TANK!
ZAP!
Poof!
HUH?!
AMAZING! I MUST HAVE WOUND UP IN A FAMILY OF WITCHES!
WHAT A JERK!
PLUNK
ZAP
Poof!
4

I TAKE IT YOUR DATE WITH SABRINA'S HISTORY TEACHER DIDN'T GO SO WELL?!
YEP! THAT KNOW-IT-ALL DIDN'T BELIEVE MY STORY ABOUT TWO BARMAIDS STARTING THE WAR OF 1812!
I NEVER HEARD THAT!
IT'S TRUE! WE WERE THE BARMAIDS!
THOSE BRITS SHOULD'VE KEPT THEIR HANDS TO THEMSELVES!
WHY DON'T WE GET SOME SLEEP! THINGS WILL SEEM BETTER TOMORROW!
I'LL NEED PLENTY OF REST TO FACE MR. HASTINGS AGAIN!
GOOD NIGHT, FISH!
GOOD NIGHT, WITCHES!
Z Z Z
yum yum
SOON...
AHHH, FINALLY! A CHANCE TO STRETCH!
SPLOINK!
MEANWHILE...
I CAN'T SLEEP!
MAYBE I'LL GO TAKE ANOTHER LOOK AT THAT TASTY FISH!
5

OH, MY STARS!
A MERMAID!
HUH?
SO, CAT, YOU'VE DISCOVERED MY SECRET!
I CAN'T RISK YOU PASSING ON MY PLAN TO YOUR MISTRESS...,
...HOW I PLAN TO TURN HER BOYFRIEND INTO A MERMAN!
AND JUST HOW DO YOU PLAN TO STOP ME, FISH-STICKS?
LIKE THIS!
I MAY NOT BE A WITCH, BUT I DO HAVE LIMITED POWERS!
SPLOINK!
EEP! I'M A... CATFISH?!
YES! HOW DO YOU LIKE YOUR NEW FORM? IRONIC, ISN'T IT?
GIGGLE
SPLOOOSH!
YOU'LL NOTICE YOU CAN NO LONGER SPEAK! SO MY SECRET'S SAFE WITH YOU FOREVER!
WHAT HAVE I GOTTEN MYSELF INTO?!
End of PART ONE
6

Sabrina in "Danger from the Deep"
PART TWO
BYE, AUNT ZEE! I'M RUNNING LATE FOR SCHOOL!
OKAY, BUT CAN YOU TAKE THESE COOKIES TO THAT SWEETIE, MR. HASTINGS?
ZAP!
sigh
BUT I THOUGHT...
WHO AM I KIDDING? I'VE GOT TO FIND A HUBBY! HECK, I'LL JUST ZAP ON SOME CLOTHES AND DELIVER THEM MYSELF!
ZAP
THE OTHER WITCH MUST STILL BE SLEEPING!
NOW IS THE PERFECT TIME FOR ME TO ATTEND SCHOOL, TOO!
SLAM
SPLOINK
7

THERE! I'M SET TO MAKE MY MOVE ON HARVEY!
SPLOINK
WOW! NICE LEGS FOR A FISH!
STAY OUT OF TROUBLE, CAT!
...I DON'T PLAN TO!
POOR HARVEY! AND I'M POWERLESS TO HELP!
SOON...
HARVEY! QUIT STARING AT ME!
SORRY, SABRINA! YOU'RE JUST SO BEAUTIFUL! LIKE YOU HAVE A SPELL ON ME!
NOW THAT'S FUNNY!
CLASS! I'D LIKE YOU TO MEET SOMEONE!
FRANCE
SANDY SHORE, OUR NEW STUDENT!
HELLO!
HEY, MY 'SPELL' SEEMS TO BE BROKEN!
SANDY, WHY DON'T YOU SHARE SOME OF YOUR FAVORITE INTERESTS WITH US?
LET'S SEE, I LIKE MIDNIGHT SWIMS, WATER SPORTS AND SEAFOOD!
8

AFTER CLASS...
SANDY, I'M HARVEY! YOU SHOULD CONSIDER GOING OUT FOR THE GIRLS' SWIM TEAM! I'M ON THE GUYS'!
THANKS, CUTIE! I'LL LOOK INTO IT!
HMMPH!
LATER...
TEAM TRIALS TODAY
SANDY WINS AGAIN!
TWEET
IT LOOKS LIKE THE SCHOOL'S GOT A NEW STAR!
?
THAT EVENING...
I TELL YOU, AUNT HILLY, THERE'S SOMETHING FISHY ABOUT THAT NEW GIRL AT SCHOOL!
IF ONLY YOU KNEW!
OH, REALLY?
SLAM!
ZAP
VROOM
NEXT DAY...
HARV, DO YOU WANT TO HIT THE SMOOTHIE SHOPPE AFTER SCHOOL?
SORRY, SABRINA...
I PROMISED SANDY I'D DO A LITTLE EXTRA SWIMMING PRACTICE WITH HER!
I HOPE YOU DON'T MIND, SWEETY!
YEAH, OKAY, WHATEVER!
SOON...
HERE KITTY, KITTY!
SLAM
Lucky
9

WHAT'S GOING ON?
WE JUST REALIZED WE HAVEN'T SEEN ANY SIGN OF SALEM LATELY!
HE DIDN'T SAY HE WAS GOING AWAY!
WE'VE BEEN LOOKING EVERYWHERE!
I'M HERE! IF ONLY I COULD LET THEM KNOW!
ZAP
IT'S ALMOST DUSK! WE'LL GO OUT FOR AN AERIAL VACUUM SWEEP OF THE NEIGHBORHOOD!
I'LL KEEP LOOKING AROUND THE HOUSE!
MEANWHILE...
CAN I WALK YOU HOME, SANDY?
ER... NO, HARVEY, I'M FINE!
NO RUNNI
POOLSID
BUT HOW 'BOUT I MEET YOU AT YOUR PLACE LATER AND GO TO A MOVIE?
THAT SOUNDS FUN!
Tickle Tickle
I THINK IT'S TIME I WENT FOR THAT KISS AND GOT THIS CHARADE OVER WITH!
NOW, BACK TO WITCH CENTRAL!
OMEN
MEN
10

SOON...
LOOKS LIKE I'M JUST IN TIME! HERE COMES OUR TEENAGE WITCH!
SPLOINK
I THINK I'LL FEED MY FISH! A GIFT FROM WHEN HARVEY WAS STILL MINE!
WELL, LOOK AT THAT! A LITTLE CATFISH! HILDA MUST'VE PICKED IT UP TO KEEP THE AQUARIUM CLEAN!
BUT SABRINA, IT'S ME!
FISH FOOD
:SIGH!: IT LOOKS LIKE HILLY AND ZEE AREN'T HAVING ANY LUCK FINDING SALEM!
BUT I'M RIGHT HERE!
IT'S NO USE, KITTY!
BRRRING
FISH FOOD
HI, HARVEY! WHAT'S THAT? YOU'RE GOING TO A MOVIE WITH SANDY TONIGHT?!
I KNOW SHE'S NEW! BUT I'D RATHER YOU DIDN'T!
NO, I DON'T WANT TO COME ALONG! GOODBYE!
GRRRR! :HUFF: I NEED A SNACK!
SORRY TO EAT AND RUN BUT THAT'S MY CUE! I'VE GOT A DATE!
GOOD RIDDANCE!
END OF PART 2
11

Sabrina "Danger from the Deep!" PART 3

OH, YEAH? IT'S GONE AGAIN! THERE'S JUST THAT STRANGE CATFISH YOU PICKED UP!

I DIDN'T GET HIM! I THOUGHT YOU DID!

12

CATFISH?! YOU DON'T THINK...
ZAP!
OH, MY!
GET ME OUTTA HERE! I'M WATERLOGGED!
SALEM! WHAT HAPPENED?
POOF
THAT CARNEY GOLDFISH OF YOURS IS REALLY A NASTY MERMAID!
WHAT?!
ONCE I GOT WISE TO HER, SHE ZAPPED ME INTO A CATFISH!
A MERMAID?! I'VE HEARD THEY CAN TAKE FISH FORM!
THUP THUP
SHE CAN TAKE HUMAN FORM, TOO, AND SHE'S OUT FOR A MERMAN!
AMAZING! LET'S CHECK MY MYSTICAL CREATURES REFERENCE BOOK!
ZAP
AH-HAH!... "TO FIND A SUITABLE MATE, A MERMAID WILL TRANSFORM A HUMAN TO A MERMAN WITH A KISS!
BUT WHO'S SHE AFTER?
Mystical Creatures
13

I THOUGHT YOU'D REALIZE BY NOW! SHE'S BEEN GOING TO YOUR SCHOOL AND IS AFTER HARVEY!
SANDY?! NO WONDER SHE'S SUCH AN AWESOME SWIMMER!
ALL IT WILL TAKE IS A KISS AND HE'S HERS FOREVER!
KISS KISS KISS
OH, NO! THEY'RE AT THE MOVIES!
IN THE DARK!
WE'D BETTER HURRY!
NEXT STOP, THE MULTIPLEX!
ZAP!
GREAT! I COULD GO FOR SOME POPCORN!
POOF!
SOON...
TWENTY-FOUR SCREENS?! THIS COULD TAKE A WHILE!
LET'S SPLIT UP! THERE'S NO TIME TO LOSE!
BUZZ BOY
MR. FUNNY
SCARE
Bijou 24
MEANWHILE...
I WISH SABRINA COULD'VE MADE IT!
Z
NO, THIS IS THE WAY IT SHOULD BE! JUST THE TWO OF US!
BUT SANDY, SABRINA AND I ARE INVOLVED!
JUST ONE KISS AND YOU'LL REALIZE I'M THE ONE FOR YOU!
UH-OH! THERE THEY ARE!
14

TWEET
I HOPE THE OTHERS HEAR ME!
HUH?
SAY, ISN'T THAT SABRINA'S CAT?
OH, FORGET ABOUT HIM AND KISS ME NOW!
EEP!
AH-HAH! JUST AS I EXPECTED...
SMOOCH
BONK!
...SOMETHING FISHY IS GOING ON HERE!
YOU'RE TOO LATE! I'VE KISSED HARVEY!
GROAN!
NOT! YOU KISSED THE PLEXIGLASS I ZAPPED BETWEEN YOU TWO AT THE LAST SECOND!
WHAT'S GOING ON? I BONKED MY HEAD!
wrap wrap
YOU'RE COMING WITH US, GILL GIRL!
WHERE ARE WE GOING?
ON A LITTLE BOAT TRIP!
Lucky
15

...TO THE MIDDLE OF THE ARCTIC OCEAN!
YOU'LL BE TOO BUSY TRYING TO KEEP WARM TO THINK ABOUT BOYS!
ZAP
GRR! FINE, I KNOW WHEN I'M OUT-WITCHED!
YOU'LL BE ONE COLD FISH, BABY!
ZAP
ZAP
Lucky
POOF!
YOW! THAT REALLY HURT! WHAT HAPPENED?
MY AUNTS SPOTTED SANDY ON THE USA's MOST WANTED SHOW!
THEY'RE TURNING HER IN! SEEMS SHE'S A NOTORIOUS THIEF!
A BOYFRIEND THIEF, THAT IS!
WHOA! HOW WEIRD IS THAT?
THE LAST THING I REMEMBER IS SHE WAS TRYING TO KISS ME!
THAT'S OKAY, HARVEY...
oooh, Popcorn!
...SHE'LL SOON REALIZE THERE ARE OTHER FISH IN THE SEA!
SABRINA, YOU HAVE ME HOOK, LINE AND SINKER!
THE END

Originally presented in **Sabrina #47**, September 2003

Abby Denson • Holly G! • Al Nickerson • Vickie Williams • Jason Jensen

YOU KNOW I'M VERY WELL BEHAVED!
WELL, GLAD TO HAVE YOU ALONG! ESPECIALLY SINCE YOU LEFT US SOME SANDWICHES!
munch! munch! munch!
PHEW! IT'S HOT!
HERE, HAVE SOME SUNSCREEN SO YOU DON'T BURN UP!
GOOD IDEA! SABRINA'S SKIN IS SO SENSITIVE TO THE SUN!
DON'T REMIND ME! I DON'T NEED ANYMORE FRECKLES! HAND IT OVER!
OH, NO! IT'S EMPTY!
I'LL BURN TO A CRISP!
Orange
2

WHY DON'T YOU CONJURE SOME MORE SUNSCREEN UP...OR BETTER YET, HOW 'BOUT A NICE, BIG, SHADY BEACH HAT?
A PURRR-FECT IDEA!
WELL, WHILE YOU DO THAT, I'M GOING FOR A SWIM!
HAVE FUN!
HERE AND THERE, THIS AND THAT...
'BRINA NEEDS A NEW SUN HAT!
BOING
GREAT JOB!
IT'S FABULOUS!
3

THE COOL THING ABOUT THIS SPELL IS THE HOTTER IT GETS, THE BIGGER THE HAT GETS!
SLURP
WELL, NOW THAT THAT'S SORTED OUT, IT'S NAP TIME!
I'LL JUST DO SOME LOUNGING, MAYBE TAKE A DIP LATER!
Magic Love
WHOAH! IT'S GETTING VERY HOT!
BOiiNNGGG!
DON'T YOU MEAN, "IT'S GETTING VERY HAT"? HA! HA!
EEEEK!
4

CAW?!
THIS ISN'T FUNNY, SALEM! MY HAT IS OUT OF CONTROL!
NONE OF MY SPELLS ARE STOPPING IT!
DUDE, CHECK IT OUT!
COOL!
WHOA!
Z
HA HA HA
OKAY, OKAY! WE NEED HELP! YOU WAKE HILDA, I'LL FIND ZELDA!
HURRY!
WAKE UP, AUNT HILDA! I'M HAVING A FASHION EMERGENCY!
I WAS HAVING SUCH A NICE DREAM!
poke
poke
WHOAH!
IT'S OUTTA CONTROL!
WATCH OUT!
EEK!
HELP!
5

OKAY! IT'S ZELDA TO THE RESCUE!
EEP! I CAN'T GET IT OFF MY HEAD!
HERE AND THERE, THIS AND THAT! GET RID OF THIS SILLY HAT!
THE OCEAN'S MELTING IT!
THANKS, ZELDA!
SPLASH
LET'S GO HOME! I'VE HAD ENOUGH BEACH FOR TODAY!
OKAY!
A-MEN!
A WEEK LATER...
HEY, 'BRINA, LOOKS LIKE YOU STARTED A TREND!
END

Sabrina in "Charmed I'm Sure!" Part 1

Basic Spellwork

WA-HOO! I ACED MY CHARMS EXAM!

Our Characters...

SABRINA: HALF WITCH, HALF MORTAL! STAR OF OUR COMIC!

HARVEY: SABRINA'S SWEET, CUTE AND MORTAL BOYFRIEND!

SHINJI: SABRINA'S NEW WIZARD FRIEND FROM THE OTHER REALM! HAS CRUSH ON SABRINA!

LILITH: DAUGHTER OF THE HEAD WITCH, ENCHANTRA, JEALOUS OF SABRINA, HAS CRUSH ON SHINJI!

PROF. LE CHAT: HEAD MISTRESS OF "SPELLING SCHOOL" AND SABRINA'S TEACHER!

Originally presented in **Sabrina #55**, April 2004

Holly G! • Al Nickerson • Vickie Williams • Jason Jensen

HEY, WHERE ARE YOU GOING? I THOUGHT WE WERE GOING OUT FOR SOME PIZZA?
MAYBE LATER!
A PROBLEM, MISS SPELLMAN?
sigh I THINK I JUST MADE A FRIEND FEEL BAD ABOUT THEIR GRADE, PROFESSOR LE CHAT!
SHINJI HAS BEEN STRUGGLING WITH HIS STUDIES!
REALLY? I DIDN'T KNOW! I THOUGHT HE GOT HIS "SPELLEXIA" UNDER CONTROL!
I MUST SAY, IT HAS IMPROVED SINCE HE'S PARTNERED WITH YOU...
... IT'S TRUE HIS CLASSWORK IS EXCEPTIONAL, BUT HIS HOMEWORK AND TESTING IS STILL SUFFERING!
MAYBE I CAN HELP HIM!
OF COURSE, SABRINA, THAT'S A WONDERFUL IDEA! PERHAPS IF HE COULD LEARN SOME OF YOUR STUDY SKILLS, HIS WOULD IMPROVE!
2

I'LL FLY OVER LATER TONIGHT AND TELL HIM ABOUT OUR *IDEA*!
BEST KEEP OUR CONVERSATION TO *OURSELVES*, MISS SPELLMAN!
SOME YOUNG WIZARDS ARE QUITE PROUD AND YOU WOULDN'T WANT HIM FEELING AS IF IT WEREN'T *HIS* IDEA!
GOT YA!
LATER THAT NIGHT...
I BETTER HEAD OVER TO SHINJI'S NOW!
STUDENT VACUUM PARKING
CHIRP CHIRP
OH, IT'S HARVEY!
CHIRP
HEY, HARVEY! WHAT'S UP?
HEY, 'BRINA! WANNA HANG OUT AND PLAY SOME VIDEO GAMES?
3

OH, WOW, I SORTA PROMISED I'D TUTOR A FRIEND!
UH--SHINJI--YOU REMEMBER, THAT GUY YOU MET LAST SUMMER*?
REALLY, WHO?
* SEE ISSUE #47
THAT GUY FROM YOUR PREP COURSE--OH!
SOMETHING WRONG, HARVEY?
NO! HEY, LOOK, I GOTTA GO--BYE!
CLICK
THAT WAS WEIRD!
4

LATER THAT NIGHT...
SABRINA!
HEY, SHINJI, I WAS WONDERING IF YOU'D DO ME A FAVOR?
I'M GOING TO TRY OUT AS A TEACHER'S AID AT SPELLING SCHOOL, BUT I'M REAL NERVOUS ABOUT IT!
DO YOU THINK I CAN PRACTICE MY LESSON PLANS WITH YOU?
SURE! ANYTHING FOR A SPELL PARTNER!
GREAT! MAYBE WE CAN START AFTER SPELLING SCHOOL TOMORROW!
SOUNDS GOOD!
AND SO...
SHINJI, I REALLY APPRECIATE YOU HELPING ME--OH, HOLD ON...
SPELL SCHOOL
CHIRP
5

OH-- HEY, HARVEY! NO, I CAN'T-- SORRY! YEAH... HOW 'BOUT I MEET YA LATER...
MMM! I WONDER WHO THIS HARVEY IS?
?
SOME CUTE WIZARD SABRINA IS KEEPING ALL TO HERSELF, I BET!
AT LEAST HE'LL KEEP HER BUSY, AND AWAY FROM SHINJI!
SHINJI, WE HARDLY SPOKE TODAY! YOU KNOW I JOINED THIS SPELLING SCHOOL JUST TO SEE YOU MORE OFTEN! WANNA GO MOONBEAM SURFING LATER TONIGHT?
SORRY, LILITH, BUT I PROMISED SABRINA I'D HELP HER STUDY... GOTTA GO!
ZIP
HMMPH! SO, THAT'S HOW YOU WANT TO PLAY, IS IT, LIL' MISS SPELLMAN?!
EVERYTHING OKAY, SABRINA?
YEAH, I THINK SO...
TWO WIZARDS ARE JUST TWO MORE THAN YOU NEED! IT'S TIME FOR ME TO TAKE THIS HARVEY OFF YOUR GREEDY, LITTLE HANDS!
End of Part 1
6

Sabrina in "Charmed I'm Sure" PART TWO
THAT'S IT! YOU GOT IT, EXCELLENT!
I HAVE TO SAY, MS. SPELLMAN, YOU ARE AN EXCELLENT TEACHER!
MERLIN
BUT YOU FIGURED IT OUT!
YES, I DID... FIGURE IT OUT!
!
7

UH... I THINK YOU GOT THE WRONG IDEA!
SEEMED LIKE A GOOD IDEA TO ME!
SHINJI! I DO HAVE A BOYFRIEND!
MEANWHILE...
THE MORTAL REALM? WHAT A STRANGE PLACE FOR SOMEONE TO HAVE A DATE!
PIZZA
PIZZA
BUT, THIS IS THE PLACE WHERE SABRINA SAID SHE'D MEET HARVEY!
PIZZA
WHOAH--IS THAT HIM?!
PIZZA
Italy
8

EXCUSE ME, IS THIS SEAT TAKEN?
WELL-- UM...
...WHY NOT? WHY SHOULD A BEAUTIFUL GIRL LIKE YOU BE LEFT STANDING 'CAUSE MY DATE IS LATE AGAIN?!
SO! WHAT'S A HANDSOME WIZARD LIKE YOU DOING IN THE MORTAL REALM? AREN'T YOU BORED?
MORTAL WHA-- ARE YOU SOME HARRY POTTER FAN OR SOMETHING? HOW CUTE!
OHMYSTARS! THIS GUY IS A MORTAL!!
HOW FASCINATING!
YES, I'M A HARRY POTTER FAN! MY NAME IS LILITH, WHAT'S YOURS?...
9

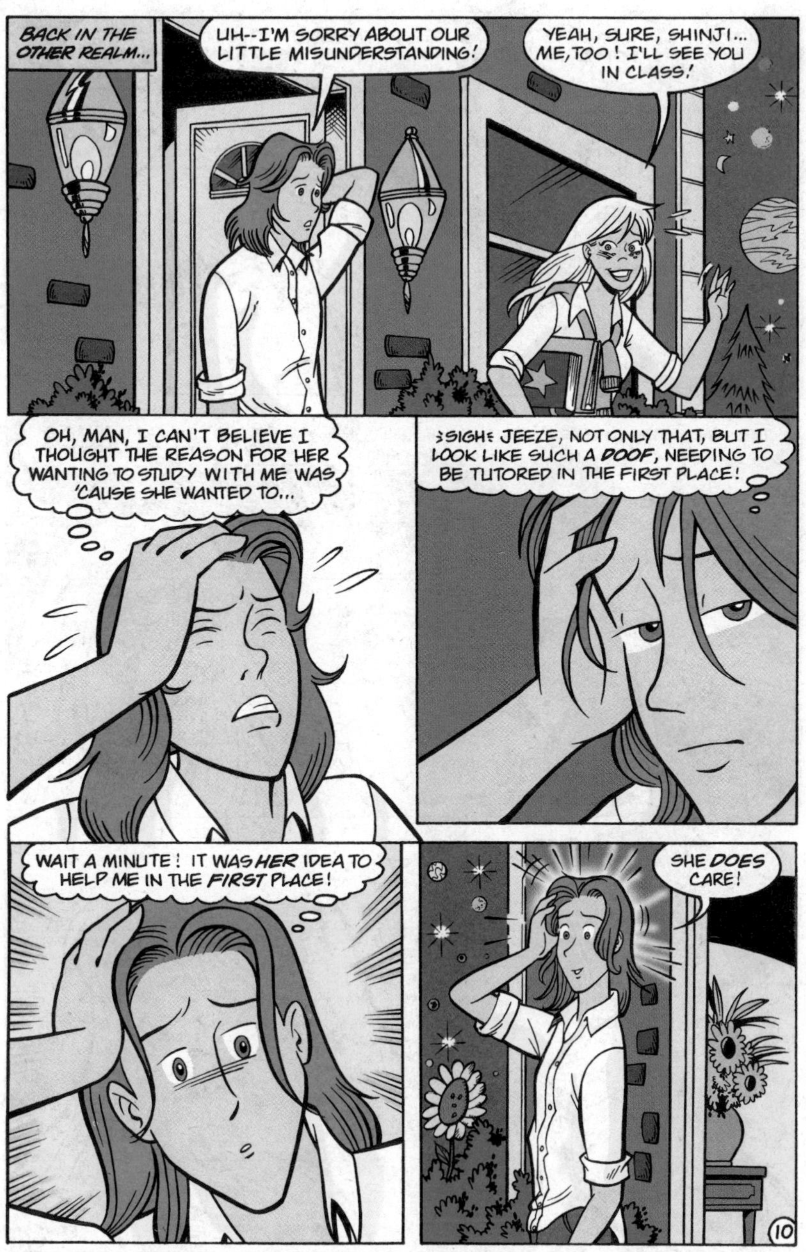
BACK IN THE OTHER REALM...
UH--I'M SORRY ABOUT OUR LITTLE MISUNDERSTANDING!
YEAH, SURE, SHINJI... ME, TOO! I'LL SEE YOU IN CLASS!
OH, MAN, I CAN'T BELIEVE I THOUGHT THE REASON FOR HER WANTING TO STUDY WITH ME WAS 'CAUSE SHE WANTED TO...
≡SIGH≡ JEEZE, NOT ONLY THAT, BUT I LOOK LIKE SUCH A DOOF, NEEDING TO BE TUTORED IN THE FIRST PLACE!
WAIT A MINUTE! IT WAS HER IDEA TO HELP ME IN THE FIRST PLACE!
SHE DOES CARE!
10

THIS HAS BEEN A *WEIRD* NIGHT ALL 'ROUND!

COFFEE Hut

I CAN'T BELIEVE *SHINJI* KISSED ME!

I CAN'T BELIEVE I LET HIM!

end

11

Spellfreeze

The very talented Tania Del Rio transforms Sabrina into a manga character, instantly making it one of my favorite comics from the 2000s. It again just shows how easy Sabrina fits into whatever genre you want her to!

✳ **Jack Copley**
Archie Historian

I remember when I read the *Sabrina: The Magic Within* manga series for the very first time. I found the first volume at a comic book shop when I was 12 years old, and I read it in one night. The next day I went back to that store to buy volume 2, and ended up finishing it just as fast. By day 3 I realized that I should just buy the last two volumes at the same time because I knew I was going to love them. That's the thing about this series, it's addicting! It's the first time we get a Sabrina series with an overarching storyline, and boy is it surprisingly complex! The way Tania Del Rio slowly releases information to the reader as the story goes along is pure genius! Every detail feels like it was planned from the very beginning. Almost every issue of this series leaves you with a cliffhanger, I can't imagine how fans were able to wait so long in between issues when the series was first being published!

✳ **Gillian Swearingen**
Archie Contributer

Salem Returns

Writing and drawing Sabrina for my manga-inspired run remains one of the brightest highlights of my career. When I reflect back on the series I'm proud of the more serious and dramatic storylines I introduced, but this issue remains one of my favorites simply because it's so silly! Salem begs Sabrina to break her self-imposed magic strike to turn him human—only for him to realize that maybe living the life of a pampered house cat isn't so bad after all. Getting to portray Salem as a grown man was a lot of fun, especially as he tries to indulge his feline habits. And even though it's a lighthearted story, it still provided an opportunity to hint at Salem's past which was later expanded upon in the spinoff series, *Young Salem!*

✳ **Tania Del Rio**
Writer/Artist

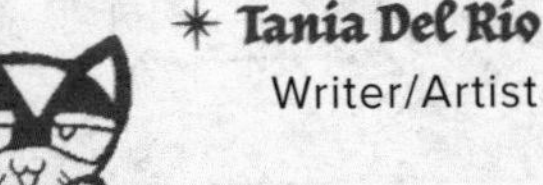

Sabrina "Manga Magic!"

WHAT ARE YOU LOOKING AT?

OH, I'M JUST CHECKING OUT SOME OF MY FAVORITE *MANGA* STORIES!

MANGA? WHAT'S *THAT?!*

DON'T YOU KNOW? IT'S REALLY POPULAR! IT'S COMICS DRAWN IN A JAPANESE STYLE!

OH, COOL!

YEAH, "MANGA" ACTUALLY MEANS "*WHIMSICAL PICTURES,*" SO IT CAN COVER A WIDE RANGE OF STYLES!

WHAT ARE YOUR FAVORITES?

COME HOME WITH ME AND I'LL SHOW YOU!

Originally presented in **Sabrina #58**, August 2004

Holly G! • Al Nickerson • Vickie Williams • Jason Jensen

WOW, SABRINA! THESE ARE REALLY COOL!
I KNOW! THEY'RE SO FULL OF ROMANCE, FASHION, DRAMA AND ACTION!
I JUST CAN'T GET ENOUGH!
I WONDER WHAT OUR LIVES WOULD BE LIKE IF WE WERE IN A MANGA!
HMM... THAT GIVES ME AN IDEA!
OH, NO, SABRINA! I DON'T LIKE THE SOUND OF THIS!
COME ON! IT WILL BE FUN! READY, GUYS?
YEAH!
HERE WE GO!
サブリナ!
HEY, 'BRINA! YOU LOOK REALLY COOL!
SO DO YOU, LLANDRA!
ACK! WHAT ABOUT ME?! I LOOK LIKE A STUFFED ANIMAL!
HEY, THAT'S A GOOD THING! NOW YOU CAN COME TO SCHOOL WITH ME AND NO ONE WILL KNOW YOU'RE A REAL CAT!
I'M NOT HELPING YOU ON YOUR HISTORY TESTS, YOU KNOW!
HA HA! ANYTHING IS POSSIBLE IN MANGA! I CAN'T WAIT TO SEE WHAT HAPPENS!
END

Originally presented in *Sabrina* #58, August 2004

Tania Del Rio • Jim Amash • Jason Jensen

WHAT A GREAT MOVIE!
I MUST ADMIT, HARVEY, I WOULDN'T HAVE EXPECTED YOU TO PICK SUCH A CHICK-FLICK!
UH...ER, ACTUALLY IT WAS THE ONLY THING LEFT IN THE NEW RELEASE SECTION...
I GUESS YOU DO HAVE A ROMANTIC SIDE!
ANYWAY, IT'S GETTING AWFUL LATE AND WE HAVE SCHOOL TOMORROW!
I WISH I HAD A SPELL THAT WOULD SHOW ME HOW HARVEY REALLY FEELS ABOUT ME!
FIRST HE RENTS A ROMANTIC MOVIE AND THEN HE ACTS LIKE HE CAN'T WAIT FOR ME TO LEAVE!
TCH! BOYS!
'BRINA! DO YOU HAVE ANY IDEA WHAT TIME IT IS? IT'S A SCHOOL NIGHT!
ZAP
IT'S NOT THAT LATE!

HOW CAN MY AUNTS BE SO COOL SOMETIMES AND SUCH...SUCH...GROWN-UPS OTHER TIMES?
ZAP
WELL, THEY HAVE BEEN AROUND A LONG TIME!
YAWN! WELL, I'M READY FOR BED, SALEM. HOW ABOUT YOU?
UH...DON'T YOU HAVE SOME BIG REPORT THAT'S DUE TOMORROW?
OH, NO! I COMPLETELY FORGOT!
IT'S GOING TO BE A LONG NIGHT...
ZAP

TURN IN YOUR REPORTS, PLEASE!
YAWN
SABRINA, WHAT IS THIS? THIS ISN'T A REPORT ON EDGAR ALLEN POE!
APPARENTLY YOU DECIDED TO WRITE ABOUT "LUCKY CHARMS AND THE SPELLS THAT MAKE THEM WORK!" SABRINA, IS THIS YOUR IDEA OF A JOKE?
OH NO! I MIXED UP MY ASSIGNMENTS! I WAS SO TIRED LAST NIGHT I DID MY HOMEWORK FOR CHARM-SCHOOL, NOT MY MORTAL HIGH SCHOOL!
HA HA!
HA HA
CHUCKLE
ARE YOU... FEELING ALRIGHT, SABRINA?
HA HA HA!
HEH HEH
NOW, LISTEN UP CLASS. WE HAVE A NEW STUDENT! HIS NAME IS SHINJI YAMAGI AND HE'S AN EXCHANGE STUDENT FROM... FROM...?
OH, HOW EMBARRASSING! THIS HAS GOT TO BE A DREAM!
OH, WHERE I'M FROM ISN'T IMPORTANT!
HOW MYSTERIOUS! LOOK AT HIS HAIR!
OOH!
SHINJI! NOW I KNOW I'M DREAMING!
SABRINA... DO YOU KNOW HIM?
OH! UH, NOT EXACTLY....

RRRRRRIIIIIIIINGGGG!
SHINJI! WHAT ARE YOU DOING HERE? I THOUGHT YOU WENT TO CHARM-SCHOOL!
I DO, AND THAT'S WHY I'M HERE!
I'M DOING A PROJECT ON MORTALS AND HOW THEY LIVE WITHOUT MAGIC! I'M GOING TO BE SPENDING SOME TIME HERE TO GET A FIRSTHAND EXPERIENCE!
AND I WANT TO GET TO KNOW YOU BETTER, TOO!
WOW, HE'S EVEN CUTER IN THE DAYTIME!
BUT YOU KNOW, SHINJI, YOU HAVE TO BE VERY CAREFUL ABOUT NOT LETTING THE MORTALS SEE YOU USING MAGIC!
SEE? YOU DIDN'T BELIEVE ME, BUT THERE THEY ARE! THERE IS DEFINITELY SOMETHING BETWEEN THEM, DON'T YOU THINK?
I...DON'T KNOW WHAT TO THINK, AMY.

YUCK!
MORTALS ACTUALLY EAT THIS STUFF?
LATER THAT DAY
NOW THESE ACTUALLY LOOK EDIBLE!
ZAP
I'M SURE NO ONE WILL NOTICE IF I JUST "ZAP" A COUPLE EXTRA ONTO MY TRAY!
IT'S TOO MUCH WORK TO FIGURE OUT THESE MORTAL COMBINATION LOCKS.
ZAP
CLICK!
SAF-T
IT WOULDN'T HURT FOR ME TO JUST "ZAP" IT OPEN...
I'M ALREADY LATE FOR CLASS AND IT'LL TAKE FOREVER TO FIGHT THIS CROWD!
I'LL JUST USE A QUICK "ZAP" TO GET ME TO CLASS ON TIME...
MAN, THIS CLASS IS DULL. I BET EVEN SABRINA WOULDN'T MIND IF I ZAPPED THE CLOCK FORWARD AN HOUR!
ZAP

CONTINUE YOUR WARM-UPS FOR 10 MORE MINUTES!
CAN YOU STEAL THE BALL FROM ME, 'BRINA?
HA! OF COURSE I CAN!
OOF!
WATCH OUT!
HEH...

WHO DOES THIS GUY THINK HE IS?
HEADS UP, SHINJI!
GASP!
SHINJI!
WATCH OUT!

ZAP
scccreeeech!
SWOOSH
HUH?
SHINJI!
TWACK!
ARE YOU CRAZY?! WE'RE IN A CLASS FULL OF MORTALS! DON'T YOU REMEMBER WHAT I TOLD YOU ABOUT USING MAGIC?
IT WAS SELF-DEFENSE!
WHAT JUST HAPPENED?
YOU'RE LUCKY NO ONE SAW YOU, SHINJI! DON'T DO ANYTHING LIKE THAT AGAIN OR YOU'LL GET US BOTH IN TROUBLE!
DID I JUST SEE WHAT I THOUGHT I SAW? THERE'S SOMETHING ABOUT THAT SHINJI...
I'M NOT SURE WHAT, BUT THERE'S DEFINITELY SOMETHING...

SLAM
UH, HELLO... AMY, RIGHT?
LISTEN, SHINJI, LET ME GET STRAIGHT TO THE POINT. I KNOW YOU'RE HIDING SOME-THING!
I...I DON'T KNOW WHAT YOU'RE TALKING ABOUT!
REALLY? WELL, THEN YOU DON'T MIND IF I TELL EVERYONE IN SCHOOL WHAT I THINK. GOSSIP SPREADS LIKE WILDFIRE AROUND HERE!
LOOK, JUST TELL ME WHAT YOU WANT!
I JUST WANTED TO LET YOU KNOW THAT I THINK YOU AND SABRINA MAKE A REALLY CUTE COUPLE.
WHY ARE YOU TELLING ME THIS?
BECAUSE, SHINJI, I LOVE HARVEY. AND I KNOW HARVEY WOULD LOVE ME BACK IF SABRINA WASN'T IN THE PICTURE! SO, IF YOU LIKE SABRINA, WHY DON'T YOU JUST GO AHEAD AND DATE HER?
THAT WAY WE'LL BOTH HAVE WHAT WE WANT AND NO ONE WILL HAVE TO KNOW ABOUT YOUR SECRET.
IF I DO EVER DATE SABRINA, IT DEFINITELY WON'T BE BECAUSE YOU TOLD ME TO!
HE'S STUBBORN NOW, BUT AS LONG AS HE THINKS I KNOW WHAT HIS SECRET IS, HE'LL DO WHATEVER I WANT!
HMM...BUT I WONDER WHAT HE IS HIDING?

I'M TELLING YOU, LLANDRA, IT WAS SO MUCH EASIER WHEN SHINJI AND HARVEY WERE IN TWO SEPARATE REALMS!
NOW I CAN'T DECIDE WHICH ONE TO SPEND MY TIME WITH! THEY'RE BOTH SUCH NICE GUYS... AND CUTE,TOO!
WELL, CAN'T YOU ALL JUST HANG OUT TOGETHER?
GLAMGAL
THAT'S THE PROBLEM! FOR SOME REASON, HARVEY DOESN'T SEEM TO LIKE SHINJI VERY MUCH...
MAYBE HE'S JEALOUS!
I WISH! LOOK, HARVEY KNOWS I LIKE HIM! IF HE LIKED ME BACK, HE WOULD HAVE ASKED ME TO BE HIS GIRLFRIEND.
BUT IF HE DID, YOU'D HAVE TO FORGET ABOUT SHINJI!
AND THAT'S ANOTHER PROBLEM! I'M GETTING A MAJOR CRUSH ON SHINJI NOW THAT I'VE BEEN SPENDING MORE TIME WITH HIM...
SOMETIMES I'M GLAD I'M JUST A CAT! SOMETIMES I FORGET HOW COMPLICATED IT WAS TO BE HUMAN!
THE NEXT DAY...
WOW! THAT IS SO COOL, SHINJI! HOW DO YOU DO THAT?
MAGICIANS NEVER REVEAL THEIR SECRETS!
WELL, IF HE WANTS TO BE SO OBVIOUS ABOUT IT, LET HIM! I'M NOT GETTING INVOLVED!

DAY 2
IT'S JUST A TRICK, BUT IT ALMOST LOOKS LIKE REAL MAGIC!
DAY 3
I TOLD YOU HE WAS GOOD!
HE'S TALENTED, AND CUTE, TOO!
THAT'S IT! THIS HAS GOT TO STOP!
DAY 4
ARE YOU SURE YOU'RE NOT JUST JEALOUS THAT HE KEEPS SHOWING OFF FOR ALL THOSE GIRLS?
SALEM, I'M HARDLY JEALOUS! I'M JUST UPSET THAT HE'S BREAKING A MAJOR RULE IN MAGIC USE BY USING IT IN FRONT OF MORTALS!
AFTER SCHOOL
Music Club
RIIIIGHT...BUT DON'T YOU USE MAGIC IN FRONT OF -
THAT'S DIFFERENT!
POW

HEY 'BRINA! HOW WAS SCHOOL?
BAD!
BAD?
IS THERE A SPELL THAT CAN **BLOCK** OTHER PEOPLE'S SPELLS?
HMM...
WELL, ***TECHNICALLY***, YES. IT'S CALLED ***SPELLFREEZE***. BUT IT'S A ***VERY*** ADVANCED SPELL, SABRINA! ONLY FOR THE ***MOST*** SKILLED WIZARDS & WITCHES.
"SPELLFREEZE," HUH?
DON'T EVEN ***THINK*** ABOUT IT! LIKE I SAID, IT'S ***VERY*** DIFFICULT.
NOT ONLY THAT, BUT IF YOU'RE CAUGHT CASTING IT IN THE ***MAGIC REALM***, YOU COULD GET IN ***BIG*** TROUBLE!
PEOPLE HAVE BEEN ***PUNISHED*** FOR USING IT UNLAWFULLY!
I SEE...
MAYBE IN THE MAGIC REALM YOU CAN GET IN TROUBLE. BUT THEY DIDN'T SAY ANYTHING ABOUT USING IT IN THE ***MORTAL*** WORLD!

HOW AM I GOING TO LEARN SPELLFREEZE? NONE OF MY CHARM SCHOOL TEACHERS WOULD EVER TEACH ME SUCH AN ADVANCED SPELL!
WELL, YOU HAVE ONE OF YOUR GREATEST TEACHERS RIGHT HERE!
YOU?
WELL, I WAS A WIZARD ONCE, YOU KNOW! AND SINCE I WAS PLOTTING TO TAKE OVER THE WORLD, SPELLFREEZE WAS AN ESSENTIAL SPELL TO MASTER!
I KNOW IT LIKE THE BACK OF MY PAW!
GREAT! TEACH ME HOW TO DO IT!
WELL...SINCE I CAN'T ACTUALLY CAST SPELLS ANYMORE, I CAN'T REALLY DEMONSTRATE IT...SO... IT WILL BE A LITTLE DIFFICULT...
YOU DON'T REMEMBER IT, DO YOU?
WELL IT HAS BEEN MANY YEARS...
THANKS FOR NOTHING.
HEY! I STILL KNOW WHERE YOU CAN FIND THE SPELL-BOOK WHICH CONTAINS THAT SPELL! OF COURSE...IT COULD BE A LITTLE DANGEROUS...
THEN WHAT ARE WE WAITING FOR? OFF TO THE MAGIC REALM WE GO!

MAYBE THIS ISN'T SUCH A GREAT IDEA AFTER ALL...
YOU'RE NOT GETTING COLD FEET NOW, ARE YOU?
YOU DIDN'T TELL ME IT WAS BURIED IN A CREEPY, UNDERGROUND CRYPT!
LET ALONE ONE THAT HAPPENS TO BE HOME TO A VICIOUS BEAST...
I ALREADY TOLD YOU THE BEAST AND ME ARE COOL! KAIBUSTU WAS GONNA LEAD MY ARMY OF HENCHMEN DURING MY BID FOR WORLD DOMINATION.
IF YOU SAY SO...
IT'S AWFUL QUIET IN HERE... MAYBE YOUR BEAST FRIEND DOESN'T LIVE HERE ANYMORE.
THERE IT IS! THE SPELLBOOK OF DARK AND DASTARDLY ARTS! JUST LIKE I REMEMBERED!
YOU WOULDN'T HAPPEN TO REMEMBER THE PAGE NUMBER, WOULD YOU?
RRRRGGGGHH
WHAT WAS THAT?
JUST KEEP LOOKING!
WHO KNOWS WHAT ELSE MAY HAVE MOVED INTO THIS CRYPT IN THE LAST 100 YEARS!

I FOUND IT! NOW TO COPY IT DOWN...
WHO DARES TO ENTER MY CRYPT AND PLACE THEIR FILTHY HANDS UPON MY ANCIENT SPELLBOOK OF DARK AND DASTARDLY ARTS?
S-SALEM? TH-THIS IS YOUR OLD FRIEND, RIGHT?
KAIBUTSU! IT'S ME! YOUR OLD BUDDY!
I HAVE NO KINSHIP WITH ANY HOUSECATS!
YOU FORGOT YOU WERE A CAT AGAIN, DIDN'T YOU?
YOU? DO NOT MOCK ME! THE SALEM I REMEMBER WAS A POWERFUL AND MIGHTY WIZARD POISED TO TAKE OVER THE MAGIC REALM! YOU ARE JUST A STUFFED ANIMAL!
RRRRGGGGGHHH
UH, SABRINA- WE'D BETTER LEAVE!
I'M WAY AHEAD OF YOU, SALEM!
KRRRRSSH

THAT WAS A CLOSE ONE!
THE IMPORTANT THING IS, DID YOU MANAGE TO COPY DOWN THE SPELL?
POOF
I THINK SO...BUT I WAS RUSHED! I WON'T BE ABLE TO PRACTICE IT ON ANYONE, SO I'LL JUST HAVE TO HOPE IT WORKS WHEN I USE IT ON SHINJI!
THE NEXT DAY
THERE HE IS! IN THE ART ROOM AND SHOWING OFF AS USUAL. NOW'S MY CHANCE TO BLOCK HIS SPELLS AND TEACH HIM A LESSON!
OOH!!
HEH
NOW, LADIES, THIS NEXT TRICK I HAVE IS REALLY COOL!
READY?

MAHOU NO CHIKARA DE KATAMARE! *
WOW SHINJI, YOU WEREN'T KIDDING WHEN YOU SAID THIS TRICK WAS COOL!
YEAH, THAT'S, LIKE, YOUR BEST TRICK YET!
OH, NO! I MUST HAVE DONE SOMETHING WRONG! THE SPELL WAS SUPPOSED TO FREEZE SHINJI'S SPELL, NOT HIS BODY!
RIIINNNG...
YOU CAN STOP DOING THAT NOW, SHINJI! IT'S TIME FOR CLASS!
YEAH, WE GOTTA GO! SEE YOU LATER!
MMPH!
* = "BY THE POWER OF MAGIC, BE FROZEN" - ED

SHINJI, CAN YOU HEAR ME? I'M SO SORRY! I DIDN'T MEAN FOR THIS TO HAPPEN!
MKAY, I... PR-MISE... NO..MRRE...SPELFF!
MOW...PREASE ...UMDO...ME!
OH, SHINJI, I DON'T KNOW HOW TO UNDO IT! BUT I'LL FIND A WAY! JUST...STAY HERE!
I DON'T REALLY HAVE MUCH OF A CHOICE...
LOOK, CLASS! SOMEONE LEFT THIS LOVELY STATUE FOR US TO SKETCH TODAY!
AUNTIES!
SABRINA! WHAT'S WRONG? WHY AREN'T YOU IN SCHOOL?

NOW YOU SEE WHY WE TOLD YOU NOT TO TRY AND USE THAT SPELL!
I KNOW YOUR INTENTIONS WERE GOOD, BUT WE'RE STILL DISAPPOINTED IN YOU!
I KNOW! LOOK, I'M SORRY. BUT CAN'T YOU JUST TELL ME HOW TO UNDO IT?
HEH.
THE ONLY THING THAT CAN MELT THIS ICE IS A KISS.
WHAT?
IT'S TRUE.
THEN CAN ONE OF YOU PLEASE COME BACK AND DO IT FOR ME?
WELL, SHINJI IS CUTE, BUT HE'S A FEW CENTURIES TOO YOUNG FOR ME!
SABRINA, SINCE YOU CAST THE SPELL, IT'S YOUR RESPONSIBILITY TO UNDO IT.
GIGGLE
GIGGLE
THIS IS SO EMBARRASSING!
HEY, IT MAY NOT BE SO BAD!
YEAH BUT IF HE'S FRIGID, DON'T TAKE IT PERSONALLY!
PAT PAT
THIS ISN'T FUNNY!

IT'S NIGHT-TIME AT LAST. I HOPE SHINJI'S ALRIGHT...
IT'S ALL LOCKED UP AND NO ONE SEEMS TO BE AROUND. I'LL JUST ZAP MYSELF INSIDE..
GREENDALE HIGH
SHINJI!
MRRRMPH! 'BRINA!
POOF
I'M SORRY I MADE YOU WAIT ALL DAY, BUT I COULDN'T RISK UNDOING THE SPELL DURING SCHOOL HOURS - SOMEONE MIGHT HAVE SEEN US!
...
YOU SEE, I HAVE TO... KISS YOU... TO UNDO IT.
TOO STUNNED TO SPEAK
I KNOW IT'S KIND OF WEIRD...BUT IT'S THE ONLY WAY. AND IT'S NOT LIKE IT MEANS ANYTHING... RIGHT?
MIGHT AS WELL GET IT OVER WITH.

IT WORKED!
ALRIGHT! THE ICE MELTED!
OKAY, I LEARNED MY LESSON.
LET'S NEVER TALK ABOUT THIS AGAIN!
DEAL!

Well, diary, I did it! I broke the spell on Shinji. he was blushing so hard, he could almost have melted the ice himself!
But I must admit...it was nice
but what about Harvey? I've liked him ever since we were in middle school! the poor guy doesn't have any clue about the magic that Shinji and I have,,,, er, I mean, use.
...even if it didn't mean anything.
Well, the important thing is, I learned my lesson. my aunts may seem young but they've been around way longer than I have and they're a lot wiser.
next time I better listen to what they say...
...and ignore Salem!
END

Originally presented in **Sabrina #69**, October 2005

Tania Del Rio • Jim Amash • Jeff Powell • Ridge Rooms • Jason Jensen

OKONOMIYAKI
PANCAKE PIZZAS!
WHAT'S WRONG WITH SHINJI LATELY? HE SEEMS SO GRUMPY. YOU WOULD THINK HE'D BE LOOKING FORWARD TO FOUR-BLADES DAY. AFTER ALL, HE HAS THE FOUR-BLADES EMBLEM MARKED ON HIS CHEST!*
YUM!
THANKFULLY HE DOESN'T KNOW THAT I SAW IT. HE DOESN'T REMEMBER ME PULLING HIM OUT OF THE WATER... OR KISSING ME. LLANDRA WOULD FREAK OUT!*
ARE YOU OKAY, SHINJI? YOU'VE BEEN KIND OF QUIET TODAY.
I DON'T KNOW. I GUESS THE EFFECTS OF THAT SIREN THAT ATTACKED ME ARE STILL WEARING OFF.*
*LAST ISSUE -ED.
I STILL CAN'T BELIEVE YOU WENT OUT ON THE MAGIC BEACH AT NIGHTTIME! DIDN'T I TELL YOU IT WAS DANGEROUS?
WELL? IT WAS WORTH IT AFTER THAT GORGEOUS MERMAID SAVED ME.
SHINJI! ENOUGH WITH THE MERMAID. I DON'T WANT TO HEAR ABOUT YOUR NEW LITTLE CRUSH ANYMORE!
AW, LLANDRA, YOU KNOW YOU'RE STILL MY #1 GIRL!!

I CAN'T BELIEVE SHINJI THOUGHT I WAS A MERMAID! WHAT WOULD THEY BOTH THINK IF THEY REALIZED I'M THE ONE THAT SHINJI'S BEEN OBSESSING OVER?
HE SAID I WAS GORGEOUS!
SIGH...
HE FOLLOWING WEEK...
THIS IS FUN, HUH? TOO BAD HARVEY'S A MORTAL AND CAN'T COME TO THE MAGIC REALM.
ANYWAY WHERE'S YOUR BOYFRIEND? ARE WE GOING TO MEET UP WITH HIM?
NO. SHINJI'S STAYING HOME. HE SAYS HE WANTS NOTHING TO DO WITH THE FESTIVITIES. I DON'T GET IT.
NOT THAT IT MATTERS ANYWAY. I HAVEN'T HEARD FROM HIM ALL SUMMER. HE PROBABLY LOST MY ADDRESS OR SOMETHING. I CAN'T WAIT TO SEE HIM BACK AT SCHOOL, THOUGH!
HIS LOSS!

OOH, LOOK! THIS IS FOR THAT PLAY THAT HILDA'S HELPING TO ORGANIZE.
This Sun-day, 9:00pm, A Theatrical Re-enactment Of The Origin Of Four-blades Day, Sponsored By The Magic Council And The Drama Club Of The Southern Flame Charm School.
COOL! I HEAR THAT THE SOUTHERN FLAME SCHOOL HAS A REALLY GOOD DRAMA PROGRAM. IT SHOULD BE FUN TO SEE.
SABRINA! WHAT A COINCIDENCE! I WAS JUST LOOKING FOR YOU!
HILDA! HILDA! LOOK AT THE GRIFFIN I WON! COOL, HUH? DID YOU KNOW I USED TO HAVE A WHOLE FLEET OF REAL-LIVE GRIFFINS BACK IN MY WIZARDING DAYS?
This Sun-day, 9:00pm, A Theatrical Re-enactment Of The Origin Of Four-b ades Day, Sponsored By The Magic Council
UH, THAT'S GREAT, SALEM. BUT I NEED TO TALK TO SABRINA.
WHAT'S UP?
WELL, THINGS HAVE BEEN CRAZY. OUR LEAD ACTRESS FELL ILL AND WON'T BE ABLE TO PLAY HER PART. WE'VE BEEN SCRAMBLING TO FIND A REPLACEMENT BUT QUEEN SELES HASN'T BEEN HAPPY WITH ANY OF THE GIRLS WHO HAVE TRIED OUT.
THAT'S TOO BAD. BUT, UH, WHAT DOES THIS HAVE TO DO WITH ME?

NOW, I KNOW THIS WILL SOUND REALLY WEIRD AND RANDOM AND I KNOW YOU DON'T HAVE MUCH EXPERIENCE, BUT...
OH, NO. WAIT A MINUTE. THERE IS NO WAY THAT I'M GOING TO REPLACE THAT ACTRESS!
WELL, I'M AFRAID YOU DON'T HAVE MUCH CHOICE. THE QUEEN HERSELF HAS REQUESTED THAT YOU FILL THE ROLE. AND YOU CAN'T SAY NO TO THE QUEEN!
WHAAAAAT? ARE YOU KIDDING ME?
HILDA, DON'T YOU REMEMBER SABRINA'S PERFORMANCE IN "OLD MACDONALD" BACK IN 3RD GRADE?
DON'T REMIND ME...
...AND ON HIS FARM HE HAD A TREE! E-I-E-I-O! WITH A--
WAAAH, I CAN'T REMEMBER WHAT SOUND A TREE MAKES!! I WANT TO BE A HORSEY INSTEAD!
HMPH! WELL, JUST SO YOU KNOW, IF I WAS GIVEN THE HORSEY ROLE I WOULD HAVE MEMORIZED MY LINES PERFECTLY!
WELL, ENOUGH REMINISCING! SABRINA HAS WORK TO DO. LLANDRA, MAYBE YOU CAN HELP SALEM WIN SOME MORE GRIFFINS SO HE CAN RELIVE HIS GOOD OL' DAYS!
YEAH, GOOD IDEA!
I THINK SHE WAS BEING SARCASTIC.

SOON...
LIKE A FISH AMONG SHARKS... I'VE NEVER FELT THIS MUCH HOSTILITY.
GLARE
NOW, I KNOW SABRINA DOESN'T HAVE MUCH EXPERIENCE IN THEATRE, BUT SHE IS WHAT I LIKE TO CALL A DRAMA QUEEN!
HILDA!
THE POINT IS, QUEEN SELES PERSONALLY REQUESTED THAT SABRINA TAKE THIS ROLE, AND SO I HOPE YOU'LL ALL HELP HER ADJUST. IS THAT ALRIGHT, DIRECTOR TWILANDER?
I SUPPOSE WE DON'T HAVE MUCH OF A CHOICE, THEN.
UM, ALRIGHT, SABRINA. THE PART YOU WILL BE PLAYING IS THE ONE OF LADY HANA, ONE OF THE FOUR LEADERS OF THE RENEGADE BLADES, THE UNDERGROUND ORGANIZATION THAT TRIED TO OVERTHROW THE QUEEN ALL THOSE YEARS AGO.
LET ME INTRODUCE YOU TO HANSEL WULF, THE ACTOR WHO WILL BE PLAYING YOUR HUSBAND, LORD KAJI.

HEY.
H-HI.
ALRIGHT! LET'S REHEARSE THE FIRST SCENE!
WOW, HANSEL IS CUTE! I GUESS THIS WON'T BE SO BAD AFTER ALL!
HAVE YOU BEEN ACTING LONG, HANSEL?
WAIT TILL YOU SEE ME IN ACTION. THAT SHOULD ANSWER YOUR QUESTION.
WELL! HE SURE IS CONFIDENT.

MY RENEGADE BLADES! TOGETHER WE WILL SLICE THROUGH THE NIGHT AND THROW THE QUEEN FROM HER THRONE! WE MAY NOT HAVE A GREAT NUMBER, BUT WE HAVE STEALTH, SKILL AND INTELLIGENCE! ISN'T THAT RIGHT, MY LADY HANA?
SCRIPT
YES... MY DEAR HUSBAND. WE ARE NOT... MINDLESS DRONES WHO FOLLOW THE QUEEN WITHOUT QUESTION. WE WILL FORM A NEW KINGDOM OF FREEDOM AND HYPOCRISY.
SCRIPT
YOU MEAN, DEMOCRACY.
OOPS.
ALRIGHT, LET'S TAKE 5 SO SABRINA CAN REACQUAINT HERSELF WITH THE SCRIPT.
I NEVER KNEW ACTING WAS SO DIFFICULT! THERE ARE SO MANY WORDS TO REMEMBER.
YOU KNOW, YOU REALLY LOOK LIKE AN ACTRESS WITH YOUR CUTE BOB, FRECKLES AND BIG BLUE EYES.
TH-THANKS!
OF COURSE, JUST BECAUSE YOU LOOK LIKE AN ACTRESS DOESN'T MEAN YOU PERFORM LIKE ONE! I STILL CAN'T BELIEVE THE QUEEN WANTED YOU IN THIS ROLE.
HMPH!

2 DAYS LATER...
THEATRE
HEY, HILDA.
Four Blades Play
HOW'S SABRINA DOING WITH THE REHEARSALS?
Four Blades Play
Sun-day
WELL...SHE'S TRYING REALLY HARD. I WISH THE QUEEN DIDN'T PUT THIS WEIGHT ON HER SHOULDERS. SABRINA SHOULD BE OUT THERE ENJOYING THE FOUR BLADES FESTIVAL WITH YOU AND SALEM.
NO, NO, NO! SABRINA, THE SCRIPT SAYS "DESPERATION" NOT "INSPIRATION!" YOU'RE CHANGING THE WHOLE CONTEXT OF THE LINE!
SO-RRRY! IT'S HARD TO REMEMBER!
I'VE EVEN MEMORIZED YOUR PART! I MAY AS WELL PLAY BOTH ROLES. UNFORTUNATELY, THERE AREN'T TWO OF ME!
THANK GOODNESS FOR THAT!
I'LL BE GLAD WHEN THIS IS OVER. THAT HANSEL IS ONE BIG JERK! AND HERE I THOUGHT HE WAS CUTE! HAH!
I'LL SHOW HIM! I'M GOING TO MASTER MY LINES BEFORE SUNDAY! I CAN DO THIS JUST AS WELL AS HE DOES-- IF NOT BETTER!
GRR

SORRY, SABRINA.
SHINJI'S NOT HERE. HE SAID SOMETHING ABOUT GOING TO THE BEACH TO FIND A MERMAID. PERSONALLY, I THINK HE'S STILL GETTING OVER THE EFFECTS OF THAT SIREN ATTACK.
YEAH, HE HAS BEEN ACTING KIND OF WEIRD LATELY. HE DOESN'T EVEN WANT TO CELEBRATE FOUR BLADES DAY.
YES, WELL, THAT HOLIDAY IS QUITE OVERRATED. NOW, I HAVE TO GET BACK TO WORK. GOODNIGHT.
SLAM
HUH.
MAN, I REALLY WANT TO INVITE SHINJI TO MY PLAY TOMORROW NIGHT. I GUESS I'LL HAVE TO TAKE A LITTLE TRIP DOWN TO THE BEACH.
I'M STILL A LITTLE SHAKY ON THE BROOM, BUT...
ZAP

AT LEAST I HAVE MY LICENSE, NOW!
WOOSH
I WISH THAT MERMAID WOULD COME BACK. I WANT TO THANK HER.
SHINJI!
WHA--?

HI.
AH!
SHINJI, ARE YOU *ALRIGHT?* WHY ARE YOU *LOOKING* AT ME THAT WAY?
IT'S JUST...FOR A SECOND THERE, I THOUGHT YOU WERE ***SOMEONE ELSE.***
SO, HOW HAVE YOU BEEN?
FINE, I GUESS. WHAT BRINGS YOU ALL THE WAY *HERE?*
ACTUALLY... I WANTED TO INVITE YOU TO COME SEE A *PLAY* I'M IN TOMORROW NIGHT. IT'S BASED ON THE STORY OF *THE FOUR BLADES.*
OH, REALLY? AND WHO KNOWS THE STORY OF THE FOUR BLADES WELL ENOUGH TO BASE A *PLAY* OFF IT?
THE-THE *MAGIC COUNCIL.* THEY WERE THERE! IT WASN'T *THAT* LONG AGO, YOU KNOW.

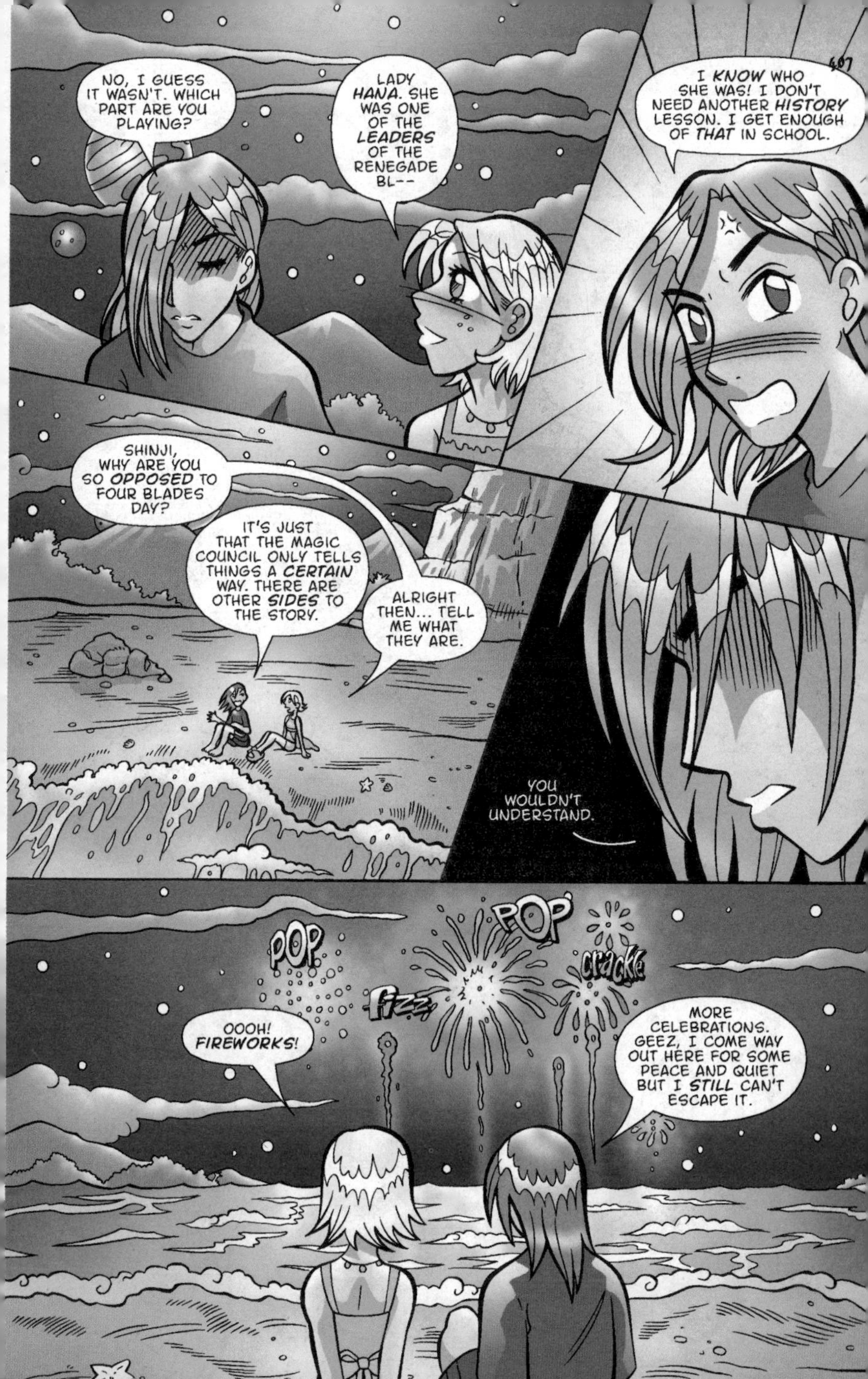
NO, I GUESS IT WASN'T. WHICH PART ARE YOU PLAYING?
LADY HANA. SHE WAS ONE OF THE LEADERS OF THE RENEGADE BL--
I KNOW WHO SHE WAS! I DON'T NEED ANOTHER HISTORY LESSON. I GET ENOUGH OF THAT IN SCHOOL.
SHINJI, WHY ARE YOU SO OPPOSED TO FOUR BLADES DAY?
IT'S JUST THAT THE MAGIC COUNCIL ONLY TELLS THINGS A CERTAIN WAY. THERE ARE OTHER SIDES TO THE STORY.
ALRIGHT THEN... TELL ME WHAT THEY ARE.
YOU WOULDN'T UNDERSTAND.
POP
fizz
POP
crackle
OOOH! FIREWORKS!
MORE CELEBRATIONS. GEEZ, I COME WAY OUT HERE FOR SOME PEACE AND QUIET BUT I STILL CAN'T ESCAPE IT.

I DON'T GET IT SHINJI! YOU SEEM TO TAKE THE HOLIDAY SO PERSONALLY! WHY?
I WANT TO ASK HIM ABOUT HIS SCAR BUT PART OF ME DOESN'T EVEN WANT TO KNOW THE TRUTH BEHIND IT.
THE MAGIC COUNCIL IS BRAINWASHING THE PEOPLE TO THINK A CERTAIN WAY, SABRINA. THERE WAS A REASON THE RENEGADE BLADES WANTED TO CREATE A NEW GOVERNMENT.
THE MAGIC COUNCIL TELLS EVERYONE THAT THE FOUR BLADES WERE BANISHED FROM THE MAGIC REALM AND NOW LIVE IN COZY SUBURBAN HOMES IN THE MORTAL REALM WITH NO MEMORIES OF THEIR MAGICAL LIVES.
WELL? WHAT'S WRONG WITH THAT?
IT'S NOT TRUE.
YOU'RE CREEPING ME OUT, SHINJI! I JUST CAME TO INVITE YOU TO MY PLAY! IF YOU DON'T WANT TO COME BECAUSE OF YOUR WEIRD POLITICAL... WHATEVER, THEN FINE! SORRY I ASKED!

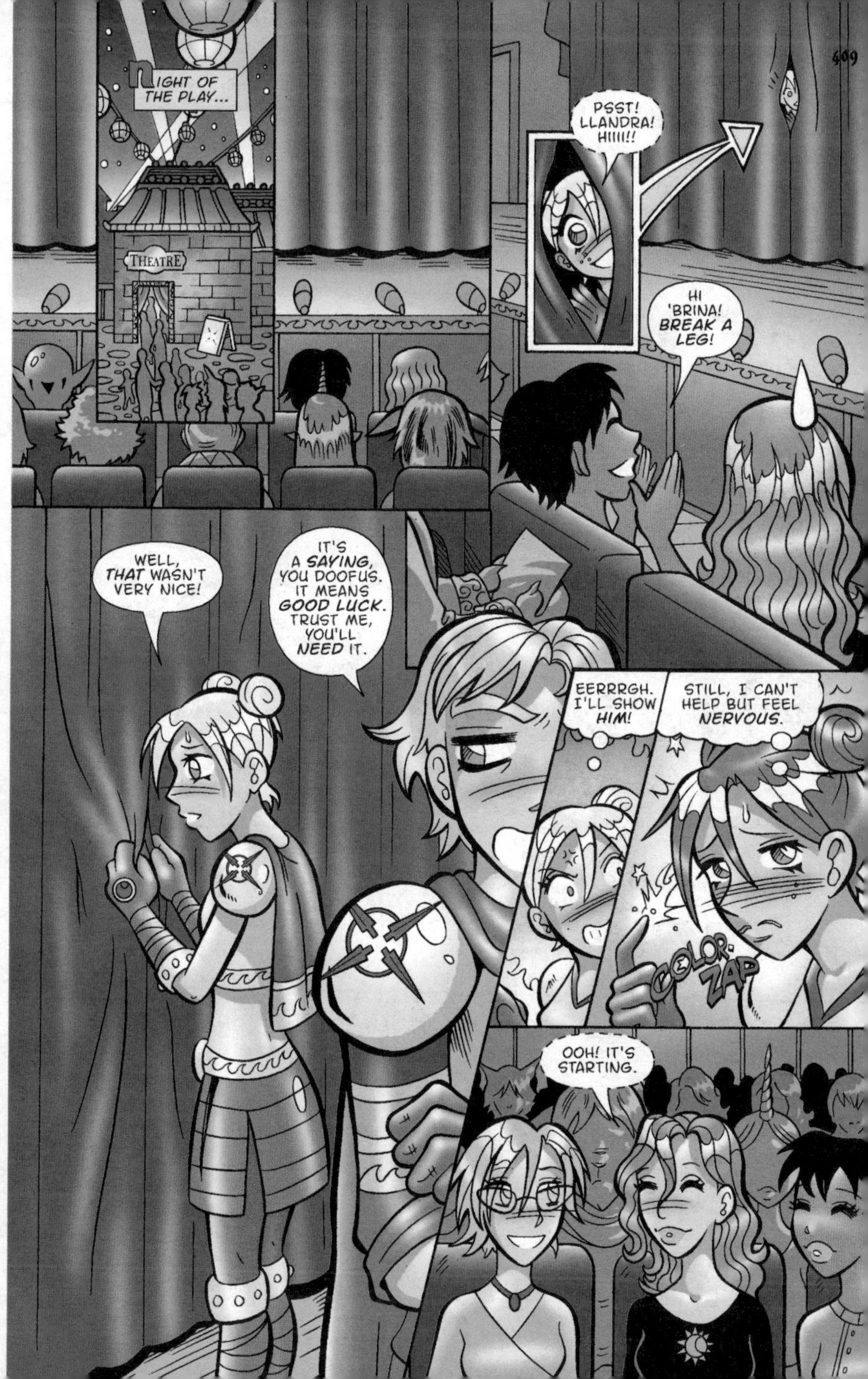

NIGHT OF THE PLAY...
THEATRE
PSST! LLANDRA! HIIII!!
HI 'BRINA! BREAK A LEG!
WELL, THAT WASN'T VERY NICE!
IT'S A SAYING, YOU DOOFUS. IT MEANS GOOD LUCK. TRUST ME, YOU'LL NEED IT.
EERRRGH. I'LL SHOW HIM!
STILL, I CAN'T HELP BUT FEEL NERVOUS.
COLOR-ZAP
OOH! IT'S STARTING.

I, DIRECTOR TWILANDER, AM PLEASED TO PRESENT A PLAY PUT TOGETHER BY OUR ILLUSTRIOUS MAGIC COUNCIL AND THE TALENTED DRAMA CLUB OF THE SOUTHERN FLAME CHARM SCHOOL.
THIS PLAY IS BASED ON THE FATEFUL EVENTS THAT TOOK PLACE EXACTLY 12 YEARS AGO. IT SERVES AS A REMINDER OF WHAT HAPPENS TO THOSE WHO WRONGFULLY THREATEN OUR WONDERFUL QUEEN, AND HOW THEIR SELFISH ACTIONS AFFECT THE ENTIRE MAGIC REALM. ENJOY.
CLAP
CLAP
CLAP
CLAP
MY DEAR WIFE, HANA. I HAVE QUIT MY POST AS GUARDSMAN TO THE QUEEN.
WHY IS THAT, MY LOVE?
HANA! TERRIBLE NEWS - THEY'VE THROWN ME OUT OF THE QUEEN'S GUARD!
NO! WHAT HAPPENED?

I THINK THE QUEEN HAS BEEN A QUEEN FOR TOO LONG! IT'S TIME FOR A CHANGE!
A CHANGE? YES, MANY PEOPLE WOULD AGREE. AND YOU'D MAKE AN EXCELLENT KING! BUT HOW WILL IT COME TO PASS? THE QUEEN IS IMMORTAL AND THE MOST POWERFUL SORCERESS IN THE REALM - SHE WILL NEVER LEAVE HER POST WILLINGLY!
I LEARNED SOME TROUBLING INFORMATION ABOUT THE QUEEN. THEY'RE AFTER ME, HANA. THEY'LL DO ANYTHING TO PREVENT THIS INFORMATION FROM GETTING OUT.
I UNDERSTAND. WE'LL HAVE TO GO INTO HIDING. I'LL GET THE BOYS READY AND PACK SOME OF OUR THINGS.
THEN, WE WILL HAVE TO USE FORCE! I HAVE BEEN SPEAKING WITH OUR GOOD FRIENDS FREYA AND SCALES - THEY AGREE THAT IT'S TIME TO TAKE ACTION. TOGETHER, THE FOUR OF US WILL CREATE AN UNDERGROUND RESISTANCE! PEOPLE WOULD FIGHT BACK IF THEY COULD DO SO WITHOUT FEAR OF BEING CAUGHT!
THANK GOODNESS THAT FREYA AND SCALES HAVE OFFERED THEIR HELP. IF WE CAN JUST REACH THEIR PLACE WITHOUT BEING CAUGHT!
WE CAN'T STAY IN HIDING FOREVER, KAJI. WE'LL HAVE TO FIGURE OUT A PLAN SOONER OR LATER!
MOMMY, I'M SCARED!
splash
splash
LORD KAJI AND LADY HANA SOON MET WITH LORD SCALES AND LADY FREYA AND THEIR PLAN WAS SET INTO MOTION. THEY BECAME... THE FOUR BLADES!
KAJI, WE HAVE TO FIGHT BACK. THE THINGS YOU LEARNED ABOUT THE QUEEN? THE WHOLE MAGIC REALM COULD BE IN DANGER!
BUT WE'LL HAVE TO BE CAREFUL. TOO MANY PEOPLE WILL TRY TO SILENCE US BEFORE WE CAN WARN ANYONE.

HAIL THE FOUR BLADES!
HURRAH!
SHHH...
CLANG
ZAP
SCALES!
URRRGK!
CLANG
WHIMPER

HANA, MY LOVE! DON'T GIVE UP!
PERHAPS THIS IS ALL IN VAIN... COUGH, COUGH PERHAPS WE WERE WRONG! IF WE EVER HAVE CHILDREN, THEY'LL GROW UP HAPPIER IN A PLACE WHERE THE QUEEN RULES. WE'VE JUST BEEN CAUSING WAR AND DEVASTATION!
HANA!
KAJI! NO MATTER WHAT HAPPENS, DON'T GIVE UP! I DON'T WANT OUR CHILDREN TO GROW UP UNDER A CORRUPT KINGDOM. WE HAVE TO STAND BY OUR BELIEFS!
SIGH... PERHAPS YOU ARE RIGHT. THE QUEEN IS JUST TOO POWERFUL. I UNDERESTIMATED HER AND HER FOLLOWERS.
HANA! NOOO!
WAAAAH! MOMMY!
WE MAY HAVE TO SURRENDER, HANA, ESPECIALLY SINCE SCALES AND FREYA HAVE ALREADY BEEN CAUGHT. BUT I'LL ALWAYS LOVE YOU - EVEN IF WE ARE IMPRISONED FOR LIFE!
WHAT IS HE DOING?? A KISS ISN'T IN THE SCRIPT!
INNER SABRINA
AHHH! MUST...NOT... PANIC. MUST... STAY...IN... CHARACTER!

THERE YOU ARE! KAJI, YOUR RESISTANCE IS OVER! YOUR FOLLOWERS HAVE ALL SCATTERED OR BEEN CAUGHT! SURRENDER NOW AND ACCEPT THE QUEEN AS YOUR LEADER!
... I SURRENDER TO YOUR AUTHORITY. I SEE NOW THAT THE QUEEN AND HER FOLLOWING ARE TOO STRONG! I... WAS WRONG.
LUCKY FOR YOU, THE QUEEN IS MERCIFUL. YOU DESERVE A WORSE PUNISHMENT THAN MERE BANISHMENT.
DRAG
YOU WERE ONE OF MY BEST GUARDS, KAJI, AND I TRUSTED YOU. BUT YOU'RE GOING TO REGRET PRYING. PRAY THAT YOUR CHILDREN DO NOT KNOW THE TRUTH- FOR THEIR SAKE ALONE. YOU... ARE ALREADY DOOMED.
AND SO THE FOUR BLADES WERE BANISHED TO THE MORTAL REALM FOR A MUNDANE EXISTENCE - SEALED AWAY FROM THE MEMORIES OF THEIR CRIMES. QUEEN SELES HAS CONTINUED HER BENEVOLENT RULE EVER SINCE THAT FATEFUL DAY.
MAY WE NEVER FORGET WHAT HAPPENED WHEN HER KINGDOM WAS THREATENED AND BE THANKFUL FOR THE STRENGTH OF THE GLORIOUS MAGIC COUNCIL! LONG LIVE THE QUEEN!
CLAP
CLAP CLAP
CHEER
WHISTLE

I DID PERFECTLY! I DIDN'T FLUB A SINGLE LINE!
OH! SHINJI CAME AFTER ALL!
CLAP CLAP CLAP
HE'S... CRYING?
fssh
YOU DID A GREAT JOB, SABRINA! YOU LOOKED LIKE A PROFESSIONAL ACTRESS!
YEAH! THAT KISS SCENE WAS SO AUTHENTIC LOOKING! WOW!

THANKS, GUYS!
HANSEL HASN'T SAID A WORD TO ME SINCE THE PLAY ENDED. GUESS I SHOWED HIM!
heh heh heh
THIS CAME IN THE MAIL YESTERDAY. I WANTED TO SURPRISE YOU WITH IT AFTER YOUR GREAT PERFORMANCE. IT'S FROM HARVEY!
ZAP
WOW! HE WROTE, FINALLY!
"DEAR SABRINA, SORRY IT'S TAKEN ME SO LONG TO WRITE. I'VE BEEN SO BUSY THIS SUMMER HANGING OUT WITH MY RELATIVES AND GOING TO BBQS AND BALLGAMES. I'VE ALSO BEEN THINKING A LOT."
"AND I'VE REALIZED SOMETHING. I THINK MAYBE WE RUSHED INTO THINGS BEFORE I WAS TOTALLY READY. I REALLY CARE ABOUT YOU A LOT, BUT I JUST DON'T KNOW IF I CAN BE THE KIND OF BOYFRIEND YOU WANT ME TO BE. I STILL WANT TO BE FRIENDS... PLEASE DON'T BE MAD. SINCERELY, HARVEY."
I... DON'T BELIEVE IT... HE'S BREAKING UP WITH ME!
WHAT DID I DO WRONG?

Originally presented in *Sabrina* #82, March 2007

Tania Del Rio • Jim Amash • Jason Jensen • Teresa Davidson

EVER SINCE I STOPPED USING MAGIC, I'VE BEEN SO RELAXED! AND I'M BACK WITH HARVEY, TOO! I'M FINALLY A NORMAL TEENAGER!
I'M GLAD SHE LOOKS SO HAPPY. SHE SEEMS LIKE A DIFFERENT PERSON, IN SOME WAYS. LIKE SHE'S NOT HOLDING BACK OR KEEPING SECRETS FROM ME LIKE SHE USED TO...
BUT I HOPE SHE DOESN'T THINK I'M LIKE HER FULL-FLEDGED BOYFRIEND OR ANYTHING. I DON'T THINK I'M READY FOR A SERIOUS RELATIONSHIP LIKE THAT...
CHIRP
CHIRP

WHY, HELLO, SABRINA.
IF YOU'RE TRYING TO IRRITATE ME, IT'S NOT GONNA WORK. I'M IN TOO GOOD OF A MOOD!
EXCELLENT! THAT MEANS YOU'LL BE HAPPY TO HELP ME OUT WITH A LITTLE SOMETHING.
DOES IT HAVE TO DO WITH MAGIC? SALEM, HOW MANY TIMES DO I HAVE TO TELL YOU GUYS? I'M A MORTAL NOW!
I THOUGHT YOU SAID YOU WEREN'T GOING TO GET IRRITATED. FINE, I'LL JUST LEAVE. BESIDES, MORTALS SHOULDN'T BE TALKING TO CATS ANYWAY.
SIGH...

WAIT, SALEM. TELL ME WHAT YOU WANT.
IT'S JUST THAT, I'VE BEEN STUCK IN THIS KITTY CAT BODY FOR 1,010 LONG YEARS NOW...
YOU KEEP SAYING YOU WISH YOU WERE A NORMAL TEENAGE GIRL, BUT WHAT ABOUT ME?
heh
SOMETIMES I WISH I COULD BE A NORMAL HUMAN WIZARD LIKE I USED TO BE!
POUNCE
I'M SORRY ABOUT THAT, SALEM, REALLY. BUT THERE'S NOTHING I CAN DO ABOUT THAT. IT'S YOUR ETERNAL PUNISHMENT FOR TRYING TO TAKE OVER THE WORLD!
BUT HASN'T THIS PUNISHMENT GONE ON LONG ENOUGH? I DON'T WANT THE WORLD ANYMORE-- I JUST WANT OPPOSABLE THUMBS!
ANYWAY, ALTHOUGH YOU MAY HAVE THE POWER TO GIVE A MER-MAN LEGS AND TO BRING DEAD PLANTS BACK TO LIFE, TURNING A CAT INTO A MAN IS COMPLETELY BEYOND YOUR SKILL. IT'S SILLY TO EVEN THINK YOU COULD.
WAIT A MINUTE. I MEAN, THEY DO SAY I'VE GOT SOME SPECIAL MAGICAL ABILITIES. I BET I COULD DO IT IF I REALLY WANTED TO. BUT IT WOULDN'T BE RIGHT!
AND, BESIDES, YOU'RE A MORTAL NOW, ANYWAY. MORTALS CAN'T DO ANYTHING AS IMPRESSIVE AS THAT.
...RIGHT.

WELL, I GUESS I'LL GO GET SOMETHING TO EAT. CHEWING HARD, DRY KIBBLE USUALLY DISTRACTS ME FROM REMEMBERING WHAT HUMAN FOOD TASTED LIKE.
WAIT, SALEM. ARE YOU SERIOUS ABOUT THIS? DO YOU REALLY WANT TO BE HUMAN AGAIN? BECAUSE I BET I COULD MAKE AN EXCEPTION THIS ONCE!
OF COURSE I'M SERIOUS! BUT, SABRINA, THERE'S NO WAY YOU CAN CHANGE ME BACK. YOU MAY HAVE TALENT, BUT YOU CAN'T DO THE IMPOSSIBLE!
WHO SAID IT WAS IMPOSSIBLE?
I CAN COMBINE TWO DIFFERENT SPELLS TO MAKE A NEW SPELL. NO OTHER WITCH OR WIZARD CAN DO THAT!
I BET I CAN FIND A WAY TO MAKE YOU HUMAN. IN FACT, I KNOW I CAN!
A-ARE YOU SURE? I MEAN, I DON'T WANT TO TROUBLE YOU OR DISTRACT YOU FROM YOUR MAGICAL STRIKE.
SALEM, I CAN AT LEAST TRY. I'LL FIGURE SOMETHING OUT!
WOW, SABRINA! THANKS, I CAN'T WAIT!
WELL, THAT WAS EASY.

LATER...
hmm
SABRINA! ARE YOU ACTUALLY READING THROUGH SOME SPELL BOOKS?!
DON'T GET TOO EXCITED. IT'S JUST A ONE-TIME THING!
WELL! SALEM MUST HAVE SAID THE RIGHT THING. I WONDER WHAT SHE'S RESEARCHING?
I HOPE IT'S NOTHING BAD...

Ahhh. TIME FOR A WELL DESERVED NAP.
SALEM! I THINK I GOT IT FIGURED OUT!
WHAT? ALREADY? THAT WAS FAST!
I'M JUST TALENTED, THAT'S ALL.
SAVE THE PRAISE UNTIL AFTER YOU ACTUALLY SUCCEED.
FINE, YOU READY?
WAIT, WAIT, WAIT! NOT SO FAST!
WHAT'S WRONG? I THOUGHT YOU WANTED THIS!
I DUNNO, SABRINA. ARE YOU PLANNING ON PLAYING A TRICK ON ME? IT'S NOT LIKE YOU CAN FIGURE OUT AN IMPOSSIBLE SPELL IN LESS THAN AN HOUR!
SALEM! WHAT KIND OF A PERSON DO YOU THINK I AM? I'M USING MAGIC ESPECIALLY FOR YOU AND YOU ACCUSE ME?

SORRY. OK, GO AHEAD, I JUST *HOPE* YOU CAN FIND A *CURE* JUST AS EASILY IF SOMETHING GOES *WRONG*...
WOOOSH
CLATTER
CLINK
CLATTER
CLINK
CLINK
CRASH
ZAP

SHOOOM
AAAAAHH!! SALEM!! PUT SOME CLOTHES ON!!
AAAAAHHH!! YOU DIDN'T GIVE ME ANY!!
YANK
O-OPPOSABLE THUMBS!!
SABRINA! YOU DID IT!

WHAT IS ALL THE COMMOT--
AHHHHH!
FSSSH
FSSSH
INTRUDER! ZAP HIM!
ZAP
WHY ARE YOU WEARING OUR CURTAINS, YOU WEIRDO?!
FSSH
WAIT! STOP!
IT'S SALEM! I MADE HIM HUMAN AGAIN!
I DON'T BELIEVE IT...

SABRINA! WHAT HAVE YOU DONE? IF THE COUNCIL FINDS OUT ABOUT THIS--
THEY DON'T HAVE TO KNOW! SALEM ISN'T TRYING TO TAKE OVER THE WORLD ANYMORE. HE'S LEARNED HIS LESSON! HE JUST WANTS TO BE NORMAL!
WHAT AM I GOING TO DO WITH HER? SHE HAS TOO MUCH POWER! IF SHE'S NOT CAREFUL WITH IT...
YOU KNOW, YOU'RE NOT A BAD LOOKING HUMAN, SALEM!
ZELDA?! GROOOSSS!
SIGH
I'VE DREAMED ABOUT THIS FOR SO LONG. I NEVER THOUGHT IT WAS POSSIBLE. I DON'T EVEN KNOW WHAT TO DO FIRST! RIDE A BIKE! USE A FORK! GET REVENGE ON THE DOG DOWN THE STREET!
NO, SALEM. NO REVENGE. THE FIRST THING YOU NEED IS A SHOWER AND A DECENT SET OF CLOTHES. YOU MAY LOOK LIKE A HUMAN, BUT YOU SMELL LIKE KITTY LITTER!
A SHOWER? BUT I HATE WATER! DO I HAVE TO?!
YES!

WOW, WHAT A DAY. I CAN'T BELIEVE I ACTUALLY CAST THAT SPELL SUCCESSFULLY ON MY FIRST TRY! BUT IT'S BACK TO BEING A MORTAL NOW. I'M NOT DOING ANYTHING LIKE THAT AGAIN!
=SIGH=
OWw!
SALEM! WHAT ARE YOU DOING?! YOU'RE LAYING ON MY FEET!
BUT I ALWAYS LAY ON YOUR FEET!
BUT NOW YOU WEIGH 200 POUNDS! OWWW, GET OFF!
SHOVE

B-BUT WHERE DO I SLEEP? I DON'T FIT IN MY CAT BED ANYMORE!
I DUNNO, BUT YOU CAN'T SLEEP IN HERE. IT ISN'T RIGHT NOW THAT YOU'RE A GROWN HUMAN. TRY THE COUCH OR SOMETHING.
I DON'T REMEMBER BEING THIS TALL...
THE NEXT MORNING...
CHIRP
CHIRP
WHAT ARE YOU GOING TO DO TODAY, SABRINA?
I'M GOING OUT WITH HARVEY.
MILK
Ahhhh, MY BACK. NO... LONGER... FLEXIBLE...
MORNING, SALEM.
SHUFFLE
SHUFFLE

SLURP
RUSTLE
...
CRUNCH CRUNCH
YES, SALEM?
FOOD! WHERE'S MY BREAKFAST?
YOU'RE A GROWN MAN, SALEM. GET YOUR OWN BREAKFAST. UNLESS YOU WANT TO EAT DRY KIBBLE AGAIN.
WHAT?! NO!
HUMAN CEREAL IS A LOT LIKE KIBBLE, HUH? I BET IT TASTES BETTER THOUGH! I'LL TRY THAT!
MILK
SPLASH

SALEM! GROSS! YOU CAN'T DO THAT! YOU DIDN'T EVEN ADD THE CEREAL!
SLURP SLURP
LATER...
ZZZ
VRRRRR
SALEM! MOVE IT!
VRRRRR
OWWWW!
SALEM, YOU CAN'T JUST LAY AROUND LIKE THIS ALL DAY!
SLAM!
VRRRR
WHY NOT? I ALWAYS TAKE A NAP IN THIS SUNSPOT!
BECAUSE YOU'RE A HUMAN NOW. IF YOU WANT TO LIVE HERE WITH US, YOU'LL HAVE TO BE PRODUCTIVE. GET A JOB, OR SOMETHING.
A J-JOB?!

WHAT A GREAT IDEA, SALEM. I'M GOING DOWNTOWN FOR A BIT. YOU CAN COME WITH ME AND PICK UP SOME JOB APPLICATIONS.
URRRGH...
I FORGOT HOW HARD IT IS TO WALK ON ICE WITH ONLY TWO LEGS!
HAHA, YOU'LL GET USED TO IT.
WOBBLE
RUB RUB
SALEM! WHAT ARE YOU DOING?!
I HAD AN ITCH!
YOU HAVE HANDS, SALEM. USE THEM.
AH!

POUNCE
DARN! I MISSED!
I CAN HARDLY BELIEVE YOU WERE EVER A THREAT TO THE MAGIC REALM.
IT WAS 1,010 YEARS AGO. GIMME A BREAK!
SALEM, YOU REALLY HAVE TO MAKE AN EFFORT NOT TO GIVE IN TO YOUR FELINE INSTINCTS. YOU'RE MAKING PEOPLE NERVOUS!
SORRY. SORRY.
SOON...
Thank You
BAT BAT

WE DIDN'T EVEN MANAGE TO GET ANY JOB APPLICATIONS.
I GUESS IT'S STILL TOO EARLY FOR YOU TO HANDLE SOMETHING LIKE AN ACTUAL JOB, THOUGH.
SPLASH
OH, GEEZ. THANKS A LOT!
LICK LICK
I CAN'T WAIT TO GET HOME.
SALEM THE CAT WAS BARELY TOLERABLE, BUT SALEM THE MAN IS EVEN WORSE!
I'M SORRY... I JUST WANTED TO SEE IF I COULD DO IT...
SABRINA, I WISH YOU WOULD THINK THESE THINGS THROUGH BEFORE YOU DO THEM.
WELL, HE'LL GET USED TO HIS HUMAN BODY IN TIME, I'M SURE.
ZZZ

THE NEXT MORNING...
AHHHH!
AH! WHAT HAPPENED?!
I WOKE UP LIKE THIS! THE SPELL MUST HAVE WORN OFF!
WHAAAT?! BUT IT WAS SUPPOSED TO BE PERMANENT! THERE WAS NO TIME LIMIT ON THE SPELL!
ACTUALLY, YOU KNOW WHAT? IT'S OKAY. I THINK I PREFER BEING A CAT AFTER ALL.
BUT... BUT, HOW CAN THIS BE? I THOUGHT THE SPELL WAS PERFECT! I THOUGHT I HAD FIGURED IT OUT!
WELL, THANKS FOR TRYING ANYWAY, SABRINA. I GUESS IT'S BETTER THAT YOU STAY MORTAL AFTER ALL.

I FAILED. I THOUGHT I HAD THE SKILL TO DO THE **IMPOSSIBLE**, BUT SOMEWHERE I **FAILED!** I DON'T BELIEVE IT!
MY MAGIC MUST NOT BE **STRONG** ENOUGH FOR A PERMANENT SPELL LIKE THAT. BUT IT LASTED ALMOST 48 HOURS! THAT'S **SOMETHING**, RIGHT?
I BET IF I KEPT **PRACTICING** MAGIC, I COULD DO IT FOR **LONGER**. FOR **WEEKS! MONTHS**, EVEN. I BET I COULD MAKE IT PERMANENT AFTER A WHILE.
ZELDA AND HILDA ARE RIGHT. I HAVE A **SPECIAL** TALENT AND I SHOULDN'T TURN MY BACK ON IT.
I'M CAPABLE OF SO MUCH. IF I CAN BREAK SALEM'S CURSE, I CAN DO **ANYTHING!**
BEING A MORTAL WAS FUN WHILE IT LASTED. BUT NOW, IT'S **SHOWTIME!**
End

Sabrina in Transformation Traumas

AUNT HILDA!
WH-WHAT'S HAPPENING TO YOU?! SHOULD I CALL THE P.N.P.M.S?!*
NO NEED TO OVERREACT, SABRINA! EVERYTHING'S FINE!
* PARANORMAL PARAMEDICS - EDITOR

SINCE I DON'T UNDERSTAND WHY YOU SPEND SO MUCH TIME WITH MORTALS--
KWA-PWOOF
--I WHIPPED UP A LITTLE DISGUISE SPELL!

I CAN NOW JOIN YOU AT THE LAKE AND WON'T STAND OUT AMONG YOUR FRIENDS!
OH, YEAH! YOU'LL FIT RIGHT IN!
IF WE EVER DO A SWIMSUIT CALENDAR!

1

Originally presented in **Betty And Veronica Double Digest #234**, August 2015

Tom DeFalco • Gisele • Rich Koslowski • Jack Morelli • Digikore Studios

EVERYONE'S STARING AT ME, SABRINA!
I MUST LOOK EVEN MORE HIDEOUS THAN I THOUGHT!
YEAH, THAT'S WHY THEY'RE STARING.
LET'S GO JOIN HARVEY AND AMY.

HARVEY KINKLE AND AMY REINHARDT, THIS IS MY... uhhh...
COUSIN HILDY!
WOW!
CHARMED.
AS IF SABRINA WASN'T ENOUGH COMPETITION FOR HARVEY!

I HOPE YOU AREN'T NAMED AFTER SABRINA'S AUNT HILDA!
SHE'S A NASTY OLD CRONE!
FLATTER!
WHAT KIND OF SPELL ARE YOU BREWING?

SOME PEOPLE THINK I MAKE THE BEST CHILI IN RIVERDALE!

BLECHK!
YOU NEED TO UPGRADE YOUR SOCIAL CIRCLE. I PREFER MY CHILI--
ZAP

--WITH A LOT MORE BITE!
EEP!
CHOMP
WH-WHAT HAVE YOU DONE?!
I JUST SPICED THINGS UP A BIT!
YOU BEAUTIFUL MAIDENS ARE WASTED ON HARVEY AND DESERVE MUCH BETTER!
AND WHO WOULD THAT BE?
REGGIE MANTLE --AT YOUR SERVICE!
REALLY? THEN TAKE OUT THE TRASH--
--STARTING WITH YOURSELF, OF COURSE!
GIGGLE!
COME WINDSURFING WITH ME, LADIES. YOU'LL BE GLAD YOU DID!
WE SHOULD GO, HILDY.
WHAT ABOUT SABRINA?
3

SHE ALREADY HAS HER HANDS FULL!

I HATE TO DISAPPOINT YOU PRETTY LADIES-- BUT THERE ISN'T ENOUGH WIND TO SURF TODAY!

YOU SHOULD HAVE PLENTY WITH YOUR MOUTH--
--BUT I LIVE TO PLEASE!
MYSELF!
ZOK

HAHAHA!!
WHOOOSH
EEEYIII!!
4

WE SEEM TO HAVE A LOT IN COMMON, HILDY!
HOW CLOSE ARE YOU TO YOUR COUSIN SABRINA?
WHY DO YOU ASK, AMY?
I WAS WONDERING IF YOU'D LIKE TO PLAY A PRACTICAL JOKE--
--AND HELP ME STEAL HARVEY FROM HER.

MY, MY, WE DO HAVE A LOT IN COMMON!
WE'RE BOTH TWO-FACED!
KA-ZAM
POOF
I GET IT, SABRINA. I FINALLY GET IT!
I NOW UNDERSTAND WHY YOU SPEND SO MUCH TIME WITH MORTALS!

THEY'RE ALWAYS GOOD FOR A LAUGH!
GAHHH!
ACK!
YIII!!
GRRRR!
END

Jughead #10

While not the title character, Sabrina zapped her way into a few excellent issues of the 2016 *Jughead* series written by Ryan North with art by Derek Charm. We may not be able to fit in the entire string of stories in this collection, but I think it's important to share a portion of her guest appearance for the hilarity alone. Where else have we seen Sabrina in a giant hamburger costume while attempting to capture the affections of Jughead? That's right. Nowhere! It's fun, it's cute, and the characters are written and drawn exactly the way they should be.

✶ **Vincent Lovallo**
Archie Art Director

Sabrina the Teenage Witch #1

What I love about all the different iterations of Sabrina is that her core basically remains the same; she's a person growing into her abilities while trying to maintain a normal life. Putting the magic spells and cauldrons aside, that's very relatable. We all have our strengths and weaknesses, and we all have our obstacles to overcome to strive for a happy life. The 2019 *Sabrina* series written by Kelly Thompson with art by Veronica and Andy Fish does a great job of showcasing that relatability, keeping all the aspects of Sabrina that we're familiar with and incorporating new elements and characters to keep it refreshing for today.

✶ **Vincent Lovallo**
Archie Art Director

The latest *Sabrina* series was like reading old Sabrina's stories with the perfect amount of modernisation. It's definitely something I would have read and gotten obsessed with as a kid (which I'm not going to lie, I still did). Sabrina's new to Greendale High, where she is struggling to balance her life as a teen and as a witch. There are of course a lot of supernatural events happening so this is the perfect combination of scary and colorful.

✶ **Sweeney Boo**
Artist

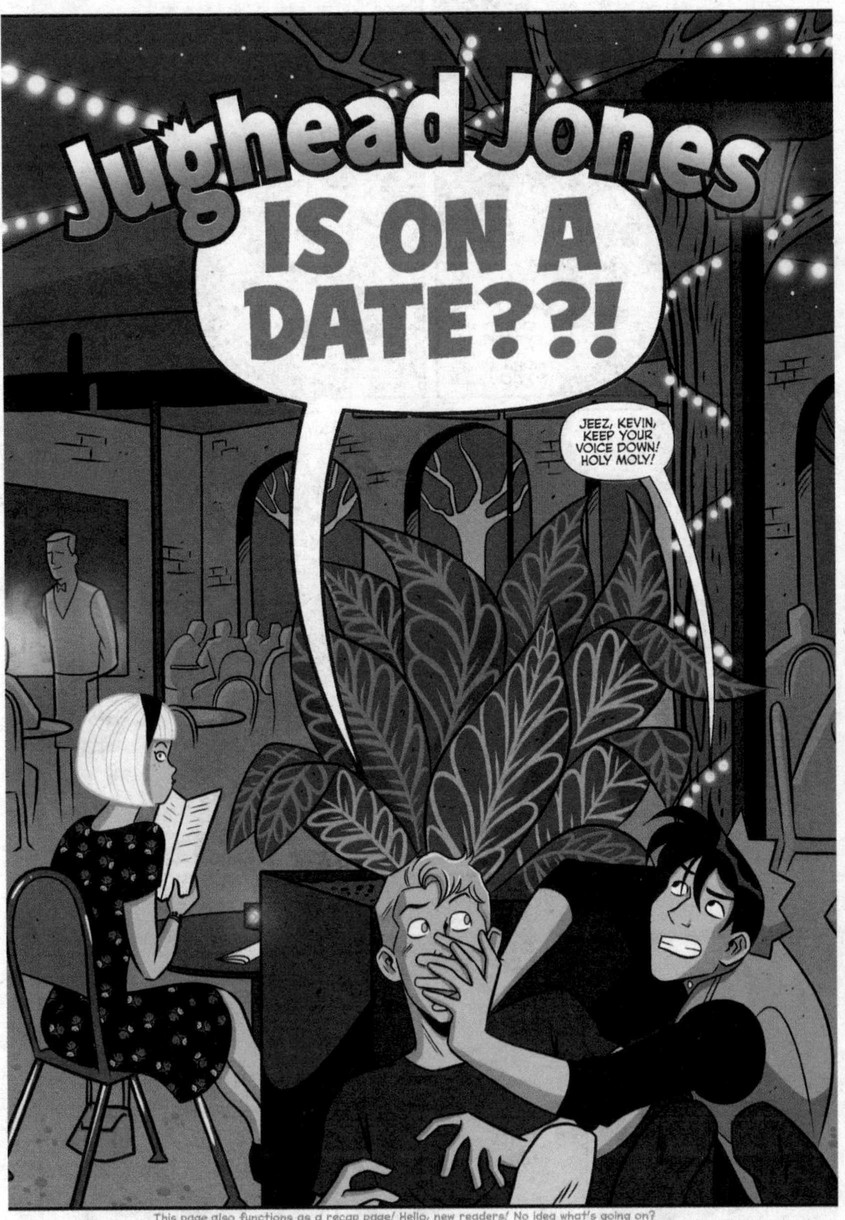

This page also functions as a recap page! Hello, new readers! No idea what's going on?
Well Jughead Jones is on a date and we're all about to see what happens next. *Whaaaaat???*

Originally presented in *Jughead* #10, December 2016

Ryan North • Derek Charm • Jack Morelli

JUG, WHEN YOU CALLED ME YOU SAID IT WAS, AND I QUOTE "AN EMERGENCY, AND YOU HAVE TO GET HERE RIGHT AWAY OLD BUDDY OLD PAL." I HAD PLANS TONIGHT.
THIS IS AN EMERGENCY! I HAVE NO IDEA WHAT TO DO HERE!

DUDE, PLEASE. THIS IS JUST "GO TO A BLAND RESTAURANT THAT'S TOO EXPENSIVE AND THEREFORE FANCY": A.K.A., BORING HETERO-SEXUAL ACTIVITY #202. YOU GOT THIS.
I DON'T HAVE THIS! I'M IN WAY OVER MY HEAD!

JUST GO BACK TO YOUR TABLE AND RELAX. ENJOY YOURSELF! DATES ARE SUPPOSED TO BE FUN!
"FUN"? "FUN"? SHE'S GOT EXPECTATIONS, KEVIN! SHE WANTS DATE ACTIVITIES!

JUGHEAD, YOU'RE EMBARRASSING YOUR-SELF AND THIS POOR WOMAN. GO.
NOBODY CARES ABOUT MY EXPECTATIONS
NOBODY CARES THAT ON SOME PRIMAL LEVEL I JUST WANTED TO HANG OUT WITH A GIANT BURGER

EVERYTHING OKAY? YOU WERE IN THE BATHROOM FOR, Uh, A WHILE.
Oh! YES! JUST WANTED TO, Um...
...I JUST WANTED TO MAKE SURE I DID A REALLY GOOD JOB??

Nobody cares that in MY fantasies me and the giant burger get into sitcom-level hijinks on the regular, and that I think about it happening all the time

Someone might tell you that the opposite of a burger isn't an inside-out burger but rather a kale salad, but 100% of the time it's just because they're trying to sell you a used kale salad.

SABRINA, KEVIN IS A MORE RECENT ARRIVAL TO RIVERDALE TOO. YOU HAVE THAT IN COMMON!
THE TOWN'S PROBABLY A BIT DIFFERENT THAN YOU WERE EXPECTING, Huh?
YOU HAVE NO IDEA.

SO DO YOU KNOW JUGHEAD FROM SCHOOL, OR...?
I'M NOT SURE I KNOW HIM AT ALL, ACTUALLY. THE JUGHEAD I THOUGHT I KNEW WOULDN'T BE SUCH A JERK ABOUT THINGS.
HAH! KEVIN THE KIDDER! THIS IS A JOKE WE PLAY, WHERE WE STEAL EACH OTHER'S PHONES AND THEN PRETEND WE DON'T DO THIS ALL THE TIME! JUST A ZANY GAG BETWEEN THE GUYS!!

I'M SORRY. IT WAS VERY NICE TO MEET YOU, SABRINA.
GOODBYE, JUGHEAD.

JUGHEAD, IF YOU WANNA GO HOME, I'M NOT GONNA BE MAD. WE DON'T HAVE TO--
Hah Hah, WHAT? NO WAY! WHAT? I'M HAVING A GREAT TIME!
AREN'T YOU?

I MEAN--IT'S THE MOST UNUSUAL DATE I'VE EVER BEEN ON, BUT THAT'S NOT TO SAY THERE AREN'T CERTAIN... UPSIDES TO IT...
Uh...

I JUST REMEMBERED I WAS MORE COMFORTABLE IN MY ORIGINAL SEAT!
Hah Hah!
WHAT A SILLY THING TO FORGET!
ZOOP

The Jughead I *THOUGHT* I knew also wasn't so good at pickpocketing things from his friends. How did you develop this skill, Jughead? How, and also, why?? Also, can you maybe teach me; it looks fun??

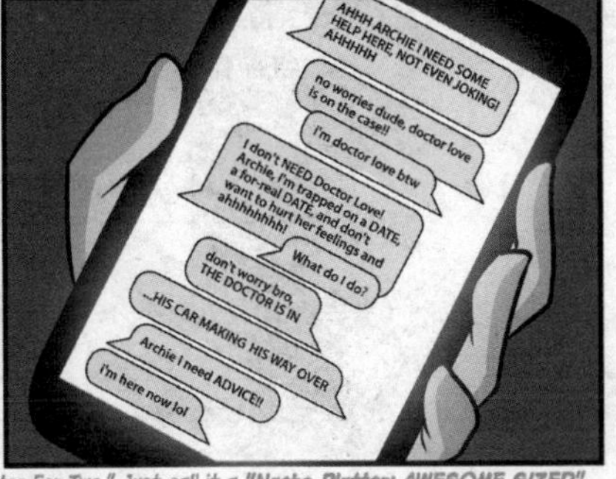

I hate when restaurants give things names like *"Nacho Platter For Two."* Just call it a *"Nacho Platter: AWESOME SIZED"* and then *MAYBE* I won't feel so judged when I order two of them while dining alone *(THEY'RE AMAZING; NO REGRETS)*

Hah Hah, TEXTS, AM I RIGHT? WHY ARE THEY SO ANNOYING, MIGHT I ASK??
JUGHEAD, CAN WE BE HONEST WITH EACH OTHER?
Y-YES?
LOOK, CARDS ON THE TABLE: I LIKE YOU, JUGHEAD. I THINK YOU'RE FUN AND FUNNY, AND YOU'RE SMART, AND YOU KNOW YOUR WAY AROUND FOOD. I LIKE ALL OF THAT.
BUT YOU'RE SO ***NERVOUS!*** AND I THINK I UNDERSTAND WHY.
...YOU DO?
YOU THINK YOU HAVE TO ACT A CERTAIN WAY TO IMPRESS ME, BUT YOU DON'T. I'M ***SOLD***, JUGHEAD. JUST BE YOURSELF, OKAY?
NO STUNTS, NO PULLING FRIENDS OVER, NO TRICKS, NO GAMES, JUST--JUST GIVE ME JUGHEAD. THAT'S WHAT I WANT.
AND I ***PROMISE*** WE'LL HAVE A GREAT TIME.
SABRINA...THERE'S SOMETHING YOU SHOULD KNOW. I--
'ALLO ZERE, YOUNG LOVAIRS! Ahh, EET IS SO NICE TO SEE "L'AMOUR" HERE!
I AM MONSIEUR CHEF AND I WANTED TO SEND OVAIR ZIS MILKSHAKE, COMPLEMONTS OF ZHE 'OUSE! BUT TRISTEMENT, WE 'AVE ONLY ZE ONE GLASS LEFT!
ZHEREFORE YOU MUST SHARE ZIS DRINK, LOVAIRS, WHICH WILL BRING YOUR FACES CLOSAIR TOGETHER, WHICH AS WE ALL KNOW EEZ THE FIRST STEP TO KISSING! AND NOW I MUST GO! AU REVOIR!!
EXCUSE ME.

This isn't even a French restaurant. ***ARCHIE WHAT ARE YOU DOING***

KA-BAM

OKAY, SABRINA: TIME TO FACE FACTS.
THIS DATE IS A DISASTER.

BUT YOU'RE GONNA PULL IT OFF, OKAY SABRINA? THIS IS GONNA BE ONE ENCHANTED EVENING...

...EVEN IF IT **DOES** COST ME SOME EYE OF NEWT AND TOE OF FROG.

ALL WE REALLY NEED IS SOME AMBIANCE. LUCKILY, IF THERE'S ONE THING WITCHES CAN **ALWAYS** DO, IT'S CONJURE UP SOME **FRIGGIN' AMBIANCE.**

KA-ZAPP
AND JUGHEAD WON'T KNOW WHAT HIT HIM.

Oh, if this is your first Archie comic I should mention that Sabrina is a witch! She is a ***TEENAGE WITCH*** and yes, nothing could possibly go wrong by combining supernatural power and teenage feelings. ***NOTHING***

Oh, JUGHEAD! DID I MISS ANYTHING UNUSUAL WHILE I WAS IN THE BATHROOM??
♫♪♪
SERIOUSLY??

Guys who shave their heads will tell you it's so they look cool and tough, but the truth is they're just real afraid of witches.

So we'll, uh...get them in a to-go bag then?

I HAVE HAD IT WITH THIS DATE, JUGHEAD! I HAVE HAD IT.
I'M THROUGH WITH YOU, AND HOW YOU'RE BEHAVING, AND THIS DATE, AND WITH THIS WHOLE FRIGGIN' TOWN OF RIVERDALE, EVEN THOUGH IT'S SURPRISINGLY FULL OF TEENS MY OWN AGE!!

THIS WAS, WITHOUT EXAGGERATION, THE WORST DATE OF MY ENTIRE LIFE. I THOUGHT ONE NIGHT OUT WOULD BE FUN, YOU KNOW? JUST ONE NIGHT WITH A CUTE BOY.
BUT INSTEAD I GET MISTER "SURE I'LL ASK YOU OUT, AND THEN I'LL ACT WEIRD WHENEVER THINGS GO WELL, AND I WON'T EVEN NOTICE WHEN SEABIRDS DUMP ROSE PETALS ALL OVER THE PLACE"??

Oh, I WAS JUST LOOKING UP IF PELICANS NEEDED MEDICAL ATTENTION AFTER SPEWING FLOWERS OUT OF THEIR BEAKS, BECAUSE EATING FLOWERS IS WEIRD FOR BIRDS AND THOSE ROSE PETALS CLEARLY AREN'T SITTING WELL--
ARRGH!!

YOU HAVE CHEESED OFF THE WRONG WOMAN, JUGHEAD JONES!!
BAH!

I have *HAD IT* with this *WHOLE TOWN* full of *RAD TEENS*, any number of which could sustain books detailing their *OWN UNIQUE ADVENTURES* for at least 75 years, *MINIMUM*??

Messages
Betty, Veronica
Edit
hey guess what babe!! all this beauty around me made me think of you specifically, and only you!! wish you were here!!! <3 <3 <333
Duuuude.

Yes, that's a group text, and yes, both Betty and Veronica will be able to see that fact!
ARCHIE, AGAIN I AM REDUCED TO ASKING: WHAT ARE YOU EVEN DOING

THE NEXT DAY...
RIVERDALE HIGH SCHOOL

MATH CLASS.
JUG, DO YOU HAVE ANY IDEA WHAT SHE'S TALKING ABOUT? WHAT'S AN *"IMAGINARY NUMBER"*?
NO IDEA, ARCH!

ZAP
PERFECT. HE DIDN'T STUDY, SALEM!
MAKE HIM ANSWER EVERY QUESTION! THAT'LL TEACH HIM TO MESS WITH YOU!
TO PUNISH YOU FOR ALL YOUR DATING SASS / RAISE HAND TO EVERY QUESTION IN THIS CLASS!

SO A NUMBER IN THE FORMAT OF (A + Bi), CAN BE THOUGHT OF AS...
...JUGHEAD?
A PAIR OF NUMBERS (A AND B) REPRESENTING A POINT ON THE COMPLEX PLANE?
Riverdale

CORRECT. AND THE "i" REPRE-SENTS... JUGHEAD AGAIN?
THE SQUARE ROOT OF -1: A NUMBER WHICH DOESN'T EXIST IN THE REAL PLANE, BUT BY DEFINING THAT NUMBER AS "i", WE CAN DO OPERATIONS WITH IT ANYWAY! MATH IS AMAZING!
AGAIN: ENTIRELY CORRECT. EXCELLENT WORK, JUGHEAD.

I THOUGHT YOU SAID YOU DIDN'T KNOW THIS STUFF!
I READ AHEAD BUT I FELT WEIRD MENTIONING IT, BECAUSE IT FELT LIKE BRAGGING! I DIDN'T WANT TO HURT YOUR FEELINGS!
AW! I APPRECIATE HOW CAREFUL YOU ARE WITH OUR FRIENDSHIP, BUD!!
Riverdale

WHAT.

Q: How can you tell someone has written a character's spells in iambic pentameter?
A: *DON'T WORRY, THEY'LL TELL YOU*

BIOLOGY CLASS.
Sigh
THIRD ROW, YOU CAN BRING YOUR HOMEWORK UP NOW.
HOW THO?
ALWAYS!

NOW'S YOUR CHANCE, SABRINA!
YOUR HOMEWORK WILL HAVE MORE THAN JUST MISTAKES / WITH BACKPACK FULL OF NEWTS AND FROGS AND SNAKES!
HERE'S MY HOMEWORK, MISTER ZD--
SNAKES?! YIPE!!

NOT JUST SNAKES: FROGS, SALAMANDERS--ALL SORTS OF ECTOTHERMIC TETRAPODS!
INCLUDING MANY NOT NORMALLY SEEN IN THIS REGION!

RIVERDALE'S HERPETOCULTURAL LEARNING LAB WILL GREATLY APPRECIATE THIS DONATION, FORSYTHE. OUTSTANDING WORK.
BIOLOGY
HOW THO?
CLASS, THIS IS THE KIND OF ABOVE-AND-BEYOND ATTITUDE YOU SHOULD ALL CULTIVATE.

AND WHILE I KNOW WE DO HAVE A TEST SCHEDULED TODAY, WHAT WOULD YOU SAY TO CANCELLING THAT, TAKING THESE DOWN TO THE LAB, AND LEARNING HOW TO SET UP PROPER HABITATS FOR THESE ANIMALS INSTEAD??
WOOO!!

JUGHEAD! JUGHEAD! JUGHEAD!
...Huh.
ALRIGHT, THAT ONE WAS KIND OF ON ME.

And your homework's here too, under all these frogs! You've made an old herper very happy today, Jughead. A+s all around!!

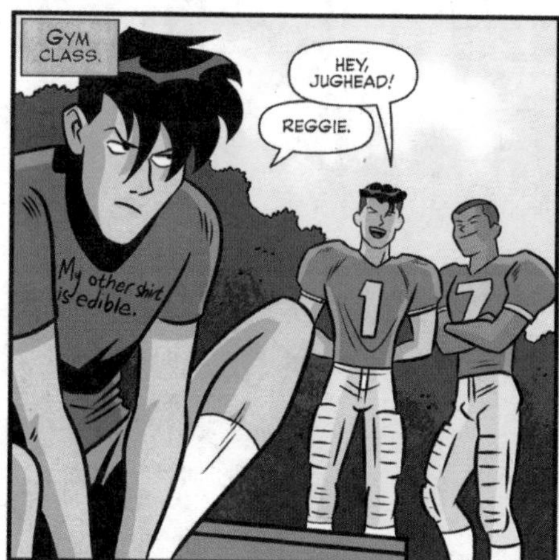

GYM CLASS.
HEY, JUGHEAD!
REGGIE.
My other shirt is edible.

HEY JUGGIE, WHAT SORT OF CAKE DO YOU PREFER?
COME ON MAN, WE DON'T HAVE TO--
UPSIDE-DOWN CAKE, OR POUND CAKE?

sigh

REGGIE, I KNOW YOU'RE JUST TRYING TO IMPRESS YOUR GYM BUDDIES HERE, BUT IF YOU'RE INTERESTED IN A REAL ANSWER, THE SWEDISH MAKE A "SMÖRGÅSTÅRTA" OR "SANDWICH CAKE," WHICH--
POUND CAKE IT IS!!

OOF!
HAW! HAW!
REALLY, GUYS? REALLY?

OF COURSE! JUGHEAD MAY BE ABLE TO TURN MY CURSES INTO BLESSINGS, BUT THERE'S NO WAY ANYONE CAN TURNING HANGING OUT WITH A JERK INTO A GOOD THING!
THIS HEX WILL SURELY GET YOURSELF A WEDGIE / FOR ALL DAY LONG YOU WILL HANG OUT WITH REGGIE!

I know you all want to hear more about this Swedish sandwich cake, so here it is: it's like a giant sandwich except with more toppings, you cut it like a cake, and you sprinkle the top of the cake with some extra toppings so everyone knows what kind of sandwich cake they're about to eat. ***IT'S AMAZING.***

BUT THEN IT TURNED INTO A JUGHEAD/REGGIE

FRIENDSHIP MONTAGE INSTEAD

BUT HANGING OUT TONIGHT HAS BEEN ***GREAT.*** WE NEVER GET TO DO THINGS, JUST THE TWO OF US-- AND SPENDING THIS TIME TOGETHER, AND HAVING IT GO SO GREAT--

--WELL, IT MEANS A LOT TO ME. I LEARNED A LOT ABOUT MYSELF TODAY, JUGHEAD. IT GIVES ME CONFIDENCE, YOU KNOW? INCLUDING THE CONFIDENCE TO THINK THAT MAYBE, ***JUST MAYBE,*** I DON'T HAVE TO BE SUCH A JERK ALL THE TIME.

Great things happen when you're relaxing on a dog! Dogs: Great Things Happen When You're Relaxing On One™.

SABRINA, YOU'RE A *LITERAL WITCH*. HOW ARE YOU FAILING TO TAKE REVENGE ON A *SINGLE* COOL TEEN?
I DON'T KNOW! IT'S SO CRAZY!!

I THINK IT'S TIME TO BRING OUT THE TOP-TIER SPELLCASTING. THE MOST ELDRITCH MAGICKS. *THE BIG GUNS.*
SNAP
I'M ALL FOR IT, SABRINA, BUT... YOU KNOW WITCHES AREN'T ALLOWED TO REVEAL THEMSELVES TO THE MORTAL WORLD.

TRUE, BUT...THERE IS *ONE* WAY WE CAN DO THAT AND NOT BREAK THE RULES.
ARE YOU THINKING WHAT I'M THINKING, SALEM?
DEFINITELY.

AMNESIA SPELL!
ENSURING THERE ARE NO SURVIVORS!
I MEAN, *AMNESIA SPELL!*

SALEM.
I'M JUST SAYIN'.

KRRRRRRTTT
UH...ARE YOU SURE YOU CAN *HANDLE* THI--
SALEM, BACK! *BACK!*

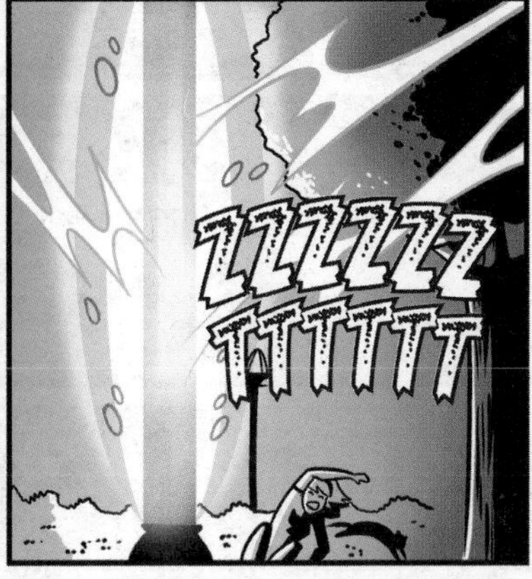
ZZZZZZZ
TTTTTTT

IT'S GETTING LATE: WE'D BETTER HEAD HOME, MAN. GRUNDY TAKES ATTENDANCE FIRST THING IN HOMEROOM, AND I DON'T WANNA BE LATE TOMORR-

KRRRAASSSHHH

Oh...

MY...

Get the whole story in the Jughead Vol.2 Graphic Novel

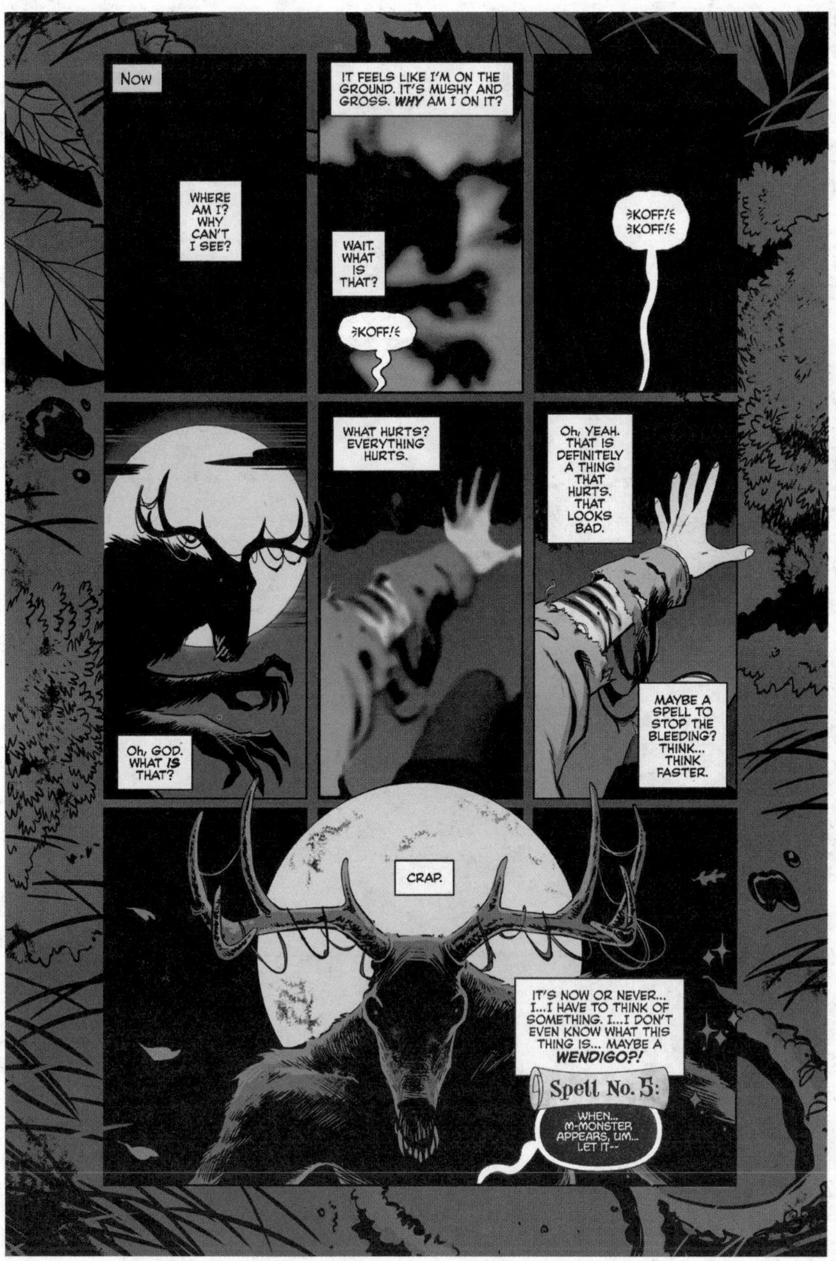

Originally presented in *Sabrina* #1, May 2019

Kelly Thompson • Veronica Fish • Andy Fish • Jack Morelli

SABRINA SPELLMAN'S HOME.
THIRTEEN HOURS AGO.
Mmmmm...
SALEM! REALLY?! YOUR BUTT RIGHT IN MY FACE? BEFORE 8AM?
THINK OF IT AS A WAKE UP CALL WITH PUNCH.

YEAH, BUT ***I'M*** THE ONE GETTING PUNCHED.
WITH CAT BUTT.
BEING TRAPPED IN THE BODY OF A CAT HAS FEW ADVANTAGES. I INTEND TO USE THEM ALL.

Spell No. 1:
ALL THIS HAIR SO BRIGHT AND WHITE... SOFTEN UP TO PALE SUNLIGHT.
Oh, I SEE. SO WE'RE JUST CHUCKING ALL OUR PROMISES AT THE FIRST SIGHT OF THE SMALLEST TROUBLE?
IT'S BEEN A LONG TIME SINCE YOU WERE A TEENAGER, SALEM... THEY'RE AWFUL... ANYTHING THAT MAKES YOU DIFFERENT MAKES YOU--
INTERESTING?
--A *TARGET*.
MY PEERS ARE MONSTERS, SALEM.
MONSTERS? Oh, CHILD, IF ONLY THOU HADST SEEN WHAT I HADST SEEN.

HADST? DON'T PRETEND TO BE FANCY, SALEM. YOU MAY HAVE BEEN FANCY ONCE, BUT YOU'RE JUST A CAT NOW.
I'M STILL FANCY.

IT'S JUST A HARMLESS LITTLE GLAMOUR ANYWAY. BESIDES, I NEVER SAID I WASN'T USING ANY SPELLS EVER. I SAID I WAS GOING TO BE MORE CAREFUL, THAT I DIDN'T WANT THINGS GOING PEAR-SHAPED THIS TIME.
BUT THAT DOESN'T MEAN I CAN'T DO ANYTHING. OTHERWISE WHY EVEN BE A WITCH?
PFFFT. THINGS ALWAYS BEGIN SMALL, SABRINA. BUT THEY HAVE A WAY OF CATCHING UP TO YOU...

...PERHAPS TAKE ADVICE FROM THE CAT THAT WAS ONCE A POWERFUL WARLOCK, YEAH?
YEAH, YEAH, YEAH.

GOOD MORNING.
MORNING!
MORNING.
GREENDALE GAZE

...
...

SABRINA WHAT ON EARTH--

WHAT?
--Uh. WHAT ON EARTH MAKES YOU THINK YOU CAN BE SO LATE ON YOUR FIRST DAY?

SINCE WHEN DO YOU CARE ABOUT THE "TEDIOUS RULES OF MORTALS"?
...YOU AREN'T THE ONLY ONE TRYING TO TURN OVER SOME NEW LEAVES IN OUR NEW TOWN, SABRINA.
NOW DRINK YOUR JUICE. I MADE IT SPECIAL TODAY WITH CINNAMON FOR EXTRA PROTECTION AND LOVE.

...

Shhhh! SECRET POPTART!
THANKS, HILDA.

YOU ALL RIGHT?
...YES.
OKAY, BECAUSE YOU'RE LOOKING AT THE WORLD BEYOND THE PORCH AS IF IT'S A HELL DIMENSION INTENT ON SWALLOWING YOU WHOLE.
RIGHT. IT'S NOT?

IT'S NOT. AND YOU'LL BE OKAY, SABRINA.
RIGHT.

EXCEPT IT IS A HELL DIMENSION... OR MIGHT AS WELL BE.
HERE I'M JUST ME... AND I'M MORTAL AND WITCH...AND WE'RE ALL FINE WITH THAT. OUT THERE, I'M...HIDING... TRYING TO BLEND IN, TRYING TO NOT BE THE VERY THINGS THAT I AM.
Sigh
IT'S KINDA A LOT.
ALSO BOYS.
AND ALSO I HATE MORTAL HISTORY CLASS. IT'S SUCH CRAP.
BUT I'LL BE FINE.

BECAUSE... BECAUSE I'M SABRINA FREAKING SPELLMAN.

RIGHT.
YUP. I'M STILL SABRINA FREAKING SPELLMAN. I STILL FEEL SUUUUUUPER CONFIDENT.
GREENDALE
GREENDALE

OOF!

BUMP

NOT A GREAT START, NEW GIRL. YOU BETTER GET IT TOGETHER.

GREEN

DON'T CURSETHEMEAN GIRLSABRINA DON'TCURSETHE MEANGIRLSABRINA DON'TCURSE THEMEAN--

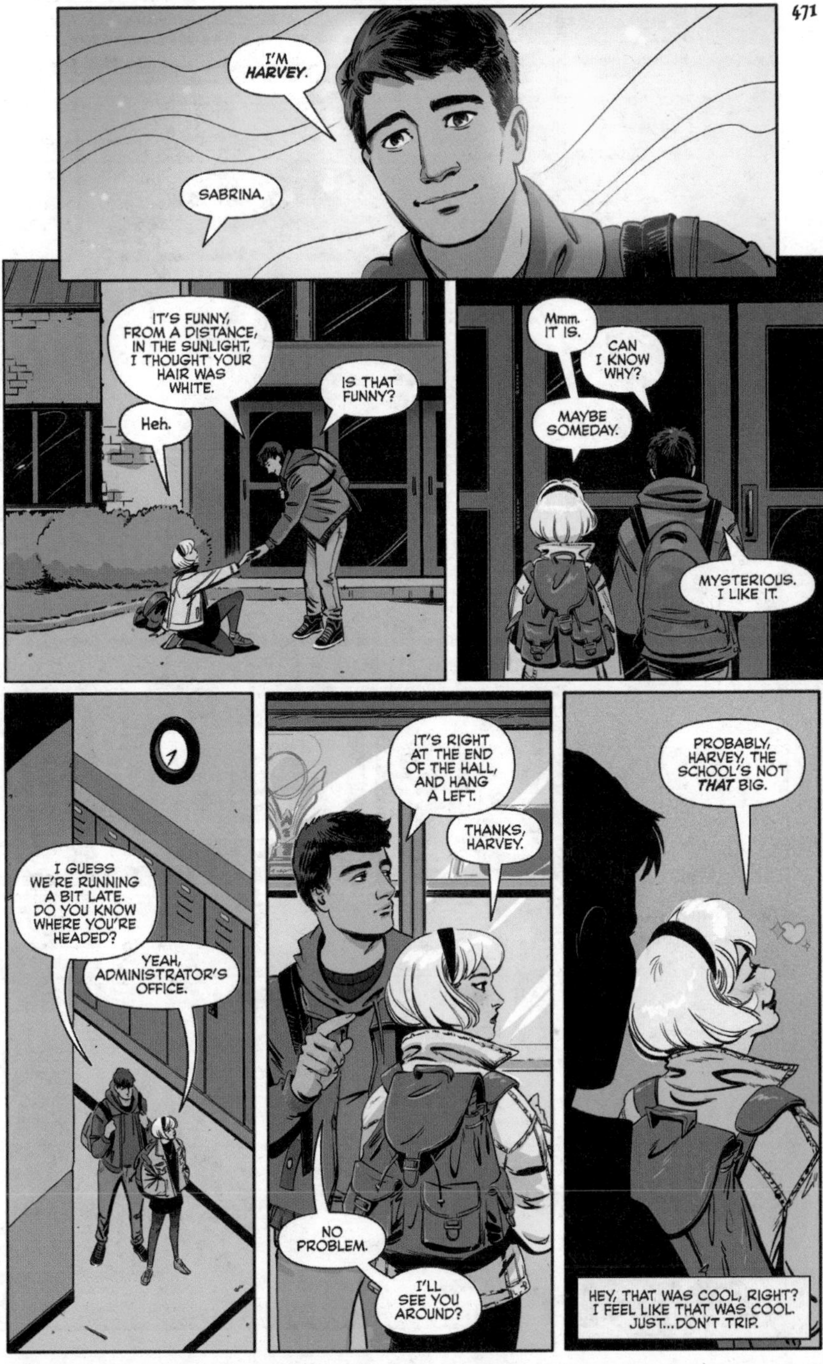

I'M *HARVEY*.
SABRINA.

IT'S FUNNY, FROM A DISTANCE, IN THE SUNLIGHT, I THOUGHT YOUR HAIR WAS WHITE.
Heh.
IS THAT FUNNY?

Mmm. IT IS.
CAN I KNOW WHY?
MAYBE SOMEDAY.
MYSTERIOUS. I LIKE IT.

I GUESS WE'RE RUNNING A BIT LATE. DO YOU KNOW WHERE YOU'RE HEADED?
YEAH, ADMINISTRATOR'S OFFICE.

IT'S RIGHT AT THE END OF THE HALL, AND HANG A LEFT.
THANKS, HARVEY.
NO PROBLEM.
I'LL SEE YOU AROUND?

PROBABLY, HARVEY, THE SCHOOL'S NOT *THAT* BIG.
HEY, THAT WAS COOL, RIGHT? I FEEL LIKE THAT WAS COOL. JUST...DON'T TRIP.

UGH. I'M CURSED.

I CANNOT BELIEVE I HAVE AMERICAN HISTORY AS MY FIRST CLASS FOR THE WHOLE SEMESTER.

I PREDICT A LOT OF ACCIDENTALLY SLEEPING IN THIS SEMESTER.

HERE'S THE THING ABOUT "HISTORY"...IT'S WRITTEN BY BY THE POWERFUL. AND THOSE PEOPLE AREN'T ALWAYS RIGHT. OR HONEST.

IF YOU'LL ALL TURN TO PAGE NINETEEN... I'D LIKE TO DIVE RIGHT IN TODAY.

AND I DON'T EVEN BLAME THIS GUY...THIS ***MR. COLLINS***...

I MEAN, HE'S JUST A COG IN A WHEEL.

AND NOT THAT EVEN UPDATED TEXTBOOKS ARE RIGHT, BUT SURELY THEY'RE MORE RIGHT THAN THIS ONE WHICH WAS PUBLISHED IN...

...1998?!?!

YEAH, I CAN'T LET ***THAT*** GO.

Spell No. 2:
SAVE THE YOUTH, TURN THEIR FADED TOMES TO TRUTH.
Ahhh. THAT'S MORE LIKE IT.
HEY...MY BOOK...
Uh...
WHOA.

SHE LOOKS LIKE SHE'S HOPING A HOLE WILL OPEN IN THE EARTH AND SWALLOW HER UP.
GODS, THIS POOR GIRL.
BOiNK
WHICH, Y'KNOW... FEELS FAMILIAR.
MAN, THIS ALPHA "MEAN GIRL" CHICK REALLY GETS AROUND.
MAYBE I SHOULD DO SOMETHING... I MEAN, I KNOW I STARTED THE DAY SAYING I WASN'T GOING TO CURSE THE MEAN GIRL, BUT SHE'S REALLY ASKING FOR IT.
I'M GOING TO OFFICIALLY GIVE HER THREE STRIKES...AND THIS IS STRIKE TWO.
YOUR APPLE, MISS.
Hmmm. MY AUNTIES ALWAYS DID TELL ME TO BE WARY OF TAKING FRUIT GOODS FROM SNAKES OR HANDSOME STRANGERS.
BUT THAT LEAVES OPEN A WHOLE WORLD OF POSSIBILITIES THAT YOU CAN TAKE FRUIT GOODS FROM...
...HANDSOME NON-STRANGERS HANDSOME SNAKES, UN-HANDSOME STRANGERS...
BUT WHY BOTHER WITH ALL THOSE WHEN IT'S QUITE OBVIOUS YOU FALL INTO THE HANDSOME SNAKE CATEGORY?
OOF. YOU WOUND ME.
MAYBE WITH ENOUGH TIME...
ALL ELSE MAY BE OFF TODAY, BUT SOMEHOW MY FLIRTING GAME IS SERIOUSLY ON POINT.
DID YOU KNOW APPLES ARE LIKE... ONE OF THE MOST POWERFUL AND SYMBOLIC FRUITS? AND I'M NOT JUST TALKING SNAKES AND BIBLE STORIES.
SO WE'RE TALKING SNOW WHITE, THEN?

NATURALLY. BUT SERIOUSLY, APPLES *ARE* ALL OVER FAIRY TALES AND FOLKLORE, NOT TO MENTION THE GODDESSES APHRODITE AND FREYJA. AND THEY CAN REPRESENT EVERYTHING FROM LOVE TO IMMORTALITY.
I HAD NO IDEA TEENS WERE SO INTO APPLES.

YES, WELL, I HAD A LOT OF SPARE TIME ON MY HANDS WHEN I WAS YOUNGER...BEFORE I BECAME SO DEVASTATINGLY HANDSOME.
DEVASTATINGLY? REALLY?
REALLY.

I CAN'T COMPETE WITH YOUR WEIRDLY EXTENSIVE APPLE KNOWLEDGE... EXCEPT I KNOW ONE COOL THING. ARE YOU READY TO BE WOWED?
I AM.
THERE'S AN... OLD SPE--Uh, OLD WIVES TALE...IF YOU PEEL AN APPLE SKIN IN ONE PEEL, THE PEEL WILL FORM THE FIRST LETTER OF THE NAME OF YOUR TRUE LOVE.
SO IN YOUR CASE...?

REN.
REN. SINCE YOU'RE SO IN LOVE WITH *YOURSELF*, SOUNDS LIKE IT WILL BE AN "*R*."

JUST IN CASE THOUGH... WHAT'S *YOUR* NAME?
SABRINA.

Spell No. 3:
GIVE THE BOY A LITTLE SUCCESS, MAKE HIS PEEL INTO AN *S*.

UGH. MANDATED "PHYSICAL EDUCATION."
MAYBE EVEN WORSE THAN MORTAL HISTORY CLASS?
ALL RIGHT! EVERYONE PARTNER UP!
I MEAN, THE CLOTHES ARE DEFINITELY WORSE.
YOU WANT TO PARTNER UP?
SERIOUSLY?
IS THIS... AM I BEING PUNK'D? IS THAT STILL A THING?

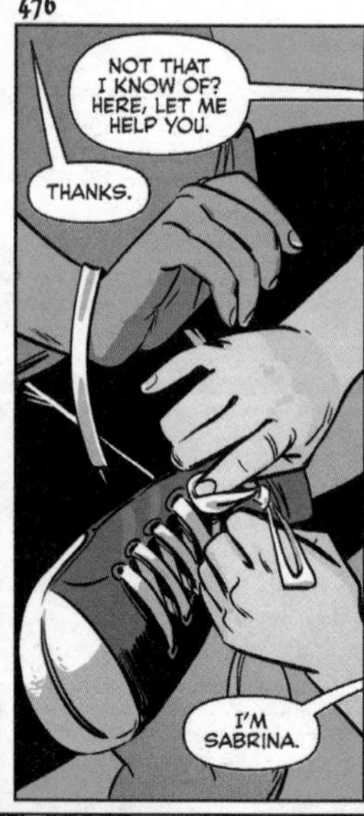
NOT THAT I KNOW OF? HERE, LET ME HELP YOU.
THANKS.
I'M SABRINA.

I'M JESSA CHIANG.
NICE TO MEET YOU.
THANKS FOR TAKING PITY ON ME. P.E. IS THE LITERAL WORST WHEN YOU'RE NEW.
ISN'T IT THE WORST ALL THE TIME?
YES... YES, YOU'RE RIGHT.

NEW GIRL...I LET YOU KNOW YOU WERE OFF TO A BAD START THIS MORNING. AND HERE YOU ARE, STILL MAKING BAD CHOICES.
STOMP

I'M PRETTY HAPPY WITH MY CHOICES, ACTUALLY.
JESSA HERE IS NOT A GOOD CHOICE. DIDN'T YOU NOTICE PEOPLE GIVING HER A WIDE BERTH?
I DID. I JUST DIDN'T CARE.

Uh-OH.

BOMP
ANNNNND THAT'S THREE.
Spell No. 4:
SLIP AND FALL IS JUST THE START. YOU CAN'T HIDE YOUR EVIL PART. A TRUE SELF REVEAL, NOT YOUR FAKE IDEAL.
SLIP
SPLAT
!
...

BUT SHE PUSHED ME!
YOU KNOW HOW YOU CAN TELL RADKA'S AWFUL?
IS IT THE SCREAMING?
Heh. I MEAN, YES. BUT EVEN BEFORE THAT...HER NAME HAS THE WORD RAD RIGHT IN IT. LIKE, CAN YOU IMAGINE THE... ENTITLEMENT YOU FEEL WHEN YOUR NAME IS LITERALLY RAD?
Heh!
VICE PRINCIPAL
Remember... You have a PAL in PrinciPAL

ALSO, IT'S ALLITERATIVE--RADKA RANSOM. Pfft. SHE SOUNDS LIKE A REALITY TELEVISION SHOW CHARACTER. I MEAN, I KNOW PEOPLE THINK ALLITERATION IS COOL, BUT C'MON, IT'S A LITTLE PLAYED OUT, RIGHT?
Heh. WELL... MY NAME IS SABRINA SPELLMAN, SOOOO....

Oh. Oh, NO.
I'M SO SORRY. I TALK TOO MUCH WHEN I'M NERVOUS. YOU'RE LIKE THE FIRST NICE PERSON I'VE MET...EVER? ...AND I INSULT YOU.
DON'T BE SILLY. TELL ME MORE ABOUT RADKA. WE CAN BOND OVER HER TERRIBLENESS.
VICE PRINCIPAL

THE ACTUAL MOST TERRIBLE THING ABOUT RADKA IS THAT HER OLDER BROTHER IS LIKE, THE BEST. SUPER NICE AND DEFINITELY DREAMY...BUT HE'S LIKE TOTALLY RUINED JUST BECAUSE HE'S HER BROTHER.
WHO'S HER...Oh, NO.
REN. REN RANSOM.

RADKA DOESN'T DO DETENTION!
Remember...

Sigh
YOU GUYS ARE DOING DETENTION, TOO. BE BACK HERE AFTER THE FINAL BELL. NO COMPLAINTS.
YES, SIR.

I MEAN, I GET THAT DETENTION IS PUNISHMENT, BUT...BANGING ERASERS? WHAT IS THIS, 1950? TEACHERS DON'T EVEN USE CHALKBOARDS ANYMORE.
I KNOW. YOU'D THINK THEY COULD COME UP WITH SOMETHING ACTUALLY USEFUL FOR US TO DO.
SABRINA... I--I NEVER REALLY THANKED YOU... FOR STANDING UP FOR ME. IT MEANT A LOT.
NOT THAT IT DID MUCH GOOD. I JUST DREW HER ATTENTION FOR MORE ABUSE AND GOT US SADDLED WITH DETENTION.
NO, SABRINA, I'M SERIOUS. IT MEANS A LOT. I...I DON'T KNOW IF ANYONE HAS EVER STOOD UP FOR ME LIKE THAT. I WON'T FORGET IT.
I KNOW HOW YOU FEEL, I--
SNAP
...JESSA. WE HAVE TO RUN!
WHAT?!!

CAN'T THINK...
MY BRAIN FEELS LIKE IT'S ON FIRE.
ALL THOSE STUPID SPELLS TODAY ABOUT HAIR AND APPLE PEELS...
...AND NOW WHEN IT MATTERS...
...I'M PARALYZED!
SHRIIIIP
HNGG!
AHH!!
GROAN...

Now.
CRAP.
IT'S NOW OR NEVER... I...I HAVE TO THINK OF SOMETHING. I...I DON'T EVEN KNOW WHAT THIS THING IS... MAYBE A WENDIGO?!
Spell No. 5:
WHEN... M-MONSTER APPEARS, UM... LET IT--
GRRRRAAAAAHHHHH!!?!
WAIT. WHAT'S HAPPENING?!
I...I... DIDN'T FINISH... I DIDN'T DO ANY-THING.
Oh... THE SPELL...

GRRAAHHHHhh*
...THE "REVEAL TRUE SELF" SPELL I PUT ON RADKA EARLIER... SHE AND REN ARE THE WENDIGO?!
Get the whole story in the
Sabrina The Teenage Witch
Graphic Novel

Originally presented in **Archie #706**, September 2019

Nick Spencer • Mariko Tamaki • Jenn St-Onge • Matt Herms • Jack Morelli

CHEER UP. YOU'RE YOUNG.
NOW SUMMER IS JUST ...ME.
Pop's
THANKS.
YOU HAD AN AIR CONDITIONER THING YOU WANTED ME TO TAKE A LOOK AT?
YUP. UNIT'S OUT BACK.
OKAY, IT'S NOT LIKE EVERYONE'S DEAD. THEY'RE JUST... GONE.
DOING THEIR THINGS OUTSIDE OF RIVERDALE.
Pop's
CHOCK'LIT SHOPPE
HAMBURGERS
MILKSHAKES
HAVING A LIFE OUTSIDE OF RIVERDALE.
MEANWHILE, I'M HERE, STUCK FIXING THE LITTLE PARTS OF IT THAT NEED REPAIR.
STUCK--
GET A GRIP, ARCHIE. YOU'RE STARTING TO SOUND LIKE JUGHEAD.

SPELLMAN HOUSE...
STUCK?
WHO'S STUCK?
IT'S NOT THAT RIDICULOUS GOPHER AGAIN, IS IT? THAT GOPHER REALLY GETS MY **GOAT**.
ME. AND NOT **STUCK**. JUST. I JUST WISH--
YOU HAVE LOTS TO DO, SABRINA, IF YOU WOULD LIKE A LIST --MY LARDER IS LOW.
WISH?
NO PROBLEM, AUNT ZELDA. I'LL GO TO THE WOODS TODAY.
MAYBE NOT WISH. IT FEELS LIKE I'M...
DARK HEART TOADSTOOLS, SOME FLANNAGAN'S MOSS, A SAMPLE OF ARCHER'S EARTH.
SOME MILLER'S TOES WOULD BE NICE.
WAITING? MAYBE THAT'S IT.
HOW LONG?
WILD CHILD

I CAN GET, Uh, CHALK WHITE NOW, BUT THE, MAJESTIC IVORY IN TRUECOAT YOU WANT?
THAT WILL TAKE ABOUT A WEEK.
DAMN. I REALLY DO PREFER IVORY.
BUT OKAY.
IF JUGHEAD WERE HERE, HE WOULD GIVE ME A WHOLE SPEECH ABOUT ME DECIDING TO STAY--HAVING SOME-THING TO DO, BEING SO TIED UP IN...

...DRAMA. WHATEVER. STUFF.
THAT I CAN'T... EVOLVE, OR SOMETHING?

ARCHIEKINS?
ARCHIE?

I CAN SEE ABOUT THE PAINT. MAYBE MAX'S HARDWARE HAS IT.
THANK YOU.

WATCH YOUR FEET!

--OR A FEW OF THESE WILL LEAVE YOU WITH SOME PRETTY ITCHY PAWS, SALEM.

ROWRRRRR

HEY, IT WAS YOUR IDEA TO COME OUT WITH ME. MAYBE BECAUSE YOU'RE AS BORED AS I AM.
I DON'T KNOW, SALEM. I JUST HAVE THIS SENSE.

AND MY SENSES ARE RARELY WRONG.

INTERESTING. DARK HEARTS DON'T USUALLY BLEED.
UNLESS IT'S A SIGN.

A CRACKED SIGN.
Oh. I THOUGHT YOU WANTED IT PAINTED. Uh, YEAH. I CAN FIX THAT.
RIVERDALE HIGH SCHOOL
HAVE A GREAT SUMMER, BULLDOGS!!

NEED IT BY FALL.
I THINK.
ANDREWS

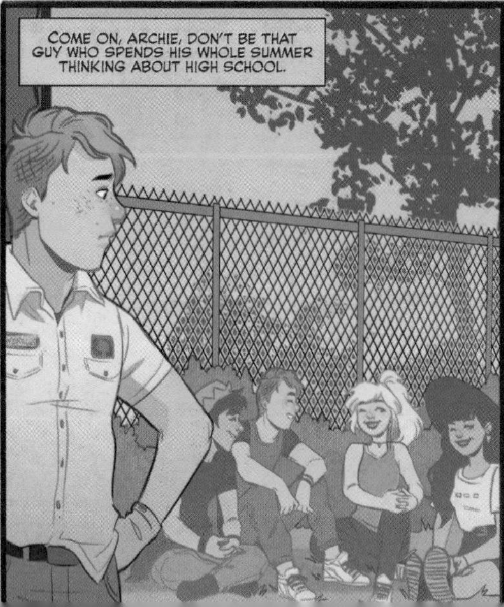
COME ON, ARCHIE, DON'T BE THAT GUY WHO SPENDS HIS WHOLE SUMMER THINKING ABOUT HIGH SCHOOL.

HEY. I NEED A PIECE OF GLASS FOR A SIGN? HELLO? A SIGN?
HEY!

I SAID, HEY LADY! YOU SEE THE SIGN?!
WHAT?

THIS IS PRIVATE PROPERTY. YOU SEEN THE SIGNS?
NO. THIS IS THE WOODS. HOW IS IT PRIVATE PROPERTY?
LOOK, TOURIST, IT'S CLEARLY MARKED, SO WHY DON'T YOU--

TOURIST?
THE ROAD IS THAT WAY.
DON'T TURN HIM INTO A TOAD. IT'S AN INSULT TO TOADS.
THANK YOU.

HAVE A NICE DAY, MARVIN.

RIVERDALE. HONESTLY, THIS PLACE. WHAT AM I DOING HERE? REALLY.

Josie
PUSSYCATS
WE'RE JUST HERE FOR THE DAY. NIGHT. WE HAVE A ONE-NIGHT GIG--
--THEN BACK ON THE ROAD FOR A FEW OUT OF TOWN SHOWS.
WHAT ARE YOU UP TO?

SIGNS.
OF INTELLIGENT LIFE? IN RIVERDALE? DO TELL.
SOME-THING LIKE THAT. JUST, YOU KNOW, KEEPING BUSY.

WELL, IF YOU'RE NOT *TOO* BUSY--

ACTUALLY, I HAVE NO IDEA IF THIS THING HAS BEEN PROMOTED SO...TELL YOUR FRIENDS.
CHERYL CALLING *AGAIN*. WHAT IS UP WITH HER?

--COME ON BY.
Josie
PUSSYCATS
SUMMER LOVIN'
GREASE
ZZZT

WHOOPS!
Josie
PUSSYCATS
SUMMER LOVIN'
GREASE
AT THE RIVERDALE THEATER

Josie and the Pussycats
Summer Lovin' Grease
at the Riverdale Theater
Josie and the Pussycats
HEY, YOU NEVER KNOW.
JUST AS WELL. NOT A LOT OF PEOPLE AROUND.
"RIVERDALE WILL SURPRISE YOU..."
"NOT OFTEN, BUT SOMETIMES."

WELL.

LOOK AT *THIS*, SALEM.
RWWWWR.

GREASE.
RWRRRR.
NO, IT'S NOT *NIGHTMARE ON ELM STREET*-- ALTHOUGH THAT WOULD BE AN ***AMAZING*** MUSICAL.
Josie
SUMMER LOVIN'
GREASE

VERY LITTLE IN RIVERDALE ***IS*** *NIGHTMARE ON ELM STREET*.

GREASE.

HAVE FUN AT YOUR BORING MOVIE INSTEAD OF STAYING HOME AND SUMMONING THE SPIRITS OF ADABASCAN WITH US!
THANKS!
THE CHEESIEST SUMMER MOVIE IN THE HISTORY OF MOVIES...

ABOUT A GUY WHO MEETS A GIRL.

A LAME GUY WHO MEETS A NEW GIRL PLAYED BY A TWENTY-NINE YEAR OLD WOMAN.

HOLY CRAP, ARCHIE ANDREWS, THE LAST THING YOU NEED...

BUT WHEN THE WIND CARRIES YOU A MESSAGE, YOU LISTEN.

...IS A NEW ROMANCE.

YOU GUYS LEAVING ALREADY? NO TIME FOR A BURGER?
NOPE, GIG TOMORROW. LIFE ON THE ROAD. LIFE OF A MUSICIAN.

WELL, GREAT SHOW.
THAT MOVIE IS SO RIDIC, I FORGOT.
Ah, IT'S GROWING ON ME.
ZZZT

SORRY, JOS, ONE SECOND.
HEY, POP?
AW, MAN! I'M SORRY. I THOUGHT THAT WOULD HOLD IT.
NO, I CAN GET THE PART. NO, IT'S FINE, POP.

JOSIE AND THE PUSSYCATS
JACK OF ALL TRADES EMERGENCY, GOTTA GO!
ARCHIE OF ALL TRADES!
HAVE A GOOD SUMMER!

HEY, IS THIS MAX'S? HOW LATE ARE YOU OPEN? **GREAT!**

Hmmm-Hmmm, SUMMER LOVIN'...
THAT WASN'T SO BAD.

I GUESS THAT'S THE KIND OF MOVIE YOU WANT TO SEE WITH A CROWD SO YOU CAN TALK ABOUT HOW RIDICULOUS IT IS.
OVER PIE OR SOME-THING.

YOU **HAVE** ONE? OKAY, HOLD IT FOR ME? I'LL BE THERE IN HALF AN HOUR. THANKS!

VRROOOOM
WHERE'S **HE** GOING IN SUCH A HURRY?

TWENTY MINUTES LATER...
YEAH, POP. I GOT IT. BE THERE IN THIRTY.

IS IT THAT IT WOULD BE NICE TO FALL IN LOVE, OR AM I JUST UNDER THE SPELL OF AMERICAN CINEMA, SALEM?
PURRRRRR

IT'S TRUE, I'VE BEEN MOONING ALL DAY.

WHAT'S THAT ABOUT?

Hmmm-
Hmmm,
SUMMER
LOVIN' H--

OHMIGOSH!

SCREEEE
NOOO!

GROOOOAN...
DAD? CAN YOU HEAR ME? DAD? I'VE HAD A... DAD?
CRAP.
GUESS THIS IS THE DIFFERENCE BETWEEN FEELING LIKE YOU'RE HAVING THE WORST SUMMER EVER, AND--
10:13 PM
DAD (CELL)
Call Failed
ARROOOOOO!

Uh...
Uh...
Oh, MY **GOD!**
SALEM?

I HAVE TO GO...
...SOMEONE NEEDS MY HELP.
Get the whole story in the
Archie by Nick Spencer Vol. 2:
Archie & Sabrina
Graphic Novel

Originally presented in **World Of Betty & Veronica Double Digest #13**, May 2022

Dan Parent • Bob Smith • Jack Morelli • Glenn Whitmore

THERE WAS A YOUNG GIRL...
HIC-UCK!
BOING
EXCUSE ME!
I'VE GOT THE HICCUPS!
SARA! SARA! WHERE DID YOU GO?!
THAT'S STRANGE! WHERE IS SHE?!!
HI, SABRINA!!
GAK!!
SARA!
HOW'D YOU GET INSIDE THAT BOOK?!
I DON'T KNOW!
HOLD ON! I'M COMING FOR YOU!!
2

I KNOW I SHOULDN'T USE MY MAGIC IN FRONT OF SARA-- BUT THIS IS AN EMERGENCY!
PER-THUNK
MY MAGIC! SOMETHING IS WRONG!
HIC!
BA-DOINK
THAT HICCUP SENT ME HERE, TOO!
WHAT A CRAZY DREAM I'M HAVING!
I MUST HAVE A CASE OF THE "WITCH-UPS"!
I HAVE TO TRY NOT TO HICCUP!
BECAUSE ANYTHING COULD HAPPEN!
GIRLS!
HURRY! YOU'RE LATE FOR THE TEA PARTY!
3

Oh, WE WERE JUST LEAVING!
NONSENSE!
WE INSIST YOU COME!
ESPECIALLY SINCE ALICE HAS DISAPPEARED FROM THIS STORY!
SO...
WE'VE GOT TO GET YOU BACK HOME, SARA!
BUT THIS IS FUN, SABRINA!
OFF WITH THEIR HEADS!
WELL, THAT'S RUDE!
NEITHER OF YOU BELONG IN THIS STORY!
NO NEED TO BE NASTY ABOUT IT.
POOF
4

IT'S DELLA, THE HEAD WITCH!!
SABRINA! I'VE DETECTED A CASE OF THE "WITCH-UPS"!
AND I'VE TRACED IT TO YOU!
THANKS, DELLA! MY MAGIC IS ALL MESSED UP!
OBVIOUSLY! LET'S GO!
OFF WITH THEIR HEADS!!
I'VE GROWN TIRED OF YOU!
ZAP
ACK!
WANT SOME COMPANY, CAT?
?
AND THEN I WAS IN WONDERLAND AT A TEA PARTY...
EVER NOTICE HOW WHEN SABRINA BABYSITS, SARA ALWAYS COMES UP WITH THE WILDEST STORIES...
END

Originally presented in **Betty & Veronica Double Digest #304**, July 2022

Tania Del Rio • Bill Golliher • Jim Amash • Jack Morelli • Glenn Whitmore

FEEL FREE TO SAMPLE ANY OF THE PERFUMES!
THANKS! AREN'T THESE BOTTLES PRETTY, VERONICA?
THEY ARE, BETTY! I'M LOOKING FOR A FRESH SUMMER SCENT-- SOMETHING UNIQUE THAT WILL TURN HEADS!
THIS ONE MIGHT WORK! THE GLASS IS NICE AND THICK!
BUT IT'S FULL OF PERFUME!
EXCUSE ME, DO YOU SELL THE BOTTLES SEPARATELY?
YES! I'LL GET YOU ONE!
OOH! NOW THIS ONE LOOKS UNIQUE! IT ALMOST SEEMS LIKE THE PERFUME IS SWIRLING IN THE BOTTLE!
SPSST SPSST
UM... THERE'S A PROBLEM WITH YOUR POTION!
OH, NO!
THAT'S NOT FOR SALE!!
LIKE I'D SPEND MONEY ON IT! IT SMELLS TERRIBLE!
KOFF KOFF
2

I THINK I PREFER FRESH AIR TO PERFUME ANYWAY!
YEAH, LET'S GET OUT OF HERE AND SEE WHAT THE BOYS ARE UP TO!
PIZZA
:Phew!: NO HARM DONE!
JUST YOU WAIT! I'D BETTER FOLLOW THEM!
BOAR
BEACH
WHOOSH
3

HOW LONG IS THE POTION GOING TO LAST? ARE YOU GOING TO FOLLOW THEM AROUND FOREVER?
HUFF! HUFF! I DON'T KNOW!
LUCKILY, THEY DIDN'T USE THE WHOLE BOTTLE!
I CAN HANDLE IT... I JUST NEED A MINUTE TO RECHARGE!

HEY, BOYS!
GET ME OUTTA HERE!!
HELP!
AHH!

RUDE!
MAYBE WE STILL SMELL LIKE THAT WEIRD PERFUME! LET'S TAKE A DIP--
--AND WASH IT OFF!!
AND MESS UP MY HAIR?!!
YOU DON'T HAVE TO GO UNDER-WATER!
PERFECT! THAT'LL WASH OFF THE POTION'S EFFECTS!

WHAT THE--?!
YOU'RE KIDDING ME! EVEN THE WATER IS AVOIDING US?!

THAT'S IT!!
WE'RE GOING BACK TO THAT SHOP TO DEMAND AN EXPLANATION!
THERE'S SOME-THING FISHY HERE--
--AND NOT JUST THE SMELL!
4

Oh, NO! THEY NEED TO GET IN THAT WATER!!

DO SOME-THING, QUICK!

ZAP

SPLOOSH

?

AAAHHH!!